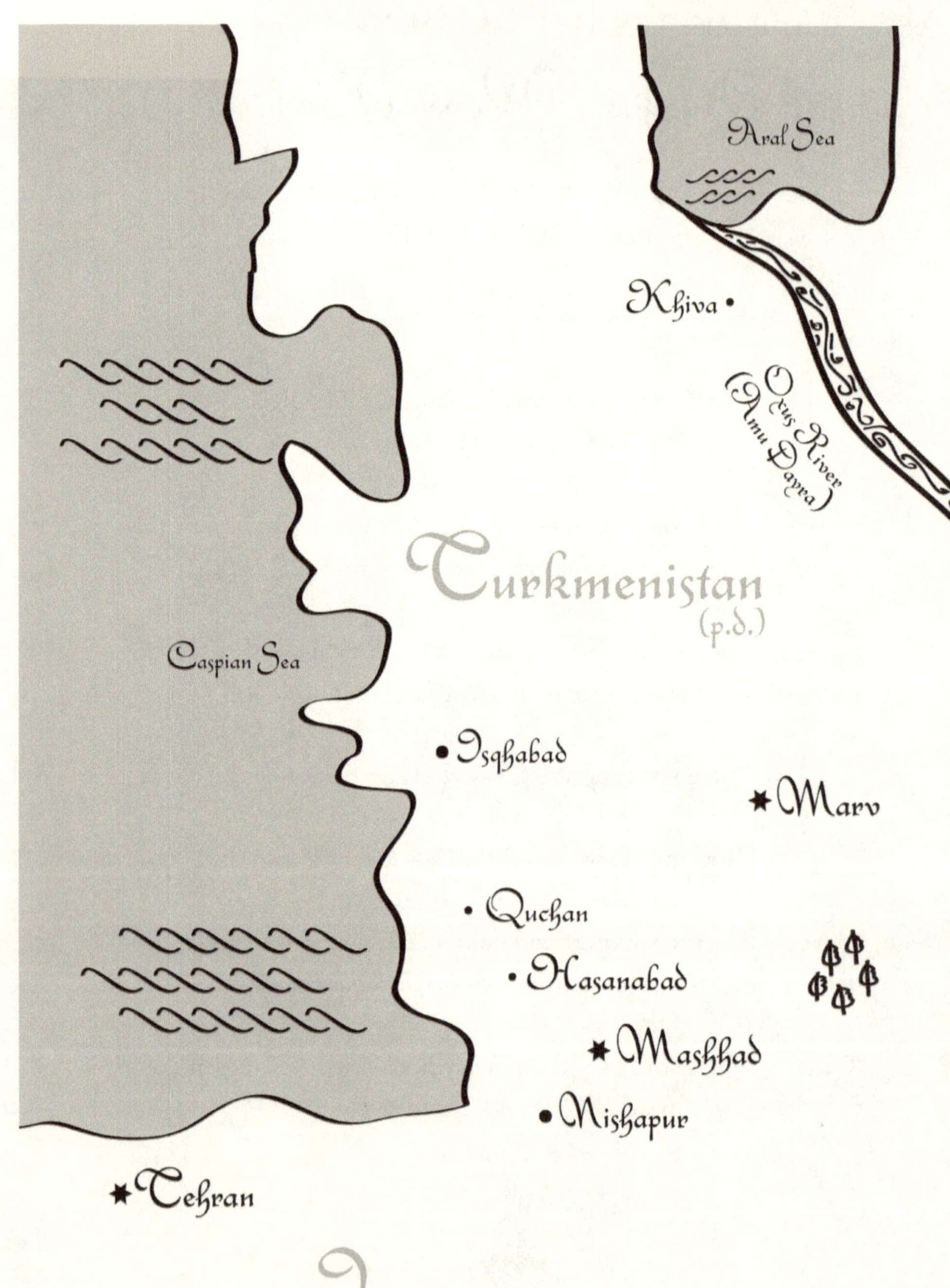

Aral Sea
Khiva •
Oxus River (Amu Darya)
Turkmenistan (p.d.)
Caspian Sea
• Isqhabad
★ Marv
• Quchan
• Hasanabad
★ Mashhad
• Nishapur
★ Tehran
Iran (p.d.)

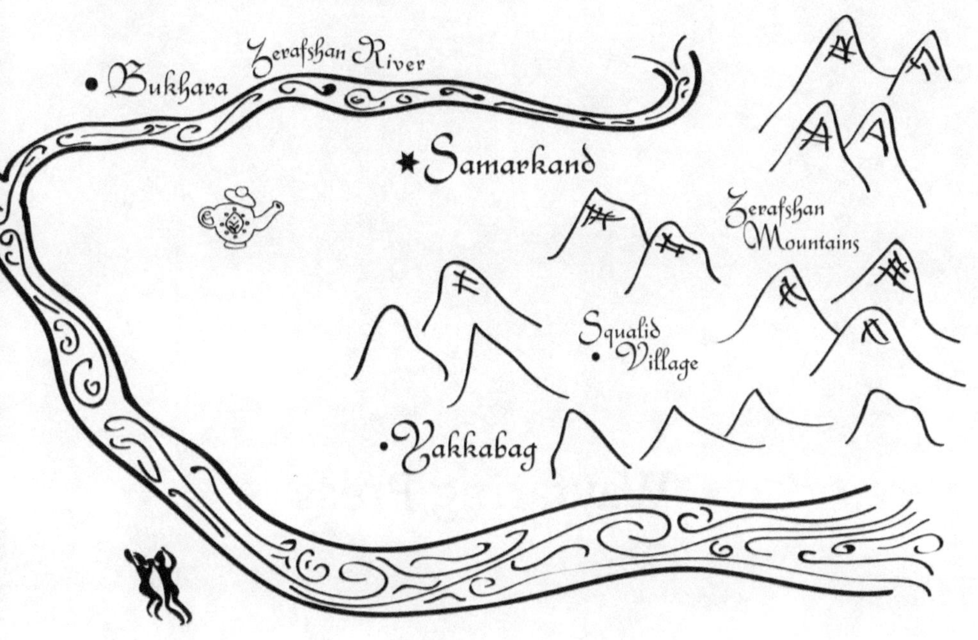

Uzbekistan
(p.d.)
Kasr-i Orifan
Bukhara
Zerafshan River
Samarkand
Zerafshan Mountains
Squalid Village
Yakkabag
Afghanistan
(p.d.)

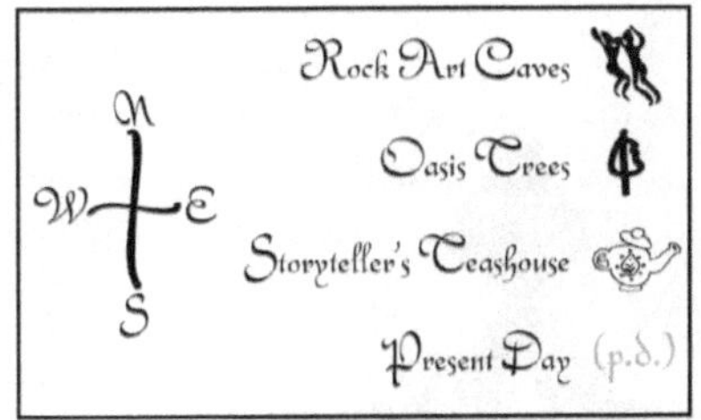

N
W
E
S
Rock Art Caves
Oasis Trees
Storyteller's Teashouse
Present Day (p.d.)
Herat

Wayfaring Press

Night Letter

MEGHAN NUTTALL SAYRES

Wayfaring Press

Spokane, Washington
wayfaringpress@gmail.com
www.meghannuttallsayres.com

Cover artwork by Rashin Kheiriyeh
Book design by Lindsey Wells

Previously published by: Nortia Press, Santa Ana, CA, 2013

ISBN: 978-1-7324741-1-6

Publisher's Cataloging in Publication Information
      1. Human trafficking—Fiction
      2. Iran—History—Qajar dynasty, 1794-1925—Fiction
      3. Muslims—Fiction
      4. Marriage—Fiction
      5. Weaving—Fiction
      6. Afshar (Turkic people)—Fiction

In memory of

Hossein Evland Ebrahimi,

whose translations of literature for young people awakened readers,
encouraged writers, and cultivated friendships, East and West.

Contents

Characters

Ali (Ah-lee)—Shirin's husband, friend to Anahita's family and tribe

Afshars (Af-shars)—Anahita's tribe

Anahita (Ah-na-hee-ta)—a semi-nomadic weaver who lives in the ficticious village of Hasanabad, Iran, and belongs to an Afshar tribe

Arash (Awe-rash)—Anahita's fiancé, a Qajar prince and the governor of Marv whose mother belongs to a Yomut tribe

Dariyoush (Dar-y-oosh)—Anahita's childhood friend, her family's hired hand, and village neighbor

Emir of Bukhara (Ee-meer of Boo-khar-a)—the ruler of Bukhara who is in need of an heir

Fatima (Fat-ee-ma)—a Hasanabad villager and friend of Anahita's family, owner of the teahouse in Hasanabad, and Naheed's niece

Farhad (Far-hod)—Anahita's father, or *baba*, the *kadkhuda* of the Afshar tribe

Habib —Anahita's violent kidnapper

Ismail (Iss-mail)—Arash's closest advisor and confidant

Kadkhuda (Kad-khoo-da)—Farhad's title, a tribal wise man and leader who resides with a branch of the Afshar tribe and is appointed by the khan

Khan (Khawn)—chieftain of the entire Afshar tribe who represents the tribe within the shah's government

Kufa (Koo-fa)—an unkind eunuch in the emir's service

Mahan (Muh-han)—an educated man turned kidnapper

Maman (Maa-mon)—the word for mother

Maman Bozorg (Maa-mon Ba-zorg)—the word for grandmother, Anahita's paternal grandmother

Mojdeh (Moje-day)—Anahita's mother, or *maman*, Farhad's wife

Muhammad (Muh-ha-med)—Anahita's presumed name for her educated
kidnapper

Mustache Man—one of Anahita's kidnappers

Naghal (Na-call)—the Sufi storyteller in the teahouse

Naheed (Nah-heed)—a free woman employed in the carpet workshops
of the emir, an old woman with Afshar connections, aunt to
Fatima

Parisa (Par-ee-sa)—a young woman sold from her home in Quchan
who becomes a member of the emir of Bukhara's harem

Pirouz (Peer-ooze)—an orphaned street kid in Marv whom Arash be-
friends

Rakhsh (Rhash)—Tamam Bas's horse

Reza (Ray-za)—Anahita's schoolmaster and tutor

Salar (Sah-lar)—a slow-witted eunuch in the service of the emir

Shahnaz (Sha-naz)—a member of the emir's harem

Shaikh Kabir (Shake Ka-beer)—a Sufi spiritual master with dervish disciples who helps Anahita

Shamsiddin (Shahms-i-deen)—a scribe in the emirs' fortress, The Ark

Shirin (Sheer-een)—Anahita's female cousin

Tamam Bas (Tah-mum Bas)—Anahita's violent kidnapper whom she nicknamed "Hawk"

Tinsmith —Dariyoush, Ismail, and Farhad's cellmate in The Ark

Place Names

Abadi-e-Golaub (Ah-ba-dee-a Go-lob)—a fictitious village on Anahita's migratory route with sandstone caves and rock art

The Ark —the fortress in which the emir of Bukhara resides

Bukhara (Boo-khar-a)—a city in present-day Uzbekistan that once belonged to ancient Persia

Constantinople —present-day Istanbul

Dar ol-Fonoon (Daa-roll-foo-noon)—a university in Tehran, sometimes spelled Dal al-Funan

Hasanabad (Hass-san-a-bod)—a fictitious village, Anahita's winter home

Herat (Her-ot)—a city in present-day Afghanistan.

Isqhabad (Ish-ka-bod)—a city in present-day Turkmenistan, once part of Persia; Reza and Pirouz traveled here when looking for Anahita in the slave markets

Kasr-i Orifan (Kaz-ree Or-fon)—a small town several kilometers from Bukhara that is home to the Naqshbandi Sufi Order and shrine; its name means "the castle of those who reached the divine truth"

Khiva (Hee-va)—a city in present-day Uzbekistan that is west of Bukhara, location of an ancient slave market

Khurasan (Koor-a-san)—a northeastern province of Iran, which includes the cities of Mashhad, Neshipur, and Quchan, as well as Anahita's winter home

Marv (Marv)—an oasis city in present-day Turkmenistan (now called Mary), home to Arash's palace; it once belonged to Persia

Mashhad (Ma-shod)—a holy city of ancient Persia in present-day northeastern Iran with shrines, caravanserais, and a marketplace that was part of the ancient Silk Route; Anahita's khan resides here

Mecca (Mek-ka)—the holy city of Islam in present-day Saudi Arabia, toward which Muslims pray and to which they are asked to make a pilgrimage at least once in their lifetime

Naqshbandi Shrine (Knock-sh-bond-ee Shrine)—located in Kasr-i Orifan, a town several kilometers from Bukhara; center of the Naqshbandi Sufi Order.

Nishapur (Nee-sha-poor)—a city in present-day Iran in Khurasan Province; the poet, astronomer, and mathematician Omar Khayyam and the Sufi poets Attar and Ferdowsi were born in Nishapur; Anahita's winter village is nearby

Persia —a kingdom that once spread from the Mediterranean to Central Asia, in which the people spoke Farsi and mostly followed the Zoroastrian religion. It is now called Iran, though its borders no longer include Marv, Isqhabad, Bukhara, or Samarkand and the country now only extends to Iraq in the west and Afghanistan in the east.

Quchan (Koo-chon)—a city in present-day Iran; this town once sold its women into slavery to pay taxes imposed by a governor of Khurasan Province

Rhud Amu Darya (Rood Am-oo Dar-ee-ya)—Oxus River

Rhud Zerafshan (Rood Zair-af-shan)—The River of Gold

Samarkand (Sam-ar-cand)—the second-largest city in present-day Uzbekistan; one of the cities in ancient Persia that served as a trading hub along the Silk Route as well a slave market

Tabriz (Taa-breeze)—a city in Iran west of the Caspian Sea

Tehran (Tear-an, Teh-ran)—the capital city of Iran, south of the Caspian Sea; seat of the former shahs

Urupa —the Farsi word for Europe

Yakkabag —a city in present-day Uzbekistan; a town along the route
Anahita travels with her kidnappers

Zerafshan Mountains (Zair-af-shan)—a range in Uzbekistan; Anahita crosses
this range with her kidnappers

There are love stories,
And there is obliteration into love.
—Rumi

MORE THAN ONE HUNDRED YEARS AGO IN THE
ancient land of Persia, a great change had begun. Trains raced across the desert replacing the camel caravans that had walked the sands for thousands of years. Wealthy landowners, eager to protect their property and its precious supply of water, no longer allowed nomads freedom to roam the desert with their sheep. Many tribes had been forced to settle. But the nomads could not survive if their animals had no access to the mountainous grasslands.

People gathered in teahouses to express their concerns and to read aloud anonymous shabnameh—night letters—grievances addressed to the Persian Qajar dynasty. Tales of injustices spread quickly, including public outcry about a tragic event that befell the Persian village of Quchan—the forced sale of women and girls into slavery in order to pay taxes after a drought. This atrocity strengthened the cause calling for a more democratic form of government.

In his luxurious court in Tehran, the shah heard only whispers of discontent. Even so, landowners, merchants, and peasants alike demanded a different kind of government, a parliamentary assembly to help make the laws for a country that would soon be known to the world as Iran.

Meanwhile, Russia sent soldiers to nibble at the borders of Iran like moths on the fringe of a saddlebag. Bandits followed, preying on villages and the newly settled nomads. The blue-tiled cities of Samarkand and Bukhara, once the northeastern frontier of Persia, had long become protectorates of Russia. And the Persian border city of Marv quaked from the peril of advancing Russian cavalry.

In the midst of such turmoil, Anahita, an Iranian Afshar nomad girl who wintered in the village of Hasanabad in Khurasan province, had held a wedding riddle contest. This event determined which of her many suitors would marry her. Arash, a Qajar prince, the son of a nomad mother and the shah, won Anahita's hand. The khan, chieftain of the Afshar tribe and a man who had lost Anahita's contest, declared that her marriage to Arash would prove too dangerous. He worried that the prince's palace in Marv would soon fall to the Russians. The day before Anahita's wedding caravan began its journey to Marv, the khan summoned Anahita's father, the headman of her tribe and the khan's second-in-command, to civil court in Mashhad. There, it would be decided whether Anahita's recent wedding riddle contest met approval from the jurists of the land.

Despite her father's absence, her caravan set off to join Arash. They would carry on as planned, regardless of the court's verdict.

Arash my *yar*,

Our caravan is only days away from Marv. Soon I'll become your wife. Still, I wanted to write. The fierce winds on the plains reflect my mood tonight.

Time has crawled by between our last letters, it feels like a summer day during Ramadan—many long hours with no food. Your dream about a jackal holding a dove in its fangs is unsettling. I dare not think about what it may mean. On a different note, I read a poem by Mowlana Rumi just last night and feel that it speaks of us.

From each heart is a window to other hearts.
They are not separated like two bodies,
Just as, even though two lamps are not joined,
Their light is united by a single ray.

You mentioned coincidences. I have had similar experiences. Often when I think of someone, they appear. Or, a letter arrives—as did yours. I find it touching that you keep a journal of such occurrences and of others for which we don't seem to have the words to explain. I look forward to hearing about them. I wonder, though, are these incidents something more than mere coincidence?

Maman, Maman Bozorg, and my cousin Shirin sewed a thousand sequins on my wedding veil. Schoolmaster Reza decided to join our caravan, too. He didn't want to miss the chance to explore Marv and celebrate with everyone. He has been a good teacher. I will miss him.

I hope that young Pirouz has given up playing with fire and that his burns have healed. It is generous and loving of you to care for him like a son. I look forward to meeting him. Most of all, I am eager to join you in our new life. You will make a fine governor. The people of Marv will appreciate your wisdom.

Forgive my briefness in saying good-bye for now. My ink runs low. May Allah watch over and protect you until we are together.

Your kindred soul,

Anahita

P.S. I am still pondering your riddle: What is sovereign and ceaselessly moves?

Kidnapped

The butterlamp's flame flickered this way and that. Cuddling beside my sleeping grandmother in our tent, the woven goat hair walls billowed in and out. As I wrote a letter to my beloved, I feared the tent stakes might loosen and we'd be blown like wheels of desert sage all the way to Arash's palace.

I startled when the tent door snapped loose. As the cool air rushed over Maman Bozorg, she stirred. I got up and fought with the flap of cloth, finally securing it. I didn't like nights like this—no nomad does—when the wind provides cover for bandits to sneak up on unsuspecting camps. Sitting again, I picked up my pen and finished my letter.

As I folded my parchment, I heard the scrape of a sandal just outside. I tucked the letter into my bodice. Again, a sudden gust intruded. Turning toward the rush of wind, I saw three men wearing black turbans. They sprang into our tent. I locked eyes with the only one wearing a mask. One seized my grandmother. Another muffled my scream, covering my mouth and nose with his large hand. I couldn't breathe.

Maman Bozorg reached for her stick and beat her assailant to no avail. I kicked and bit, but minutes later my grandmother and I lay slung over the backs of two different horses. I strained to see in the inky light, catching sight of Schoolmaster Reza amidst the fray and Dariyoush pulling a blade from his leg.

Slung over the front of a saddle, I grunted in pain when the horse took off running. The steed's spine pierced my stomach, and my face bounced off my kidnapper's knee. I heard faint gasps coming from my grandmother until the sound of thundering hooves drowned them out. Tents, bleating livestock, trees, stars, and even the earth—everything in my world—became swallowed up in the blackness and the wind.

It seemed hours before we stopped at an oasis. My captor pulled me and my grandmother from the horses and threw us on the ground. We clung to one another while our kidnappers argued.

"Why did you bring the old woman?" a voice said from behind me in the shadows with an accent I could not place.

"I wanted a girl for myself. I didn't see that she was a hag," said the kidnapper with a thick mustache standing in front of me. The largest of the three, the one at my side, laughed.

I squeezed Maman Bozorg's hand as the man with the accent led his horse to water. "The All Merciful One will protect us, Anahita," she whispered.

Mustache Man and the large kidnapper pulled my grandmother and me apart, Maman Bozorg hanging on with tremendous strength.

Mustache Man chewed on his whiskers as he tied our wrists and ankles. After, he spoke a few words to his accomplice, then jumped on his horse and rode into the desert.

I struggled to stand despite my bound ankles. It was too dark to make out my large kidnapper's features. I spat at him. "My tribe will hunt the three of you down! The governors of Marv and Khurasan will send battalions after us."

A sharp pain, like lightning, had struck my head. His blow to my cheek crackled in my ears. Maman Bozorg's plump body softened my fall, her voice a drowsy lullaby.

Daylight filtered into the cave where I lay on the cold ground. I awoke to two men arguing, rock shards digging into my thigh, and pain in my right eye. I fingered my swollen cheek as I studied my surroundings. The entrance to the cave was nearly the size of the double arch in our mosque in Hasanabad, tall enough for anyone to pass through. I turned to search the dark end of the cave for my grandmother. A lump formed in my throat when I remembered how our captors had pulled us apart at the oasis. I longed for the joyful sound of Maman Bozorg's slippers in the sand, the rosewater scent of her scarves, her touch.

I listened to the men outside as I struggled with the ropes binding my wrists and feet.

"You shouldn't have hit the girl," said the man with the accent.

"She tripped and fell. Her wrists were tied." This voice belonged to the large captor who struck me.

"She tripped, *mon derriere.* I don't—"

"*Mon derriere?* You know what you can do with that *Français* of yours?"

I heard the strike of flint, followed by the burbles of someone smoking a hookah.

"You're nothing but a washed up courtier," the man continued. "You should have stayed in Urupa. *Your derriere.*"

Smoke floated by the cave entrance. I wondered how long I'd slept. My stomach ached, my limbs shaky from hunger and fright.

"We could double our money, Muha—" the large kidnapper said.

"Bsshht! You fool, do not reveal my name."

"Our precious little darling didn't hear a thing. She's out cold."

The contours of the cave carried their voices like the whispering wall of the grand palace in Esfahan.

"You best check on her."

My chest heaved with fear when the large one came and knelt beside me. I could feel his body heat. *Allah, protect me.*

"Have we disturbed your sleep, *azizam,* my sweet helpless one?" His breath smelled like soured goat's milk. I rolled as far back into the curve of the cave wall as I could, afraid that he might hit me again. This brought laughter to the man's lips. His guttural voice—words spoken from the back of his throat, much like Arabic—confirmed it was he who had made the slip of the tongue by calling his partner, the French speaker, "Muha." He likely was going to say Muhammad. He was either careless or cunning—maybe he meant to give away his accomplice's identity.

My kidnapper leaned closer. His pistachio-green eyes narrowed like a hawk targeting its prey. "I am told that every woman hides a nightingale in her tresses."

"I'll scream if you touch me." With bound wrists I struggled to pull my scarves more tightly about myself. *Please, Allah.*

"And who would come to your rescue?" He unsheathed his *janbiya,* dagger. "Your bespectacled brave tribesman who tried to hit me over the head with a book? Or the one whose leg I crippled?"

A picture of Dariyoush gripping his thigh came back to me as my captor ran his finger across the inscription on the blade.

"How about your father, who saw no reason to accompany your entourage and protect you? Or might you have some lover whom you dream about?" He snickered, sheathing his knife. "Only I will protect you now."

He reached for my loosened braid. "Kiss by kiss, I will become that nightingale who makes a nest in your hair."

"Leave me alone!" I tried to shout, but he pressed his hand to my mouth. My muffled cry must have carried outside because Muhammad appeared at the cave entrance.

The hawk-eyed man hissed under his breath as he slowly rose. "We have many days to travel together, my lovely. My partner may not always be around to temper my impulses. Perhaps then you will think twice before shouting orders at me."

Surely no plants could grow where he stepped. I watched them leave.

On the wall opposite me, I spotted rock drawings: images of hunters, ibex, and dancing figures. Perhaps I could scratch a message for my rescuers among the markings. Surely someone would come for me. I pulled at the ropes on my ankles again, but the knots were too tight.

More hookah smoke wafted across the opening of the cave. The same two men were arguing again. Three captors had abducted Maman

Bozorg and me. Had the one who rode off never returned? With the men seemingly off guard, I scooted backwards like a caterpillar toward the pictographs, softly, so as not to make a sound. On my last effort to drag myself closer to the rock paintings, my skirts knocked two stones together on the gravelly cave floor.

"What was that noise?" Muhammad said.

I rolled back as fast as I could, biting my tongue as I flipped from stomach to back. The men's footfalls grew near. I closed my eyes. *Allah, please don't let them notice if I am not in the same place.*

The sound of metal scraped stone. A scimitar, perhaps. I shook all over as I met Muhammad's glance. This man wore a black scarf to conceal his face, but I could see his eyebrows drawn together, as if in deep thought. His long shirt hung over his loose-fitting *shalvar kameez* trousers. A leather belt with a lapis buckle hung on his hips.

Hawk knelt beside me. "Swollen eyes don't become you," he said, touching my cheek. He wore a gold ring on one finger. No wonder my face throbbed. The sharp edge of his ring had cut me. When I smacked his hand away, he grabbed my wrists. I curled into a shivering ball.

"Leave her be," Muhammad said.

The cave seemed less dark all of the sudden. But my trembling didn't subside.

The throbbing triggered thoughts of Dariyoush's injury. I hoped he wasn't suffering. If only Baba and some of the others had been with us, things would have turned out differently. I wondered why I had been kidnapped. Before we left home my father's scouts and the khan had reported that there were no bandits in the area, and no Russian cavalry, deeming the route from Mashhad to Marv safe for travel.

Hawk hovered, leering before he strode off. Muhammad stood in the cave entrance. "Get her water," he said.

A full day and night had passed since the evening of my kidnapping and my separation from my grandmother the morning after. Tears gathered behind my eyes as I thought how the men in my tribe had decorated the camels and festooned each litter in our caravan with tapestries to shade our tribe from the sun. How the women had draped themselves in their most colorful veils and painted their hands and arms with henna. I clutched the letter I'd written to Arash, which I still kept tucked in my tunic.

I just wanted to be in his arms. Like rain after a drought, my tears let loose.

Through bleary eyes, I studied Muhammad. He moved like a *pahlevan*, a champion warrior-knight of ancient Shiite Islam. I blushed remembering the glimpse of him I stole the day before. Disrobed from the waist up, he'd stood on one leg with his other bent, his right foot resting on the inside of his left thigh. Never had I seen a half-dressed man. At first, the sight of him stirred an alien kind of fright. Yet his stance resembled that of a great tree firmly rooted. His extended arms could be branches, reaching toward the sky. Though silken with sweat, he kept this position for a long while, showing great concentration—and possibly devotion. I turned my back, not wanting to see what might sprout from his limbs.

Looking up at Muhammad now, I asked him why he didn't steal any of the other women in my caravan. He fixed his eyes on mine before walking toward the mouth of the cave.

"Please," I said, wiping my tears with the back of my hand. "At least tell me about my grandmother." Surely, Moustache Man had taken Maman Bozorg to the slave markets of Isqhabad or Bukhara.

"We set her free."

Closing my eyes, I leaned my head against the cave wall. A tightness left my neck. I imagined her all alone at the oasis now.

I thanked him for telling me.

Muhammad turned to look at me, his eyebrows lifted.

I believed him because I refused to imagine my grandmother suffering. Neither could I think about my mother worried sick. Instead, I began reciting the names of the twenty constellations Schoolmaster Reza had taught me. Orion, Sagittarius, Scorpio....

Muhammad walked outside, brushing past his comrade, who had come back with a goatskin of water. Hawk tossed the leather pouch at my feet. I didn't look at him as I drank. I poured a little water on my headscarf to cleanse my wound. The coolness made it feel better. All the while, I sensed him watching me.

While he cut his fingernails with his knife, I examined the wall of rock art again, recognizing several of the geometric designs—including spirals and cloud bands—motifs the women in my tribe wove into their carpets. Stick figures of men and women appeared to be dancing. I had to think of a way to keep my captors out of the cave so that I could scratch a message into the stone. An image of a pregnant woman—legs spread and ready to give birth—painted with a blood red ochre evoked a sense of power. *Blood.* I could leave a trace of blood—another clue for my rescuers to follow.

Without looking directly at Hawk, I said, "I need rags."

"Rags?"

I nodded, looking away, embarrassed but determined. "And I need some time alone to take care of myself."

Hawk waved a hand. "Use your head scarf if you need a rag. I'd prefer you with it off, anyway."

"I don't want to soil my veil."

"Explain yourself, *dokhtar.*"

I couldn't say it.

Hawk stared at me. His mouth opened and closed. Turning, he left the cave.

I overheard my captors outside discussing the matter in hushed voices.

"Well—tear up some cloth for her," Muhammad said.

"Not from my robes."

"Then look for a sack or something to tear apart."

"This wasn't part of the bargain. I only kidnap the *jendeh.* I don't see to the bitches'…*needs.*"

I winced at the disgusting names he called me. But the men's distraction was exactly what I had hoped for. As they argued, I examined the cave wall again. If I hurried, I could scrape a message on the rock. This time I rolled toward the painted figures. Just as I reached the rock drawings, a wad of cloth came sailing into the cave. With bound wrists, I picked up a sharp stone. My fingers shook and my left hand hampered my right as I tried to imitate the dancing stick figures. I began by scratching two wavy lines that suggested my own female contours. Then I drew a spindle and thread. Beside it, I wrote in Farsi, the answer to my wedding riddle contest. Those who knew me would recognize these words as mine. If my captors saw my phrase, it would not make sense to them. Perhaps they would not suspect me as having written it.

"Anahita," Muhammad called.

I dropped my stone, turning my back to hide my work.

"Your meal is…"

Allah, The All Merciful, keep them from coming in here.

"There is food here at the mouth of the cave," Muhammad said.

As his footsteps receded, I took a deep breath. Turning to my work again, I hurried to scratch the finishing touch on the spindle. Then I grabbed the rag. Squinting, I picked open the scab forming on my cheek. How it stung! I felt faint, sucking in air as I dabbed the cloth against my cut to absorb the blood.

I scooted to the food so that they wouldn't wonder why I was not eating. That, and my stomach now cried of hunger. Plain white rice—nothing like the kind my mother made with butter and saffron. Looking outside, the men were nowhere in sight. I did not recognize a single landmark on the desolate horizon.

I shoveled down the rice. After, I managed to leave the soiled rag in the blackness of the cave. It wasn't much bloodied, but it was better than nothing. Then I scooted back to my original spot on the cave floor, where I had slept. From here I could see that my etched figures looked new. Their white lines stood boldly against the brown mineral varnish on the wall. Surely, my captors would notice them.

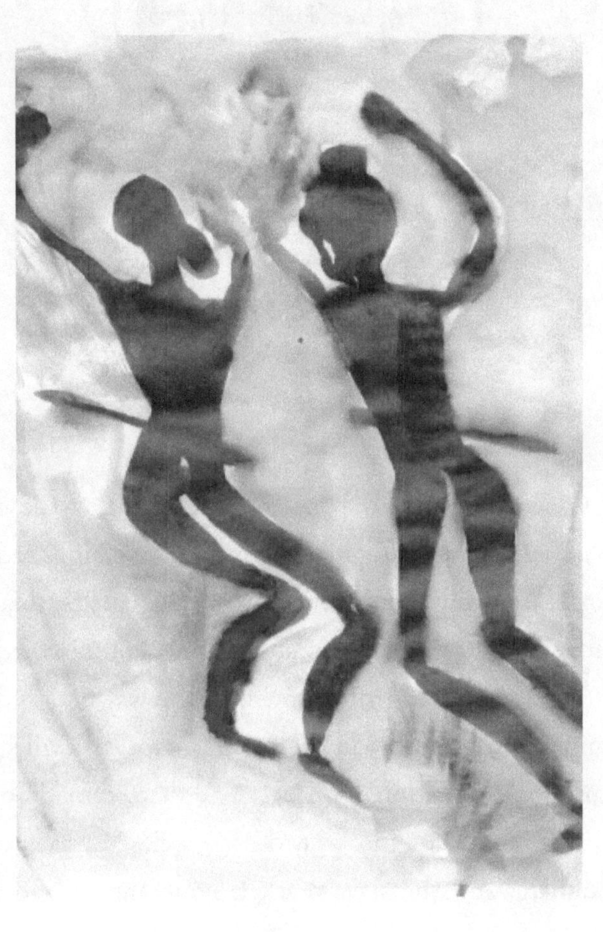

Predators

My feet unbound, I spent the last hours of the day before making camp trudging across a dusty plain, heading north by northeast. Surely my captors aimed to weaken me by this, yet it did not slow our swift pace. I contemplated escape, but the dried riverbeds and barren landscape didn't offer much in the way of a hiding place, nor food and water. I would wait for better prospects, a village perhaps.

We came to a junction with a gorge that seemed to lead due north through a gap cut into the desert rock. It was probably the road to Bukhara, and the slave market. Muhammad had instructed Hawk to ride in that direction. My spirits rose. I tread more lightly when I realized Muhammad and I would not follow him, but continue eastbound toward Samarkand.

I pictured myself safely in Marv with my mother, grandmother, and Shirin trying on bridal hats—beanies made of pure white silk and trimmed with strands of glass beads. I could feel the beads as they streamed about my face, sweeping one side of my neck, cooling my skin like tiny drops of rain. Local merchants and diplomats would attend my wedding, and Arash's father, the shah, would come. The fact that Arash was a prince still seemed like a fairytale. Upon marrying him, I would become a princess. Never had I imagined myself part of a royal family.

The sun baked my skin and my throat grew dry. Muhammad, with the water skin, rode far ahead. All too soon, Hawk came thundering up behind me. I should have realized that he probably rode off to elude anyone who might be tracking us. Reining in his Arabian, he slowed to my pace. We traveled in silence. Though I stared ahead, I was aware of his gaze on me. With him near, each step seemed heavy. After a while he sang, "If a Hasanabad Afshar maid would take my heart into her hand, I'd give Bukhara for the mole upon her cheek—or Samarkand."

Perhaps because I did not look at him, he said, "This is all just a love contest, and I never lose. Now you have another good reason to spend more time with me."

I wanted to say that his modification of Hafiz's poem ruined it, that a person who espoused hate had no right to utter the beloved Sufi's words. But I couldn't bring myself to speak with the irreverent man.

"If I spare your life, will your Baba give me all his money?"

Whipping my head toward Hawk, fists clenched, I shouted, "What made the two of you think that my family is rich? Did you see expensive trappings in my tent when you kidnapped me? Are these clothes I am wearing made of silk?" My family couldn't raise enough money to pay ransom. The khan of our tribe would not help my parents; he was no friend of my father's. Even if he did, he would demand my hand in marriage in return.

Hawk snickered.

I burned. "Perhaps if your songs were of something other than distant places, lost princesses, and imagined treasures, you might have known that no ransom comes with a poor nomad girl."

Hawk grinned. I sensed the pleasure that he reaped from the moment. I vowed not to talk to him anymore. I wouldn't allow his hate to constrict my heart. I wondered if Allah somehow blundered, how a handsome man could be so ugly inside?

"Oh, azizam, how you make this journey a holiday for me. It will be such a shame to leave you with…" He did not finish.

"Leave me with whom?" I asked. Maybe he'd slip up again and give me more information.

"Ah, now that is not for your ears, my fetching nomad girl." His eyes roamed my body, lingered on the curve of my throat. "But perhaps if you would muster up that look you give my partner and bestow it on me, I might let you in on a little secret."

I didn't know what he meant.

"Don't look so puzzled, azizam. Do you not realize that you look at him with interest?"

Interest? Perhaps I triggered this impression because I have looked at Muhammad when spoken to, but refuse to look at Hawk at all. Only a man who has never experienced the loving gaze of a woman could confuse acknowledgement for romantic interest. "Secrets never pass my lips." I faked a smile, feeling sick inside.

"It is not ransom for which you are destined—at least not according to *my* plans—but *sigheh*."

"Sigheh!" I spun toward him. "Did you say——?"

"With a prominent man in Bukhara. It will be a much more profitable arrangement for both of us than what my partner has in mind for you. But it will take our mutual cooperation." He stared at me and spit on the ground. "Mention this to him and your fate will be far less attractive." He ran a finger across his throat, as if slitting it.

We had long passed the fork in the road to Bukhara, so I didn't want to believe him. Walking on, I realized my mistake. I should have played up my family's riches because it might have persuaded them to ransom me. Then they would not dare to dishonor me, to defile me. I pressed my knuckles to my forehead. I could hardly breathe.

Hawk pulled on his reins, stopping his horse. A step later, what he said had finally sunk in. Dear Allah, I will be married to a stranger in Bukhara. Sigheh was supposed to be voluntary, a temporary marriage in which the woman determined the duration and bride price of the nuptial agreement. What Hawk spoke of wasn't true sigheh at all.

I began to lose balance and reached toward a boulder to steady my fall. I sat with my head between my knees for only a minute before Hawk slid off his horse.

When he looked over his shoulder for Muhammad, I understood his intentions. My adrenaline surged, and I took off running toward Muhammad. Hawk caught me by the arm. I whistled as loudly as I could as he yanked me toward him.

He pulled off my headscarf, his fist tangled in my hair. "Do that again and you'll regret it."

I heard the hoof beats on the sand before I saw Muhammad approach.

Hawk snorted. "You won't escape the inevitable."

"Take your hands off her. We gave our word. If they suspect she's been mistreated, you will be killed," Muhammad said.

Hawk held steady, his eyes boring into mine. Then he tossed me away, and I stumbled. "And what about you?" he said. "They'll kill you right along with me."

"I find your conjectures tiresome." Muhammad got off his horse. "We'll rest here."

As I walked past Hawk, he clicked his tongue in a lewd gesture. I sought a rock to sit on as far from them as they would allow. Alone, my adrenaline subsided, and I began to tremble.

On my left, I discovered the scat of a snow leopard, and told them. While Hawk had refuted my claim, Muhammad examined the droppings and scanned the horizon. There was no mistaking that the dung contained ibex fur, a tooth, and bits of weeds.

I was glad Muhammad decided to make camp here because I desperately wanted to respect evening *azan*. The prayer ritual would help me forget about what had just happened, and help me forget about sigheh.

Performing my cleansing ablutions with sand, I washed my feet, hands, and forearms. Then, standing, kneeling, and touching my head to the ground, I prayed that The Compassionate One would save me. Though I performed this ritual just as I would at home, holding each position until tranquility filled my heart, that solace never came. When an odd howling disrupted my meditation, I looked up.

"It's just a wolf," Hawk called from the other side of camp.

He watched my every move. But his comrade Muhammad did not pay me much mind. He held a touch of mystery—especially because he stayed masked. From what I could see of his eyes and brow and the bridge of his nose, he resembled someone I knew, but couldn't name.

Out of the corner of my eye a small, beige animal bounded away from me, running from behind a nearby boulder. Turning, I saw that it looked like a cub—a leopard cub. Perhaps we had awakened it.

Hawk came crashing down on the animal, thrashing and rolling in the brush until he stood holding the little creature trapped in his saddle blanket. It hissed and squirmed with much force to free itself. Looking at me, Hawk held the sack higher, grinning.

"You'll lead its mother right to us!" Muhammad yelled.

"This little fellow's pelt is going to make me rich," Hawk said.

"We'll be dragging no bloody carcasses with us. We'll attract a trail of predators."

Hawk held tight to his treasure.

In three great strides, Muhammad faced Hawk and kicked his leg up high, knocking the cub from Hawk's grasp. The animal let loose a tremendous hiss when it thudded on the ground and the blanket fell open. Before the cub could get onto all four of its feet, Muhammad placed a punch to the back of its head. Unconscious, the cub's wet tongue slipped to the side of its mouth. Its soft white underbelly gleamed in the light. I shut my eyes, caught my breath, and fought back nausea.

Hawk reached for his rifle and I scrambled for cover. Muhammad spun around. With the flash of his arm and the turn of his heel, he sent the gun wobbling into air and Hawk sprawling to his knees.

My whole body shook as Muhammad knelt beside the leopard and stroked its fur. I tasted the morning's dates coming up in my throat.

"Let's get going. The mother won't likely leave the cub to follow us," Muhammad said.

"I don't intend to walk away from money that's lying right in front of me."

"We aren't killing any snow leopards." Muhammad picked up his saddle.

"Did they teach you that *jujitsu* at Dar-ol-Fo—I mean, that fancy school your benefactor sent you to? Or did you learn that in Urupa?" Hawk said, getting up, brushing sand from his elbows.

Dar-ol-Fonoon was the name of the school where my Schoolmaster Reza had studied. Muhammad glared at his comrade and then looked my way. "You ride with me."

I hesitated. *Allah, deliver me from these violent men.*

"Bia, come on," Muhammad said. I walked from behind the rock and climbed onto his gray stallion. I could hardly grip the horse's girth, my thighs and calves so jittery. When we had galloped far enough away from Hawk, I told Muhammad what Hawk had said to me back in the cave, that Muhammad might not be around much longer to protect me. But I didn't mention Hawk's plans for sigheh. If I kept this secret from Muhammad, perhaps Hawk would disclose more. When I finished speaking, I stayed quiet, swaying in rhythm with my captor as we rode. I waited for a lecture about the dangers of meddling, but to my surprise, Muhammad said, "Thank you." His two civil words calmed me.

My mind reached back to a morning at home during Arash's last visit. We had been strolling through my village, Arash stopping now and again to give resting camels the treats he often carried with him. After a game of Leap Over The Camel with our neighbor's children, news of Arash's playfulness radiated throughout Hasanabad, and we soon had a passel of girls and boys in tow. He told me about his wise dervish friend, a spiritual seeker, and how he'd never met a dervish with whom he could not trust his innermost secrets. I confessed that waiting more than a month to travel to Marv for our wedding would seem an eternity, but that I was also afraid to leave my life in Hasanabad behind. Taking hold of my shoulders and peering into my eyes, Arash said, "Do not wish the time away with your family and friends, but appreciate the moments you have together. The present is all we have."

He was right, I thought, leaning back to avoid bumping Muhammad's back as we rode. To dwell in the past or the future is to live in a state of destruction. I took stock of my current fortunes: I was not hurt, just a little bruised on the cheek. One of these men was indifferent toward me and not so threatening. And, Allah willing, I had a whole tribe looking for me, and possibly two, if Arash's people had been informed.

Anticipating Anahita

Arash saw that Ismail, his advisor and closest confidant, waited for him just outside the weaving room in the governor's palace in Marv. Arash had recently renovated this room as a private *atelier* for Anahita. Signaling Ismail to enter, a fabric merchant carrying several bolts of silk and linen squeezed past. "I'll return in a fortnight with oodles of choices for the bride-to-be," the man said with a flourish of his hand. He bowed deeply before leaving, honored to have been chosen to serve the new prince-governor.

Inside, Ismail spun around slowly. "It's stunning."

"I like how the rosewood warms the room," Arash said, tucking into his sash the pink beaded *janbiya* he had just purchased for his fiancé. The dagger was crafted with a fine Damascus blade. Anahita would need it for safety in Marv.

The two sat side by side on a brand new daybed that was situated in front of a fireplace. Arash hoped Anahita would enjoy her new room, be it for weaving, visiting privately with her new friends, or as a retreat when she wanted to be alone.

Ismail scanned a list of tutors he'd interviewed and handed it to Arash.

Arash read the first name. "Master Mozafarri."

"Nice but uninquisitive," Ismail said.

Arash nodded. "Master Ravanipur."

"Energetic but overeager. A bit of a *chaploose*." A brown-noser Ismail said.

Arash nodded again. "Master Dayani."

"Ah," Ismail said, stroking his chin. "Now this man struck me as intelligent…creative…"

"Exceedingly attractive," Arash added.

Ismail nodded.

"Too utterly attractive," Arash continued. That deep, sweet ache of missing Anahita arose.

The two turned to the sound of someone running down the hall. Without stopping to announce himself, young Pirouz, the street boy Arash had befriended upon moving to Marv, skidded into the room. "*Agha! Agha!* Anahita has been kidnapped!"

Arash sprung to his feet and grabbed Pirouz by the shoulders. "What? Where did you hear this?"

"Among the *bazaari*. They said that three men stole a woman and her granddaughter while they were camping. They took them to an oasis to be sold as slaves, each to a different owner." Pirouz's chest rose and fell, still panting as he continued. "Before their fates became unknown, they were given one more minute together." He lowered his voice. "They hung on to each other the way a soul clings to Allah."

"This cannot be true!" Arash stepped away, turned again to Pirouz and shook him. "What makes you certain that it was Anahita?" *Allah, let him be mistaken!*

"Your scouts met up with those from Anahita's tribe."

Arash fixed his eyes on the boy's. "I'm not convinced. Why have you and half the bazaar been informed, and yet I had not!"

Three palace scouts filled the threshold. "Agha, we bear urgent—"

"Enter at once! Tell me what you know about this…'this kidnapping.'" Heat spread through his body, *I've not hired topnotch men.*

"The Afshars believe that she will be taken to Bukhara."

Arash felt as if a horse had given him a swift kick just beneath his lungs. "How many men raided their camp?" He gripped the frame of the daybed.

"Three."

Arash straightened. "Where was she abducted?"

A scout stepped forward. "A two-day ride northeast of Abadi-eh-Golab, near Quchan."

They could go any number of routes from there, Arash thought. Had it been farther north, it would have eliminated a few possibilities. "Only three men?"

One of the scouts nodded.

Arash strode to the window and smashed his fist against the casing.

"It doesn't sound like the work of a slave trader," Ismail said.

"No. Her captors must want ransom." If someone abducted Anahita with the intent of asking ransom, no harm would come to her.

He sent for a scribe and demanded bulletins posted in every corner of the province announcing that he will pay a high ransom to anyone who returns Anahita. One of Arash's scouts nodded and left the room.

"What is this news about a grandmother?" Arash listened as another scout explained, then questioned him further. "So, Anahita was targeted. But why? By whom?" Arash began to think of what enemies he might have made in the last year as well as in the last few weeks since having taken over the governorship of Marv from one of his many Qajar-prince relatives.

"When is Anahita's caravan due to arrive?"

"Perhaps three days."

"Let us make haste," Arash said. He pressed the heel of his palm against his forehead, willing himself to think faster. "My scout, send those in your charge to search the routes to Bukhara, Samarkand, and Herat."

"You might consider the routes to the west, my prince. Isqhabad, Tabriz, Constantinople," Ismail suggested.

"Consider it done," the scout said.

Arash turned to him. "I will consider it done when I hear that it has been done."

Tilting his head toward Pirouz, Arash continued. "This *boy* brought me the news before you." Then, looking into each of the men's eyes, Arash said, "When Kadkhuda Farhad arrives, follow his every wish. Any and all resources shall be at his disposal."

He turned to Pirouz. "My friend, I want gossip. From within and without the palace. Find out who might be holding a grudge against me or any news at all that pertains."

"Yes, agha."

"Get going!"

The other two scouts bowed and left with Pirouz.

"What are you going to do?" Ismail asked.

Arash took off his turban and ran a hand through his hair. He exhaled. "Am I dreaming this, Ismail? I'm supposed to be planning a wedding, not a rescue."

Ismail held his comrade's gaze. Arash could feel Ismail's worry, as if it were his own bride held captive. He appreciated that he had such a true friend—someone he could trust with his life, and with Anahita's.

"I will go to the oasis where Anahita was last seen with her grandmother and follow their tracks. If after a few days I come up with nothing, I will ride to Bukhara, in case this is actually a slave trade abduction rather than a kidnapping."

"It makes good sense."

"Ismail, what do you know about foreign slave markets?"

His advisor told him the slaves are usually brought to the auction blocks in sizeable lots. They sell whenever a shipment comes in. Prices vary according to whether the slaves are fortunes of war or famine, the talent of the auctioneer, the fluctuations of supply and demand.

Arash swallowed, gazed upon the street through the window.

Ismail pressed his lips into a thin line. "Prices also are determined by the shrewdness of the buyer, and the looks of the slave."

Arash looked down. He drew a ragged breath, feeling himself choke up. "What kind of cash would I need were I to find Anahita and have to buy her?"

"Prices for trained strong men cost in the vicinity of four to five thousand piasters. Eunuchs, healthy young males, and women suited for labor are more expensive than older men."

"What about..." Arash couldn't bring himself to ask.

"Beardless boys and beautiful women, those suitable for concu—" Ismail stopped. Perhaps he chose not to emphasize the reality of Anahita's predicament. "They can sell for as high as fifty thousand."

Every muscle in Arash's face and neck tightened. He pulled the jeweled dagger from his hip and hurled it at the target he had hung on the opposing wall for Anahita to practice her aim. *Allah, how can you have forsaken her?*

Ismail flinched when the knife hit its mark.

Arash knew Bukhara was a protectorate of Russia and that the czar insisted that the slave trade cease there, that it was considered illegal in Russian territories. Perhaps this would work to his advantage. Wiping his brow with his sleeve, Arash turned to Ismail and asked him to go to the slave market in Bukhara with one hundred thousand piasters and look for Anahita. "Let no one outbid you for her. Stay there until we meet again."

"As you wish, my prince." Ismail embraced Arash, and then turned to leave.

"Perhaps one of Farhad's men should follow suit in Isqhabad. Please see that money is set aside to buy Anahita should she turn up there." Ismail nodded and left.

Arash sat on the daybed. He grabbed the list of tutors, crumpled it into a ball, and tossed it into the empty hearth.

He stood up again and paced. He must not embark on this chase in the wrong state of mind. Anger, he knew, grew from a resistance to immediate circumstances. If he could bring himself to accept what had happened to Anahita, he could work with, rather than against, the energy that the present moment dealt him. Luck would come to his aid like a bird on wing.

The best way to clear his mind would be to set off in search of Anahita, in the mountains on his horse. Closing the door to Anahita's weaving atelier behind him, he prayed, "Allah, please allow her to one day enjoy this room…to endure…to survive the terrible ordeal she must be experiencing." As he let go of the door latch, he remembered Anahita's dagger and he went back inside to retrieve it. Tears trickled down his face as he left the room.

Arash spoke briefly with his vizier about overseeing the palace while he was gone, and instructed his scribe to send any urgent communiqués to him at the main caravanserai, inn, and animal shelter, in Bukhara. He consulted with his militia, the detachment that would leave for Bukhara and the other that was assigned to protect Marv from offensives by the Russians.

After half of the sand had dripped from the hourglass in his private quarters, Arash and two escorts wrapped their torsos with sashes made of fifteen-foot lengths of silk, a trick to prevent nausea during their journey. They mounted their stallions and rode like men chased by a demon. Toward and beyond the distant snow-covered peaks they raced, heading to a vast desert in search of fresh footprints around an ancient and time-trodden oasis.

Hidden Threads

The following afternoon Muhammad, Hawk and I crossed the Rhud Amu Darya, the ancient Oxus. Hawk rode behind me, Muhammad ahead. The sky blanched and the earth burned. A film of sweat covered my body. I wished I could peel off one of my skirts, but my hands were tied. Plodding onward, I watched for more snow leopards, and other predators.

I touched my letter to Arash through my tunic and pondered the riddle he had posed to me: What is sovereign and ceaselessly moves? Later, as I walked, I imagined Arash and myself in Marv. Dressed in wedding finery with his thick black hair glistening, he rides toward me on his stallion, its neck arched. Seated on a donkey and wearing white silk, I look at him through my veil. We meet in front of our wedding tent—the most decorated I could ever have imagined—with purple and indigo tassels, blue-green carpets, and a pink and white embroidered door. Arash tosses a ripe apple in my lap, as tradition calls for.

A mountain lay ahead. Anticipating the climb made my feet hurt. Even though a woman's honor would be maintained when she was kidnapped for ransom, few would receive offers for marriage because of the stigma attached to those who have kept unsavory company or who have spent time alone with unrelated males. Surely, Arash's royal family would refuse me. I slowed to a shuffle. Maybe Arash would, too.

Even though my captors tried to wear me down physically, I preferred walking to sitting behind Muhammad or Hawk on their horses with my hands tied around their waists. Picking up my pace, I vowed they wouldn't break my spirit.

Muhammad trotted back to me with a goatskin of water. I drank and then dampened my headscarf. The coolness soothed my skin. Though his body looked lean and less cumbersome than Hawk's, I worried if Muhammad's martial arts would triumph were they to fight.

The sun shone directly overhead as we came to a green belt of juniper and spruce that lined the base of the mountain range. A family of grosbeaks rustled in the underbrush, and mountain finches chirped overhead. While biting into a pumpkin-colored *narenj,* which Hawk had given me, I thought about leaving a message for my rescuers. If my hands weren't tied, I could scratch a note in the sand of the brook. I would write *Muhammad: Dar-ol-Fonoon,* the name of the school that Muhammad had attended. Master Reza went to that school and might know of Muhammad, as they looked about the same age. Perhaps they had attended together.

The men told me to continue walking while they watered their horses. "But stay within a dagger's throw," Hawk said. I finished my narenj and it gave me a lift of energy. As I walked through the warp and weft of the trees the cool shade helped me think more clearly. I stuffed my terror and trembling of the last few days into an imaginary *chanteh* and sewed the bag shut.

While I ambled up the trail, my skirt caught on a twig and was torn. I hated to see my beautiful skirt go to ruins. While carefully unsnaring myself, I spotted bark chips at my feet. Glancing back, I saw that the men were still at the stream. I picked up a few bark chips and began to incise clues on them with my fingernail, just as Dariyoush and I used to do as children, our letters showing up lime-colored on the undersides of pieces of wood he had whittled. We used to jumble them to see who could find the marked one first.

I carved *Dar* on one of the chips, and then let it fall to the ground. Turning, I saw Muhammad and Hawk shoring up their saddlebags. I hurried to scratch *ol-Fonoon*. As they cantered up to me a horse neighed. Hawk jumped off his Arabian and surveyed the area. I tried not to glance at the places where I had dropped the chips. He reached down and pulled a thread of my skirt from the underbrush. "What is this?" His eyes bore into mine.

I took it from him. "It looks like a thread from my skirt."

"Why would it be draped on this bush?"

"A twig snagged my clothing." Fear twined its fingers around my neck when I saw that one of my chips lay face up on the ground, the green letters in plain sight.

Hawk squinted at me. Then he looked beside the scrub oak to a low-lying fir, where he saw the bark chip. "*Dar?* Did you write this?"

I took a deep breath.

"Enough," Muhammad said. "We must cross the summit before dark." He shot Hawk an impatient glance. "Untie her."

"You're making a mistake." Hawk's eyes darted here and there for more chips. He swept up a handful and shoved them in his sash.

Muhammad pulled me onto his horse. I thought about how he did not seem to allow his comrade's contrary remarks to affect him. He seemed not only to possess control of his body, but also his emotions. I would do well to emulate him.

The horse eased into a canter. I didn't like sitting so close to this man, or care for the smell of him. But I felt glad for the rest. Just as I wondered why he had not tied my hands around his waist, he said, "No more tricks, please. This includes leaving behind a trail. If you attempt this again, things might get rougher for you than you'd like."

Hearing these words, expressed so politely—so much the way Schoolmaster Reza framed a phrase—scared me more than anything Hawk had said to me.

I palmed my chest, feeling for Arash's letter. Was my beloved, at this very instant, galloping toward me, his swords clanging as he swept across the desert? Great clouds of dust rising beneath the horses of those who accompany him: Baba, Dariyoush, Ali, and the best of Arash's battalion in Marv. Surely, Arash had found my bloodied rag, deciphered my message on stone. Soon, lime green letters would glimmer his eye.

Pursuit

Dariyoush winced as his father unraveled the bandage on his thigh and checked the stitches sewn the day before. Shirin took the soiled cloth and handed the tribe's healer a clean one. They gathered around the lip of a clay oven they used for making flat bread that was buried in the ground. Anahita's mother, Mojdeh, knelt next to Maman Bozorg on a prayer rug, a position from which Mojdeh had scarcely moved since Anahita's abduction. Her petitions to Allah had lapsed into sobs. Tears trickled down her unwashed face and her shoulders shook with grief. Maman Bozorg stroked her back.

Dariyoush and the others awaited the arrival of Anahita's father, Kadkhuda Farhad, and for more men from home to escort the caravan on the rest of the journey to Marv. Given Anahita's betrothal to a Qajar prince, Dariyoush hoped that their khan in Mashhad would ask the governor to send forth a squad of regional forces to help search for Anahita. He prayed Arash would respond to the news with a clear and focused mind.

Shaking his head, Dariyoush's father said, "The rogue missed your hamstring by centimeters. But he went deep."

"I know. I'm the one who pulled the dagger out." Dariyoush felt murderous. Who would do this to Anahita, to her family, to him? His frustration soared as he thought about his failure to save her. Their assailants had managed to unleash the livestock and horses, forcing the Afshars to retrieve the animals, thus winning time for their getaway. And, the bandits had chosen a windy night when no one would hear them coming. The cloud cover made it impossibly dark and Dariyoush hadn't heard the *ankhabis*—the louse who had slit his leg open—approaching. Not above Anahita's screams.

"You never should have ridden after them, Dariyoush," his father said. "You lost much blood."

"Yes, but we have Anahita's grandmother home safely." He winked at Maman Bozorg. "She might have perished."

"I had dates and water," Maman Bozorg said, stretching a sphere of dough between her palms. "It is you who would have perished if I had let you continue riding after Anahita."

Rinsing the blood from his hands in a bowl, Dariyoush's father asked, "Have you thanked Maman Bozorg for saving your life?"

Dariyoush looked at his hands. Hands that had recently held Anahita in his arms in a cave at Abadi-eh-Golab when they pretended she was a damsel in distress for the children who accompanied them. That this had become a reality seemed unfathomable. *If I have to crawl, I will go after Anahita,* he thought. *Upon my blood.*

Shirin's husband strode toward the group sitting around the oven. He greeted Anahita's grandmother with a bow of his head as he placed a palm on his heart. "I've come to tell you all that I will accompany Schoolmaster Reza to Mashhad. I don't think Reza would last a day alone in the desert."

Maman Bozorg sprinkled water on the dough and smoothed it against the concave wall of the oven. Within minutes it would bubble, brown, and blister. "The schoolmaster tried to hit one of those bandits over the head with his book," she said.

Shirin shook her head as she sewed a small blade, sunflower seeds, and flints for lighting a fire into Dariyoush's waist sash. A survival kit in case he was captured.

"But we must give him credit," Dariyoush said, leaning heavily on his crutch to stand. "Reza showed more courage than—" Each of them turned their heads to the sound of footfalls sprinting toward the tent. Reza announced himself and came in.

Exchanging glances with the others, Dariyoush's father welcomed him.

"A messenger has come from Mashhad. The jurists absolved Kadkhuda Farhad of any charges by the khan regarding the wedding riddle contest. He is due to arrive within a day or two. Apparently, he doesn't know about Anahita's abduction."

"You and I will inform the kadkhuda about his daughter on our way to Mashhad," Ali said.

Reza nodded. "Thank you for granting me this indulgence. I know that the maps I have of Isqhabad and Bukhara in my *manzel* in Mashhad will be helpful. They are ancient. We will learn about all the old structures, former street names, and *meydans*. The new maps are cheap imitations and show little detail, hardly worth the tomans." He fiddled with his eyeglasses. The frames had cracked during the scuffle on the night of the raid. "My colleague knows many people in Bukhara. With his assistance, we will find informants there. People who understand the ins and outs of the..." he hesitated to say what everyone in the room dreaded to think about, "of the slave trade."

Dariyoush grabbed his turban and limped outside into the hot April sun. But rather than put the headpiece on, he threw it forcefully on the ground. "I should be riding after her now," he said under his breath. Looking north, his intuition told him that something wasn't right about Reza's notion that Anahita was abducted by slave traders. Her captors did not take enough women to make it worth their while. He had better get tracking them. He'd already lost a day. *Tonight, while the tribe sleeps, I'll go.*

Maman Bozorg stoked the oven's hissing embers with a twig. "The kidnappers came straight for our tent, passing up several others from which they could have taken hostages. But they chose ours, the one in the middle."

Mojdeh lifted her head from the prayer carpet. "They knew it was a *kadkhuda's* tent."

"Hmm." Maman Bozorg lifted the steaming, fragrant bread from the oven and placed it on a tray. "The timing seems too coincidental, happening at the same time as Farhad's summons to civil court." She would have liked to have heard Farhad defend himself against the baseless grievances the khan waged over Anahita's wedding riddle contest.

Shirin, preparing another sphere of dough, asked, "Mojdeh, will you eat something this evening?"

Anahita's mother nodded, sitting back on her heels as if she couldn't relax enough to sit down completely.

Eyeing her daughter-in-law, Maman Bozorg said quietly to Shirin, "I wish the mullah were here. Maybe he could do something to ease her mind."

"Maybe the mullah would have an idea of how to find Anahita." Shirin placed the dough on the oven.

"I don't know, dear. Never in the history of our tribe has anyone been *kidnapped*."

Mojdeh turned her head. She fussed with her tunic and said, "Surely, they would not harm her if they planned to ask for money." Maman Bozorg nodded with Shirin, but did not mention that there had been no ransom note.

Maman Bozorg scraped the flatbread from the oven with too much force, tearing it. *Indigo is not as dark as my present mood.* Never in her long and blessed life had she felt so furious. She would be of little help to anyone unless she shed this emotion. She suggested the women should continue to bake bread for the tribe for the rest of that afternoon. The three of them would benefit from the meditative task.

As they worked, she recited a poem by her beloved Hafiz that would soothe the women's nerves.

How
Did the rose
Ever open its heart

And give to this world
All its
Beauty?

It felt the encouragement of light
Against its
Being.

Otherwise,
We all remain
Too
Frightened.

Under the light of the moon, Dariyoush jumped off his horse at the oasis where he had rescued Maman Bozorg. The pain in his leg caused him to suck in his breath. Shadows of date trees threw a lace-like pattern on the earth, obscuring any tracks. After a while he found signs of a single horse heading north, toward the Bukhara road. But there were three men. These could not be the right tracks.

Dariyoush circled the oasis again in the darkness, finding no leads. Drawing water from the well for his stallion, he wondered if one of the men had departed with Anahita on one horse. Even if so, the tracks of the other captors should have been evident. *Lanati!* he cussed, throwing his saddle against a date palm. No sense in riding off and wearing out his horse for a partial lead. He'd have to wait the few hours until dawn so that he would be able to see more clearly.

After wiping down the sweat-soaked flanks of his horse, he sat on the sand and redressed his bandage, taking comfort in the fact that the stitches still held. He pulled out his knife and surveyed the ground for a twig to whittle, finding a piece of camel bone as thick as two of his thumbs. He began cutting the jagged end of it, thinking about how

Anahita always liked to watch him carve figures from wood. *Just because she wove Arash's name into her wedding dowry carpet doesn't mean I can shake off my love for her.* He soon dozed off.

Awakening to his horse's whinny and sunlight, Dariyoush scouted around again. He found dead cypress branches and palm leaves that appeared crushed from the weight of horses. Nearby tracks pointed west, possibly to Isqhabad. Yet intuition told him there should be tracks leading toward Samarkand. Retracing his steps, he walked into the shade of a tree and there in the moist sand he spotted several hoof prints that confirmed his notion. He jumped on his horse, following the tracks along a familiar route east. He made good time throughout the morning, happy that his thigh tolerated the ride.

By evening he came to a sandstone escarpment with several caves. Anahita's captors would have chosen the protection of these shelters for a place to rest, so he led his stallion up a skinny trail cut into the sandy bluff. Both he and his horse stumbled from time to time when chunks of the sand fell from beneath their feet.

Before sunset, he reached the last cave. He dropped his reins and walked inside. The coolness offered relief. His eyes wouldn't adjust to the dimness so he returned to his horse for a torch, lit it, and went back inside. He inspected the space for any belongings that might have been left behind but saw none. The floor seemed to have pattern or texture to it. Kneeling, he inspected it more closely, discovering that the dirt had been disturbed intentionally, as if someone had taken a branch and swept away traces of footprints. Pacing and crawling around every inch of the area, Dariyoush finally found imperfect footprints in the dust that looked to be the size of Anahita's. The sight of them brought a rush of relief and a surge of adrenaline. Beyond the footprints lay a rag. The fabric was not the madder-colored linen Anahita had been wearing the day she was abducted. Picking it up, he saw blood. Though dry, it appeared carmine, fresh.

Turning, his torch lit up the rock drawings on the wall beside him. He stared at the wealth of images—hunters and ghostly shamanistic shapes—that covered the panel. Three figures stood out a shade lighter than the others. He rushed to the wall and knelt in front of it. He discerned curvy lines in the shape of a woman, two figures that looked like men dancing, and something written below them. He wished he understood the script scribbled before him, but he had never learned to read. If the markings were Anahita's, they might indicate that she was guarded by two men. He rummaged through his saddlebag for a piece of leather and scratched onto it the words etched on the wall. He would find someone who could tell him what it said.

Dariyoush left the soiled rag bearing Anahita's scent in the mouth of the cave in the event that Farhad, or anyone else, sent a team with search dogs. He knew they would likely follow this same route from the oasis to here, as his tracks would surely guide them.

Wasting no time, he led his horse off the bluff and continued to ride toward Samarkand. Anahita's captors must be people who wanted to settle a score with Arash, he thought. Dariyoush frowned. Anyone who was remotely related to the Qajar court couldn't be all that… clean. Princes always had skeletons in the closet.

Darkness fell. Dariyoush's leg throbbed as he rode. He nudged his horse to run faster.

6

Summiting

Clouds had gathered and began to spit rain. When my captors and I broke above the tree line, snow flurried. I had always marveled at the seemingly magical snow line that was most pronounced in the springtime. Buds blossomed on the slopes below while winter swirled at elevations above.

Sweat that formed during the day's walk now chilled me. The cold caused my eyes to tear and my nose to run.

We came upon a steep slope of scree where fallen trees and chunks of ice the size of tents indicated a recent avalanche. A thin layer of snow blanketed the slope. Our stallion labored in the thin altitude. We now had to climb the mountain on foot because the horses had begun to slip.

Snow seeped into my slippers, numbing my feet. I sat on a boulder and rubbed heat into them.

"Get up," Hawk said. "No wasting time."

"I'll never make it to the top in these slippers."

Muhammad stroked his chin before loosening the girth on his saddle and yanking the blanket beneath it from his horse. He took out his knife and sliced the tightly woven fabric in two, and then in half again. After tossing me two of the pieces, I wound the coarse material snugly around each foot, making a bootie of sorts that rode halfway up my shins. Hawk handed me twine. Then I asked if I could drape Hawk's saddle blanket over my shoulders. He hesitated, but gave it to me.

We pushed upward with Muhammad in the lead. The snow fell sporadically, between bursts of sunshine. I skimmed a handful of snow from a boulder to quench my thirst. I doubted anyone from my tribe could find me. No one would consider scaling this mountainside in this unpredictable weather. Perhaps later, in the summer, but not now.

When I tired to the point where I believed I could go no further, Muhammad called to Hawk that the spine of the mountain looked near. This news quickened my step. *Inshallah*, there would be a village tucked into the valley below. I envisioned a bowl of hot saffron rice and a fire.

I stood panting after I joined Muhammad on the summit. Around us stretched a sea of glaciated mountain peaks extending east and west. Far below, the land burst with the green of spring. Across the valley, a massive black cloud spilled over the far ridgeline, like paintings I had seen of curling waves on the Caspian Sea. Its darkness descended rapidly toward the valley below. I looked for dwellings that might be clinging to the side of the slopes or along the river that sliced the landscape. No village. Not a single house. I lowered my head, feeling defeated.

"Cheer up, azizam. We're almost to Bukhara!" Hawk said, catching up with Muhammad and me.

In the few moments that I had been standing still on the ridge top, my toes had frozen. I curled and uncurled them, hoping they'd thaw. The horses whinnied, wanting, perhaps, to be off this peak where the snow blew sideways, sending tiny biting shards of ice against their faces. Or perhaps it was the abrupt knife-edge beneath their hooves that spooked them. The summit seemed as vertical and white as a freshly warped loom. Yet the expanse before me held premonitions of dread rather than a welcome anticipation of weaving.

I wound my scarves more tightly around my face, leaving only my eyes uncovered. I looked at Hawk. "This is Yomut territory, is it not?" I hoped that he couldn't resist correcting me, and by doing so, would give away our position.

"No, my little know-it-all, it is Turkman country. The most dangerous in these parts." He snickered.

I assumed we must be as far north as, or farther north than Marv, heading to Samarkand.

Muhammad shoved Hawk forward, hissing his words through closed lips. "Start down. That cloud will ride up this side of the valley and engulf us in a manner of minutes." He had shut Hawk up, stopped him from giving me more information.

I studied the snow on the north face of the range. This slope had collected much more powder than the side we had just walked up.

"Keep to the left. Follow that narrow shoot and make for the junipers," Muhammad said. He had suggested we avoid the open snowfield, which would be more likely to slide.

When Hawk dropped into the ravine with his horse in tow,

thunder sounded. Muhammad reached out and caught my sleeve. Perhaps he wanted me to wait and see if the mountain would let loose. After a while, he gestured for me to go.

With each step I sank to my knees, the snow filling the rims of my cloth boots. After I took several strides, Muhammad dropped into the chute with his horse. Within seconds, there came more thunderous moans and a hissing. But the sounds came from the earth, not the sky.

Upslope, a fracture line split on the couloir and traveled like the arch of whip to the other side of the snowfield. *Phump!* The surface on which I had been walking sank. "It's going to slide!" I yelled.

I fell into the moving mass of snow. The roar grew deafening. The force of the avalanche swept me along, pushing me into the trunk of a small juniper tree. I raised an arm to protect my face. Snow pummeled my back, shoving me against the tree. Pieces of branches and rocks nicked me as they flew by in the fury of frozen debris. Something snagged and tore one of my headscarves, winding it around my neck.

The avalanche stopped as suddenly as it started. All fell quiet. I couldn't catch my breath. The scarf was strangling me. I gurgled. Choked. Panicked. Gasping for air, I tugged at my scarf, but the pain in my chest was so great I let go. My body was buried from the waist down. I couldn't move my legs.

The cold blade of a knife chilled my neck. Hawk slid his dagger between my throat and the scarf, and sliced it off of me. I sucked in air, but my lungs hurt badly. When I tried to pull myself from the snow, a pain pierced my ribs. I cried out.

"Careful," Hawk said. "You may have broken something." He

grabbed a split tree branch to dig me out. I'd be worth nothing dead.

I chattered uncontrollably from the cold. I'd lost my saddle-blanket cloak. The arm I used to protect my face was badly bruised.

Hawk's horse survived the avalanche, too, but it was tossing its head and rearing up. On the mountain, three quarters of the field had slid and the snow had piled high inside the narrow gully we had walked down. But I felt thankful that I had taken this path, the trees saved me. My bruises and cracked rib were worth my life.

I wondered why Hawk seemed unscathed. "Did the avalanche not harm you?"

"Missed me by the span of my hand." He spread his fingers wide and laughed. "Rakhsh, too."

My jaw dropped. He got away without so much as a scratch, the miserable wretch! Rakhsh—he had never called his horse by name before.

I looked for Muhammad.

Downslope, the cloud had consumed the valley floor. One of my feet felt extremely numb. After Hawk had dug me out, I discovered that I had lost a boot in the slide. Sitting on a felled branch, I tried rubbing my frostbitten foot, but the motion hurt my chest. "Will you please cut up the cloth to make me another boot?" I asked. Hawk scowled but helped me.

As he worked, I surveyed the area again for Muhammad. I didn't see him or his stallion. "Have you seen your comrade?" I asked.

"No." Hawk tossed me the cloth for my boots.

My stomach clenched. "He's not buried under the snow, is he?" I tried to reach my foot to wrap it, but I stopped short in pain.

"Give me those." Hawk grabbed my pieces of cloth. He sat beside me and tied them to both of my feet, none too gently. "Now let's get going."

"Won't you search for Muhammad and his horse?"

"Who? You mean Mahan? I didn't much like traveling with him to begin with."

"You can't just leave a man here to die!"

"Watch me."

Stunned, I did not know what to do next.

Hawk untethered his horse, gave the reins a tug, and descended into the thick of the forest toward the river. His rifle was no longer attached to his saddle. He must have lost it during the slide.

I stood up too fast, nearly doubling over. I could barely gather my skirts about me, the slight arm movements causing a stabbing pain. I took a few steps uphill and listened. Walking in an arc, pausing and listening again for possible cries for help, I heard nothing. The snow had hardened like rock. I recalled my father's story about an avalanche that had buried an entire caravan.

I stood for a long while, shaking. Then I began to cry. When I looked for Hawk, I couldn't see him through the dark fog that had swept up from the valley.

I clung to the warm thought that Hawk had showed a glimmer of tenderness when he called his horse by name. In the legend of Rustam and Sohrab, the great warrior Rustam's horse, Rakhsh, was so strong no elephant could match him in a fight. But deep down I knew most any rogue would call a horse by name. And my hope soon turned to ice.

Meanwhile in Marv

While Anahita's father, Kadkhuda Farhad, organized a battalion from among the soldiers at Arash's palace in Marv, Reza and Arash's servant boy, Pirouz, boarded the train for Isqhabad, a city on the Persian-Russian border. The slave market there had recently swelled with an influx of women. Reza thought it ironic that the town was named "The City of Love."

Always looking to the future, the schoolmaster seated himself facing the direction in which the train would be going. Pirouz watched out the window, excited to pull away from the platform. Reza fingered the money pouch that Arash's treasurer had given him. He wiped a bead of sweat from his brow. The responsibility of carrying so much money made him nervous. To relax, he read aloud to Pirouz from a newspaper, the *Musavat*, which he often read to his students back in Mashhad and Hasanabad.

"The Majlis are agitating the shah's regime again," Reza said. As the locomotive eased into motion, he looked up at the great billows of steam in the air.

"Will they become the seat of power?" Pirouz asked.

"Many dream of this, but the shah and his cabinet have many supporters."

"But don't the merchants have lots of money?"

"Ah, one would think that the Majlis—the merchants and professionals—have lots of money, but often their pay comes from the treasury. I myself have not been paid in months."

Pirouz pulled a string from his pouch and gave it to Reza. "Make a knot that you think I can't untie."

Reza looped the strand over and under, making a Ghiordes knot, a weaver's knot.

Within seconds Pirouz had freed the tangled string.

"You are a good magician," Reza said, wondering still why Arash's battalion officer sent this child with him to Isqhabad.

"That was too easy," Pirouz said, giving Reza the string again. "If Anahita is in Isqhabad, how will we ever find her among so many?"

Reza wished his young companion hadn't raised that possibility. He tied the boy another knot and then focused again on his newspaper.

Disembarking the train in Isqhabad, Reza and Pirouz walked past a vendor selling fur caps to the arriving passengers. Pirouz tried one on. "I want one of these," he said, pressing the earflaps against his head.

Reza removed the hat and gave it back to the vendor.

His old maps weren't going to be of much help finding the current slave market, so Reza and his young companion made their way to the noisy bazaar, where they would inquire about the...the *bazaar bardeh furushi*. The very mention of the place shamed him. In the tinsmith's stall, where a boy with blackened hands oiled engraved platters and jars, Pirouz patched together sentences in several dialects before he landed on one that the apprentice understood. The worker lowered his voice to give Pirouz directions. Reza strained to hear above the sound of the clanking pots, *samovars*, and tea trays through which customers rifled. He wondered where Pirouz learned so many idioms.

"Let's go." Pirouz tugged on the schoolmaster's arm.

Reza wanted both to find Anahita there and *not* find her there—the possibility of her being among the women for sale began to overwhelm him. He doubted whether he could stand up to the heartless men who would run a slave trade and he worried that trafficking might be illegal here, that the authorities might no longer look the other way. He and Pirouz could be thrown in jail for patronizing the slave market.

That evening they found the bazaar bardeh furushi behind closed doors. Reza hesitated, taking a deep breath before knocking. A large man opened the door but stood blocking the entryway. "May we come in?" Reza inquired.

The man with his arms crossed appeared not to have heard him.

Pirouz stood on tiptoe and whispered into Reza's ear. "Show him your money belt. Prove that you are here for business."

Reza looked at young Pirouz beside him. The boy shrugged. Reza lifted his *shalvar kameez*, showing the guard a glimpse of where his money pouch bulged from his waist sash. The man stepped aside.

The auction room, an old house and courtyard, overflowed with clusters of women, some of whom were only partially draped in cloth. Their skin appeared weathered from sun and hardship. Reza blushed, gazing at the women only long enough to discern if they were Anahita, then respectfully averting his eyes. He should not have allowed Pirouz to come with him.

The auctioneer was now selling a group of women. The prices seemed deflated, probably because of the glut of slaves for sale. Anahita did not appear among them. He overheard a man beside him whisper to a friend, "I will buy the lot of them, take them by train to Bukhara, and sell them there for twice what I would get here."

Reza took out a sketch of Anahita and showed it to the stranger beside him, explaining her story. He pressed coins into the man's hands and said, "Please send word to the governor's palace in Marv should you learn anything of her whereabouts." He repeated this tale many times over that night and the next, showing everyone he could the sketch of Anahita. He became disheartened by every blank stare, shake of the head, or eyes that filled with pity for him.

Pirouz befriended local street boys and learned how to sneak behind the slave-holding room to peer at each and every girl waiting to be sold. "Anahita?" he whispered to those who resembled her, only to have them shut their sad eyes, or turn away, as if they were too tired or too afraid to speak.

The next day, feeling exhausted and dejected—useless, even, as he was normally not one to give up until he achieved his goal—Reza boarded the train with Pirouz to return to Marv. Shoving his belongings on the shelf above his seat, he wished he had better news for Kadkhuda Farhad. But this endeavor was different than anything he had ever set out to do. He had no models from which to learn how to monitor the slave trade or track bandits. Frustrated, he snapped open his newspaper.

Eventually, Reza gave in to the lulling rhythm of the train. As it rounded a curve, he glimpsed women's headscarves blowing through the slats of the cattle car. Alerting his traveling companion, he gasped at the injustice that was taking place before his eyes.

"Pirouz, rather than disembarking with you in Marv, I will stay on. Please tell Kadkhuda Farhad I believe that these women will be sold in Bukhara. I will meet up with Farhad there."

Pirouz joined Anahita's family and Arash's battalion leader in the palace drawing room. A pet pigeon from the courier coop played on his shoulder, nibbling at his ear. They had gathered around a teak table to study maps of the land between Marv and Bukhara, including some of the ancient city maps that Reza had brought from Mashhad.

"Young man," Farhad said to Pirouz, "please cage that bird so that it doesn't soil the map." Pirouz did what he was told. Farhad tapped his finger on the parchment. "Looks as if there are many caravanserais in Bukhara. We shouldn't have any trouble finding shelter."

How silly to have to rely on a map to find one's way around a city—a bit like following instructions. Pirouz had better success navigating by the shuffles of his own feet—by the light of hookah embers, the whispers of *ouds*, or the scent of mulberry trees where he might rest his sleepy head.

Pulling the map closer, Farhad said, "The markets seem to be clustered just west of the town center. The bazaar bardeh furushi might be in or near this district."

Pirouz told them the news from Isqhabad about the slave market, but no information regarding Anahita's whereabouts. "Women were bought and sold and resold. They were chained at the ankles. Some had been made to work under the hot sun from morning until night, naked, collecting thorn bushes."

As Pirouz told the disturbing details, Farhad cleared his throat and gave him a stern look. Mojdeh squeezed her eyes shut and covered her heart with her hand. *Oh,* Pirouz hung his head in shame, beginning to understand what it must be like to have a parent who might be worried or sickened or frightened for you.

Anahita's grandmother glanced at Shirin. Tears filled the young woman's yes.

"Isqhabad isn't far from where Anahita and I were abducted," Maman Bozorg said. "But I still don't think it was slave traders who kidnapped us. After all, they took only Anahita and me and they stole no camels or sheep." She held Mojdeh, stroking her arm as she talked. "One of them, I believe, spoke with a foreign accent. I wish I could remember what he said…I think it was a word for *Stop!* He said it when one of the men intended to hit me."

"*Arrêter?* Is this the word?" the battalion officer said.

"Yes, I believe so."

"He spoke French," the officer said, pulling on his chin. "Much of the nobility of Iran speak French."

"Hmm." Farhad pressed his lips into a thin line.

Pirouz fingered the juggling balls in his satchel. *Could I practice while the adults talked?* But he held back. He'd been living in Arash's palace long enough to know that there were different rules inside compared to the freedoms he had when living on the street.

Maman Bozorg said, "I seem to recall having met an acquaintance or relative of the khan who spoke French." Everyone glanced at her, but no one concurred.

"We shall leave for Bukhara tomorrow," Farhad said to his mother. "You and Mojdeh and Shirin are to make yourselves at home here. We will send word by dispatch, daily."

Pirouz caught the furtive glance that Shirin threw Maman Bozorg, a look that suggested she had no intention of staying behind.

"These may be dangerous times, but I will die of worry should I be left here to sit idle," Maman Bozorg said. She would not take no for an answer. "Not with Anahita's life at stake. I ushered this grandchild into the world with my own hands."

"That's my final word," Farhad said, leveling his eyes on his mother's.

Pirouz wondered whose word would triumph.

The three women left Pirouz and the men to their maps. Passing through the courtyard, Shirin kicked off her sandals to dip her feet in a pool of water. "They won't be able to search the public bathhouses, weaving workshops, or infiltrate any women's circles for information."

"Or harems," Maman Bozorg added as she sat on a cushion and joined Shirin.

Mojdeh placed a palm over her heart. "Harems!"

"I'm afraid it's a possibility," Maman Bozorg said, dipping her toes in, too.

"Farhad and Ali will never agree to let us go," Mojdeh said, glancing at Shirin.

"They won't," Maman Bozorg said, "but who's going to tell them?"

Mojdeh looked surprised, then thoughtful. "Why…that's the right thing to do." She paced behind them, wringing her hands.

"Maybe it would be better if you stayed here at the palace, Mojdeh," Maman Bozorg suggested, "in case Anahita is returned to us by the grace of Allah. You could send any news you learn of her to Farhad by courier to Bukhara."

Mojdeh held her mother-in-law's gaze. "Yes…of course. Perhaps I should stay. Anahita may well make it here on her own accord. And there will be our guests from Hasanabad to look after…" She trailed off into her own thoughts.

Maman Bozorg smiled. It was the first touch of hope she'd heard in her daughter-in-law's tone since Anahita's abduction. Hope carried the light of Allah, and the more light in the world, the better for everyone.

When dawn pinked the horizon, Maman Bozorg and Shirin hurried down the hall of the governor's palace. Outside, they went to the stables where the caravan for Bukhara awaited. They tossed their satchels into the reed litter strapped atop one of the strongest camels and climbed in. It was laden with textiles for barter, but Maman Bozorg, no bigger than a child, and slim Shirin nestled themselves among the saddle bags, blankets, and rugs with room to spare. They found it spacious enough to move their limbs so that they would not become too stiff while hiding.

One by one, Farhad, Shirin's husband, Ali, and finally Ismail—carrying a leather bag and Reza's scrolls and maps—came from the palace. With them marched soldiers and scouts disguised as nomads. A wise decision, Maman Bozorg thought. In uniform, they would alarm the Bukharan militia. The two women exchanged satisfied looks as they peered at the men through the weave of the reed basket. When the battalion leader let out a whistle, Pirouz came wheeling into view to join the caravan. Slowly, the camels pitched forward and back, struggling to stand under their burdens. Rocking their heavy loads, they pulled away from the walls of the palace, and eventually, the city. The horizon turned from pale blue to white as the sun journeyed through the cloudless sky. And a secret scent—a complicity of rose water and jasmine—filled the air.

Because I Love Her

Arash and his two escorts galloped east across the plains toward Samarkand. They had made good time to the oasis, where his scouts had reported that Anahita was last seen. They rode on to the escarpment of caves, which he recognized from previous travels, suspecting correctly that the largest cave would be the one in which Anahita's captors would have taken refuge. After surveying the cave, Arash couldn't take his mind off the bloodied rag. But he took heart that the footprints he saw could have been from Anahita's tribesmen. Perhaps they had already visited the cave in their own pursuit to rescue her.

Miles beyond the caves, Arash and his men came to a junction and turned north toward Bukhara, through a gorge cut into the desert rock. They followed fresh tracks nearly all morning until they saw where the trail doubled back. Arash slowed his stallion, took off his turban and scratched his head. "Surely anyone making a false trail wouldn't have ridden this far. It must only appear that they have turned back." They continued north, but the rocky terrain made hoof prints difficult to discern. Dismayed, they turned back.

The sun shone directly overhead before they returned to the junction where they'd started. Refusing to rest, Arash took a chunk of dried yogurt from his sash and ate it as he rode. This time, toward Samarkand.

After forging the great Rhud Amu Darya, they came to where the plain met the mountains. Arash knew of a small tributary nearby. He led his stallion to water farther upstream than his men, and there he heard the neigh of an unfamiliar horse. A hundred paces away, an Arabian stood tethered to a tree. Arash pulled the janbiya from his hip and listened. The water gurgling over pebbles grew loud.

A strong body came crashing down on him from behind. Arash grunted, rolling with his assailant side over side, each grabbing for the other's knife arm. Arash strained against the man's strength. He managed to pin his assailant's wrist to the ground as his scouts ran toward them. When Arash and Dariyoush recognized one another, they both yelled, "Peace!" The two released their grips, stood up, and brushed themselves off.

"I am sorry, my prince," Dariyoush bowed. "I had fallen asleep and did not hear your approach early enough to get a good look at you."

"I am pleased you are here, Dariyoush." Looking about, Arash said, "From where did you jump to tackle me?"

Dariyoush pointed to the large boulder behind Arash. "Less chance of scorpions crawling on me up there. It's an old habit."

Arash squinted at Dariyoush in the sun's glare. "You are looking for Anahita?"

Dariyoush nodded as he limped to pick up his turban and shake the dust from it. "I am following tracks, which I believe are from Anahita and her captors."

"My scouts and I followed your tracks from the caves," Arash said, noticing the bandage on Dariyoush's leg.

"Perhaps Anahita's captors took the north fork to Bukhara and are just superb in hiding their tracks."

Dariyoush's remark irked him. "Have you found any sign of them continuing east from here?" Arash asked.

"I have yet to look. As I said, I fell asleep for a short—" He cut himself off, apparently distracted by a lizard that scurried from under the boulder and around a small bone vial lying on the ground.

Arash followed Dariyoush's gaze. The vial looked like a container that would perhaps hold *suzan,* sewing needles.

Dariyoush's face reddened when he picked it up. "It's just something I'm whittling." He tucked it in his sash and pulled out a piece of leather and gave it to Arash. "I found this in the cave."

Arash examined the scratched inscription. "'The un…' I can't make this out."

"I found this message etched on the rock wall. The scratches looked fresh," Dariyoush offered.

Arash stared at the leather again. "It's the answer to Anahita's wedding riddle. Anahita wrote this." The two men broke smiles.

"Perhaps we're on the right path," Dariyoush said.

"But where from here." It was more a statement than a question. For the better part of an hour, Arash, Dariyoush, and the scouts searched round and round for anything that might suggest that Anahita's kidnappers continued east, toward Samarkand, but the men saw nothing. Arash signaled for his men to rest.

"They might have walked their horses in the stream so as not to leave tracks," Arash said. Dariyoush nodded.

Arash looked at Dariyoush's bandaged leg again. "Where did you get that wound?"

Dariyoush explained and said, "It set me back initially, or I would be farther along this trail, perhaps would have found her by now."

"It looks bad. Do you need respite?"

"I'm fine."

Arash held his gaze before looking away. The young man's remarks seemed a bit like hubris. "Can you think of any reason why slave traders would take Anahita to Samarkand?"

"Not one, agha."

Arash pursed his lips. He looked west, from where he'd just come. "I may have missed some sign indicating that they continued on the Bukhara road. It seems logical that slave traders would go that way."

"Unless..." Dariyoush said, hesitating.

Arash turned, waiting for him to finish. "Unless what?"

"Ah, it's nothing."

He's keeping something from me, Arash thought. "There's no time to doubt hunches. Anahita could be—"

As if Dariyoush couldn't cope with hearing the rest of Arash's words, he rushed to say, "Unless the captors are not slave traders."

Yes, Arash thought, something he'd already considered.

Dariyoush sat down to change his bandage, blotting the dried blood with stream water. His wound appeared swollen and raw.

"Do you know something I do not?" Arash asked.

Rather than respond, Dariyoush tended to his bandage.

"I'm sorry." Arash said. "I can't bear to think of anything bad happening to—"

"And you think that I *can* bear such a thought?"

Dariyoush stood up. His eyes cut like a sword. He nearly whispered, "Haven't you considered the fact that having grown up with Anahita that I am…that I am deeply concerned for her welfare?"

Arash just looked at him.

After a while Dariyoush said, "Please tell me how you could possibly love her so much, when only having met her so briefly?"

Arash eyed the horizon as he gathered his thoughts. "Dariyoush, I understand that you've known Anahita your whole life, but…how can I explain this? It's the intensity of the connection that I—we—feel for each other that makes up for time."

Dariyoush held his gaze.

"I truly believe that Anahita and I share such a bond and will grow in this love."

Dariyoush turned away, kicked a pebble, and stared at Arash again.

"I love her," Arash said.

Each gesture and every expression of the young Afshar suggested that he loved Anahita, too. It was hard for Arash to witness. Mounting his horse, he said, "I have sent word throughout the province among the Yomuts and other tribes with whom we are friendly to be on the lookout for Anahita. I will continue on toward Samarkand." His horse pranced in place. "Please follow the road to Bukhara. My subjects are there now, in case she appears at the slave auctions. Let us hope that one of us finds her before it is too late." Gathering the reins, he said,

"Thank you for your help, my friend. I am indebted to you."

One of Arash's scouts mounted his stallion. The other stayed to accompany Dariyoush.

Hands on hips, Dariyoush glowered into the desert, seemingly fuming that his prince instructed him to backtrack and follow the Bukhara road. "*Hoda Hafiz*," Dariyoush said to Arash, wishing him Allah's protection. But his words rang hollow.

A Child's Promise

Hawk stood waiting with a piece of rope. Despite my cries of pain, he lifted me onto his horse. I could not see through the dense fog as he tied my hands around his waist, but I could hear the ice cracking and the torrents of water rushing in the river below us in the valley. We followed seemingly endless switchbacks. I had little strength to sit up straight. *Allah,* I cried, *I am so weak.* Arash's letter had survived the avalanche, and it crinkled against my skin whenever I bumped Hawk's back. His nearness offered some warmth.

When we came to a smattering of homes on the valley floor, my hope increased. The place appeared to be a long-abandoned settlement in which only a few unkempt children lived. It looked like the village had slid downhill with heaps of mud into its present position on the side of the mountain, as if its equilibrium had fallen off kilter—just as mine had. I now suffered vertigo from the dizzying heights, from tumbling in the avalanche, and from slogging through the fog. With no roads leading here, I couldn't imagine why anyone would live in this squalor, where even the cypress trees grew stunted. I looked about for a hint that might tell me the name of this settlement, but saw none.

Mangy dogs roamed the paths between shacks, snarling as they slinked past. A pack of children ran between buildings. I couldn't make out whether they were homes, sheds, or teahouses. Even though the air felt warmer down here, I remained chilled to the bone.

Hawk stopped in front of a woven saddlebag that someone had tossed on the ground. It appeared locked. He pulled out his knife as if to slash open the bag and caught the obvious horror on my face. Only the lowliest creature would slice open, rather than pick the lock, on a saddlebag. "All right, all right. I won't destroy the painstaking workmanship of this chanteh," he said. "Especially, if you will reward me later." He laughed.

He must have known that the bag was worth more than what he would likely find inside. But the fact that he even thought about robbing from the poor in this village repulsed me as equally as if he had cut it. I walked on, not wanting to witness his rummaging, and stopped in front of the first hovel.

Hawk caught up with me. "Say nothing to these people." Then he walked inside. I didn't follow. Instead I watched the boys and girls outside. Their round faces and big smiles seemed a gift—a reminder of the innocence in the world. But Hawk wouldn't leave me to my own thoughts. He poked his head back through the door. "Get in here where I can keep an eye on you."

We sat across from each other in the smoke-filled teahouse. The heat inside the place began to thaw me. A frayed reddish-brown prayer carpet with a well-known Bukharan design covered the floor. But rather than pointing to Mecca, it pointed north, toward a life of slavery. I shuddered. The rug was so filthy it would take a treasure hunter to dig through the layers of grime to reveal its complete pattern. Its dishevelment, like everything else in the community, suggested a world terribly out of order. I swore I heard a cackling, perhaps that of a perverted *jinn*, seep from the carpet's wool pile.

A man wearing sandals stuffed with straw stirred a pot in the kitchen. The air smelled of cardamom. He ladled two bowls of the steaming liquid, placed some *naan* on a plate, and brought the food to us. Then he left the shack. Hawk slurped up his soup, grabbed a piece of bread, and followed the man. The lentil soup soothed me. As I ate, I overheard them talking about weather and guns and the whereabouts of any caravans. I felt grateful to have survived the avalanche, despite my injuries. Thankful to be out of the wind, and for the roof overhead.

As I broke off a piece of bread, a child peered at me from the kitchen. I smiled and patted the bench beside me. The girl ducked behind the kitchen wall. Seconds later, she looked at me again. I patted the bench, and this time the child drew near. She reminded me of the children in the orphanage in Mashhad that I had visited years ago with my mother and Maman Bozorg. The poor children there starved for attention and human touch.

"Anahita is my name. What is yours?" I whispered.

The child didn't answer me. I wondered if she had a mother. I hadn't seen any women about. The girl climbed beside me on the bench, fingered my colorful but torn skirts, and touched the bangles on my wrist. I took one off and slipped it onto the girl's skinny wrist.

The child's face became like the moon when she smiled—rounded and radiant. "Keep it," I said.

"Thank you," she uttered, climbing onto my lap. The girl's action caused me much pain in my ribs, but she seemed so content that I didn't ask her to move.

"Tell me a story."

"A story? Let's see…do you like fairytales?" I asked, glancing over my shoulder at the door.

The little girl nodded, twirled the bangle around her wrist.

"Well, if a stranger comes to town and asks you where you got that bangle, be sure to tell them that a princess named Anahita gave it to you."

"You're a princess?"

I nodded, supposing that my colorful dowry skirts and jewelry made the little girl think that I might be one. "Almost. You see, once upon a time a nomad girl was betrothed to a terrible khan. But the girl refused to marry the chieftain of her tribe and wove a riddle into her wedding carpet, for she knew that whatever man could solve the riddle would be her *yar.*" I paused to think of what to tell the wide-eyed girl next. "One day she met a prince in the marketplace, but she did not know he was a prince, for he wore no royal clothing. Sadly, the two became separated and never learned each others' names or tribes. The prince spent the whole summer, fall, and winter searching for the girl, only to be told that in order to marry her, he must compete for her hand."

"Did he guess the riddle?" the girl asked, twirling her hair with her finger.

"He did indeed," I said.

"Did they have a wedding? Did the princess wear a sequined veil?"

I didn't have the heart to tell her the real ending to the tale. "The wedding is to take place very soon, and yes, the bride will wear a veil with a thousand sequins! But you mustn't tell anyone you know," Anahita whispered, "or you might break the magic spell, and she won't become a princess."

The little girl smiled. "I won't break the spell. I want her to become a princess. Could I become a princess someday?" The question nearly crushed me. I doubted the child would ever leave this valley.

"You most certainly can." I listened for the men's voices outside. "You look very smart. Will you help me?" The little girl's eyes brightened, as if surprised that a grown-up would ask her this. Just then the door creaked. "Shh. Sit absolutely still, sweet one." The child was so tiny that, were Hawk to peer inside, he would not see the girl in my lap. I broke a piece of bread, pretending to eat. I didn't dare turn my head. The moment seemed endless.

I flinched when Hawk shouted, "Have you eaten?" The little girl slid off my lap and under the table. He grabbed my arm. "We're leaving as soon as I buy a gun."

I got up and walked past Hawk to distract him from seeing the child. Perhaps I'd get a second chance to ask her for help. Stepping outside, I told Hawk I was in too much pain. I could not go on. I was tired, still hungry, my arm felt as if it were broken, and it hurt badly to breathe. Glancing about, I thought there might be one decent person here who would come to my rescue. I needed more time. I wanted to ask someone exactly where I was. I asked Hawk if we could stay the night in the village.

"No."

"While you are waiting for your gun to arrive, could you at least find me some decent footwear, gloves, and a warm cloak? I'll need them if you intend to march me over any more mountain passes." I wanted him to leave me alone so that I could tell someone about Muh…Mahan.

"What am I, your handmaid?" He crossed his arms.

"If you deliver me to your 'client' or the slave market in Bukhara and I am as beaten up or in worse condition than I am now, I don't think it will be to your advantage."

Hawk fingered a strand of my hair that strayed from my headscarf. "Damaged goods—especially when they are beautiful women—still bring high prices at the auctions."

I swatted his hand away and stepped back, letting out a gasp of pain. My ribs.

Pure amusement lit Hawk's eyes.

"We would make better time had I a decent pair of boots."

"You have been taught to look after yourself, haven't you? Quite forthright for a woman."

I turned away. A gust of wind tore a piece of parchment off a nearby shack. It wrapped itself around my calf. As I peeled the mud-splattered sketch from my clothing, an image of a Qajar official unfolded. He wore a hat with an emblem of a lion and a sun on it, and held a handful of women up-side-down by their ankles. Beside him stood a Russian. The caption read: "Asif al-Dawlah, governor of Khurasan, sells Quchani Iranians to Russians as if they were chickens." Covering my heart with my hand, I thought, this could not be true. My fellow Persians would never do such a thing.

آذربایجان
۱۹۰۷ ۱۳۲۵
نمره ۱۳
بازار خراسان

Gold Coins and Silver Bangles

Arash and his scout came to a belt of juniper and pine alongside the trail at the base of the mountains east of Yakkabag. The sweet scent of juniper lured Arash toward the summit. Riding on, his scout slowed to a halt and jumped off his horse. Arash stopped, too. The scout plucked a madder-colored thread shimmering in the waning sunlight from a branch of shrub oak and held it up. Taking the thread, Arash felt a presence. Anahita's. The air he breathed then held an added savor—a familiar trace of rose water and lanolin.

He had a choice. Follow the Yakkabag-Samarkand road or travel over the summit. Because the Samarkand road was more traveled, regional regiments often controlled the caravans that came and went. Kidnappers or slave traders would avoid taking that route. Arash turned to his scout. "Follow the main road and wait for me at the first caravanserai. If I do not come by morning, change course, and look for me at the teahouse on the Bukhara road."

"Which one, agha, there are two?"

Arash had forgotten about the new teahouse that had been built just north of the original one so as to attract the caravans traveling south from Bukhara first.

"Shall we meet at the teahouse where the owner dangles a fake spider on a string or at the place where the *naghal* tells stories?"

"The owner keeps that spider, still?" It had been years since Arash had been through this territory.

"Children beg their parents to stop there."

"Let's meet there."

Arash's scout bowed his head and spurred his horse on.

With luck, Arash could make it to the ramshackle village on the other side of the mountain by dark. Scrutinizing the slope, he knew it would be safe to walk up as the snow barely covered the rocks. However, he wasn't sure about the condition of the north face. Nevertheless, Arash began his ascent. Up and up he rode until he reached an altitude at which he became short of breath and his thoughts became hazy. He recalled the dream he'd had weeks ago—a disturbing vision of a jackal, dark as midnight, something delicate and white trapped between its fangs. And from out of the blackness—a crying, crying, crying. Perhaps a mourning dove surrendering its nest. It seemed like the worst kind of omen.

As the sun threw streaks of scarlet into the sky, he dismounted his horse for the last pitch up the mountain. When he reached the top, he saw signs of a recent avalanche. His heart thudded. Leading his stallion, he picked his way down the ravine as fast as possible alongside an outcropping of rock. The debris from the snow slide had piled high in places. Branches and whole roots of juniper trees littered the slopes. He found a piece of a saddle blanket half buried in the snow amid a cluster of spindly trees as well as a remnant of a woman's scarf. He knew this headscarf, the one with the tiny, red madder-colored tassels. *Dear Allah,* he prayed as he let go of his horse's reins to tear the remains of the scarf from the tree. Arash rushed about looking for any signs that Anahita might be buried beneath the snow. When he had explored all the possible places without finding her, he dropped to his knees. Crumpling the scarf in his fist, he held it to the heavens and shouted, "How could you have allowed this to happen! How?" Unclenching his hand, he held the scarf to his cheek and cried.

He dried his face with the scarf as he stood, then walked back up the slope to inspect a rock that appeared to move. As he came closer to it, he made out the head of a white horse with a gray streak on its snout, which lay covered with snow. Behind it, the foot of its rider broke the crust under which he lay buried.

Arash stuffed Anahita's scarf in his sash, grabbed the nearest tree branch, and began digging. The leg moved, and a muffled sound came from below the snow. He dug and dug, chipping away at chunks of ice, until he uncovered the torso of a man who lay trapped upside down. Arash debated whether to try and pull him free, risking injury to the man's back, but possibly saving him from suffocation. Since the fellow had lasted this long, he likely had a pocket of air to breathe. It would be safer to remove more of the snow around him before trying to ease him out. So he kept digging. Soon he was able to help the victim sit up. The man breathed deeply as he moved his fingers and limbs. Arash turned immediately to the horse.

"Thank you," the man finally uttered.

Arash studied him to see if he was armed, but apparently he was not. "Any false moves and I won't hesitate to kill you," Arash said. "What is your business here?"

The man rubbed his forearms to generate heat. "I am inclined to ask you the very same question, except that I owe you my life."

Arash eyed him.

The half-buried horse groaned. It might have broken its legs, otherwise it should have been strong enough to free itself from the snow. Arash continued to dig as the man he had just rescued slowly stood.

The man was now able to shake his hands and legs a little more vigorously to get his blood flowing. He appeared to have hurt his arm. Arash thought about lighting a fire for him, but the fellow would warm up as soon as he started walking down the valley. The man searched for a sturdy branch and tried to help Arash shovel the snow from around his horse, but he appeared weak. Both men squatted to feel the stallion's hind legs. Bones protruded through the skin on each of them.

The owner threw his branch to the ground. "There is nothing we can do for him." Spotting the rifle on Arash's horse, he said, "May I?"

"I will shoot him for you," Arash said. He would give his gun to no one.

The stranger knelt beside his horse and stroked his head. "You've been a good companion," he said. Then he stood and stepped back. The man's horse had a similar fire in his dark eyes to that of Arash's own horse—a kind of knowing. For a nomad to conceive of an existence without his horse or livestock is to envision certain death;

their lives were that enmeshed. Arash walked beside the lame horse, took aim and fired one shot.

As the man shoveled snow to bury the horse, Arash swallowed hard against the lump forming in his throat. This incident cut to his heart—his emotions shaken from the possibility that Anahita could also be dead nearby.

The stranger seemed to regain his strength quite readily.

"May I ask your name and why you have crossed this mountain?" Arash said.

The man did not respond initially. Arash stared at him.

"What would be my motivation to tell you the truth?"

"Perhaps this gun in my hand."

The man smiled.

This person was hoping for Arash to volunteer information first, so that the stranger could form his answer accordingly. Arash raised the gun to his shoulder and aimed it at the stranger. But the man simply stared into the barrel. Arash cocked the trigger. The two stood perfectly still. Something about the man's facial features looked familiar.

"I propose a truce," the stranger said. "I am capable of killing you without the need of any metal. But this will not help us find the young woman for whom you are looking…you are looking for one, aren't you?"

Arash said nothing.

The stranger continued. "I was hired by someone to find her. I imagine you and I are following the same signs."

"Such as?"

"The madder-colored threads on the bushes on the other side of this mountain."

"Who sent you?"

"A khan."

"From where did you begin your journey?"

"That's irrelevant. Though I have been instructed to take her to Samarkand, should I find her."

Arash couldn't think of any khan in Samarkand whom his tribe or Farhad's would have enlisted for help. "What khan?"

"An Afshar from Mashhad."

Anahita's khan! Arash stared in disbelief. Why would he hire someone to bring her to Samarkand? It made no sense.

The man continued. "The khan blackmailed me."

It didn't surprise Arash to hear that the khan from Mashhad would blackmail someone. Not wanting to waste more time talking, Arash said, "Please take your leave."

"Tell me who you are, and then I might trust that you will not shoot me in the back," the man said.

"I just saved your life," Arash said. "If you do not go, I will consider you foe."

The man turned and walked eastward down the slope, away from the village. Arash watched closely until he saw him crown the pass that led through the mountains toward the ancient city of Samarkand.

Arash stood silently listening for a sign of Anahita.

Upon entering the village, Arash found a group of rag tag children chasing hens. Without wasting time, and before any adults came, he said, "I am curious if a young woman might have come through this village in the company of one or two men?"

The children looked at one another, giggled, and ran off.

He strode to the nearest building. Not certain if it was a private or public dwelling, he pushed lightly on the door. Inside he found the filthiest teahouse he had ever seen. The door creaked shut behind him. Turning around, he saw no one until he looked down. A little girl peered around a table leg and ran away. When she reappeared, Arash caught the glint of a silver bangle on her wrist. He said, "That is a pretty bracelet you have." But the little girl—a nameless flower—faded away as a man, presumably the owner of the place, strolled out of the kitchen.

"If you've come for food, I've got lentil soup. If not, move on through town. Talk to the children again and there'll be trouble."

Arash wanted a chance to talk with the girl, so he said, "I'd like the soup." The bearded man spooned a bowl and held out his hand for coins. After Arash paid him, the cook left. The girl never returned. He drained his bowl of lentils and went to his horse. As the teahouse owner had suggested, it would be best to move on out of town, but only after he found the girl with the too-large bracelet.

Outside, a bent old man approached him. "What brings you here?"

"Just passing through." Arash swung himself onto his horse, nodded to the elder, and trotted off. He passed several shacks, catching no sign of children. At the end of the village, he glimpsed the girl crouching beside a water trough. When he stopped at the trough to let his horse drink, she skipped inside a broken shed.

No one seemed to be watching, so Arash slid off his horse and peered inside the shed. He saw the girl with the bangle. Kneeling on one knee to lower himself to her height, he said, "I've never seen such a pretty bracelet. Would you like to show it to me?" The girl hid her hands behind her back. "Did someone give you that as a gift?" he pressed. The girl merely blinked. Trying to think of a way to win her over without scaring her off, he untied a pouch from his sash. He pulled out a gold coin and held it out to her, but she wouldn't come take it from him. Arash took the coin in both hands, shook it and said, "I command you to tickle this little girl's toes." He set the coin rolling across the uneven floor. It moved swiftly toward the girl before wobbling up to her foot, touching the tip of her bare toe, and plunking on its side. The child giggled.

"Again," she said.

Arash pulled out a second coin. This time he spit on his palms, rubbed the coin between them, and set it into motion. "Tickle the toes on her other foot!" The silver piece landed exactly beside her other foot, and the girl laughed. She picked up the coins. "What is your name?" she asked.

Arash thought that telling her the truth might be the right choice. Surely the girl was too innocent to be cunning. "Arash," he said quietly, "but please don't tell anyone." The girl pulled the bracelet from her wrist and held it out to him. He crept toward her and took it, soon recognizing it as Anahita's. The tautness in his neck relaxed as relief washed over him.

"Do you know where the woman who gave you this has gone?"

The girl pointed north, down the valley toward the Bukhara road.

"How many men were with her?"

She held up one finger.

"How long ago was she here?"

The girl raised her shoulders to indicate that she wasn't certain. "Late afternoon."

Arash assumed he wasn't long behind them.

"Thank you, sweetheart. May Allah keep you." As he stood up to leave, the girl said, "She's a princess, but she looked hurt."

Arash tilted his head. "How so?"

"Her arm was black and she could hardly walk," the girl said. "I think that man she was with is a bad man."

Grimacing, Arash patted the top of her head and turned to leave.

"Are you a prince?" she asked, then shyly covered her mouth with her hand and ran away.

Arash took up the reins and jumped on his stallion. As he rode out of town, he watched over his shoulder to make sure that no one from the village followed him. The trail he chose perched higher on the ridge rather than the one close to the river. It seemed to offer a better vantage unobstructed by trees. He hoped to spot Anahita and her captor before the light left the sky. Looking back, two people traveled in the distance, high on the Samarkand road on the other side of the village. One of them could be the man whose life he had just saved, or, his own scout, who decided to come looking for him earlier than planned. He wondered if the little girl had sent him in the right direction.

Tamam Bas

The too-large boots Hawk found for me back in the village had cracked soles, but the only snow at this elevation gathered in the shady patches so my feet stayed warm. Alone with Hawk, my fear made me lightheaded. I shut my eyes for an instant and managed to bring forth Maman Bozorg's soothing voice: *Loving kindness is drawn to the saint, as medicine goes to the pain it must cure. Wherever the lowlands are, the merciful water flows.* My grandmother said knowing this allows us to love our enemies and cherish this imperfect world. Maybe those Quchani girls' lives had been perfect before they were sold. My world had been. Even before Arash.

The answer to Arash's riddle crept through the back door of my mind then, just as ideas or solutions to my weaving designs do when I'm not thinking about them.

Hours after leaving the village, Hawk stopped to allow his horse to drink and offered me raw lentils that he had bought from the cook. I ate a fistful and asked for more.

"Hungry, my little virgin of paradise?" He handed me pistachios from his grubby pocket. "You are as thin as a bow string. The emir of Bukhara may not find you so appealing."

"The emir of Bukhara?" I scuffled toward him in my ill-fitting boots. "He is seeking sigheh with *me?* How does he know of me? But you said . . . not the emir!"

Hawk watched a flock of starlings chattering overhead. "You sound like them."

I recalled my bearings on the summit. "Why had we been traveling east toward Samarkand before leaving the village?"

"Perhaps you should have asked Mahan that question before he perished." He laughed. "That plan was his and his alone. I always had my own designs for you. It is sheer fortune—or fate—that nature chose which one of us to aid."

We both turned to the sound of a stone tumbling on the mountain. An eerie sense of my own downfall resounded in that rock. "Let's go," Hawk said, picking me up. I started to squirm, but it hurt my ribs so badly that I stopped. It was futile to fight him, and my injured arm was nearly useless. A bandage packed with snow to prevent the limb's swelling could have helped, but Hawk had not allowed me to take the time.

The valley darkened with shadows as we galloped along a path that trailed gently downward, farther away from the village where I had left my hopes in the hands of a little girl. Hawk refused to stop for sunset azan, so I recited my prayers on horseback. *"La ilaha il Alla."* There is no god but God.

"You think Allah is listening to you, my azizam?"

Yes, I thought. God is The All Merciful.

When night fell, Hawk and I took refuge in a cave. He lit a fire and pulled his water pipe from his saddlebag. Then he reclined with his legs stretched in front of him, his back to the cave wall. Each time he inhaled from the mouthpiece on his pipe, the burning embers of the tobacco coals glowed fiercely, making his green eyes gleam like a night predator. Whenever his gaze fell on me, his irises seemed to darken with needs long unsatisfied. *Come . . . come . . .* they said to me, causing ripples of shaking in my shoulders and legs, and even my teeth to chatter. I normally liked the soothing burbles of a water pipe, but tonight I found his hookah menacing. Even so, I benefited somewhat as he seemed lost in thought, his smoke taking part of his attention away. Then, as if he had read my mind, he said, "Do you want to know my name?"

I was taken back.

"I said, do you want to know my name?"

His growl frightened me. Until now, he seemed only mean spirited, but this question seemed more disturbing. I could hardly see his face through the cloud of smoke about his head and couldn't read his expression.

"Yes, I would," I answered carefully.

"My name is Tamam Bas."

Surely his parents were quite odd, deranged maybe, for naming him *Enough. Finished!*

"What's the matter my little Qajar princess? Do you not like my name?"

I didn't want this conversation to continue.

"I asked you a question," he hissed. His water piped seethed, its cords entangling.

"I neither like nor dislike your name."

"Oh, that's beautiful." His laughter split the chill in the air. "You are one clever woman…or perhaps I should say, girl … as actually—" He put down the pipe's mouthpiece, not bothering to finish his sentence. "I intend to sell you to Emir Abdullah of Bukhara. He is in desperate need of a male heir and is looking for women who will enter into sigheh with him. When he sees you, he will reward you and me broadly."

"I would think that the emir would not want to enter into a temporary marriage with me since I have been abducted."

Tamam laughed loudly as he slid beside me. "Ah, yes—how fragile a woman's honor is. But purity is the emir's least concern. He is taking a different woman into his harem every week until one of them produces a son. Perhaps chastity would be more important to him were he looking for a permanent wife."

My scalp went tingly as I became starkly aware that this was to be *my* plight. I could understand how some women who were desperately in need of financial security, or someone wanting to raise her status through the bride wealth received from such a marriage, would look favorably upon an opportunity for sigheh.

Tamam drew on his pipe.

But even though sigheh empowered women by allowing them to choose their husband, negotiate their bride price and the length of the marriage, it still made me cringe. Most clerics did not support it.

Tamam rested a hand on my thigh. My whole body seized. The night air quivered—shifted like hairs on the back of a jackal. *Dear Allah, help me endure this night.*

My awareness slipped from the beast beside me to the sound outside of the wind gathering.

What a place for trials and transformation did my Lover put me, but never once did He look upon me as if I were impure… I struggled to recall the rest of the ancient Sufi Rabi'a's words, spoken after having been sold to work in a brothel.

With obvious urgency—a ruby-tinged desire—Tamam tugged at the rope that bound my ankles and tossed it behind him with a flourish. I flinched. A high-pitched tone rang in my ears, as if my mind were signaling an alarm, that it would not, could not, bear this horrific threat to its well-being. It wanted to shut down.

"Now, azizam …." he said.

Dear sisters, all we do in this world, whatever happens, is bringing us closer to God.

Squeezing my eyes shut, I imagined Arash only steps away, his temples throbbing at the sight of this man sitting so near to me.

My legs quaked. My teeth clenched. I could not work my muscles. I lay frozen. My scream was imprisoned in my throat.

I felt Tamam lean away. Exhaling smoke, he fastened the cord onto his water pipe. Intuition told me to stay still—a message traveling imperceptivly as pollen.

I heard a *wishhh* sound and opened my eyes as a dagger came flying.

A dagger came flying.

Tamam gasped, reaching for the blade that had sunk into the flank of his back. He rolled away from me and collapsed.

No. That was not fantasy. Through my tears I made out the silhouette of Arash's face, his dark ringlets of hair. Arash rushed inside and pulled me into his arms. I buried my face in his chest. "Shhh," he said, rocking me. "Everything will be all right."

But I couldn't still the ringing in my head. Nor the images: Green-eyed jackals. Emirs. Gaggles of slave women.

12

Pink Dagger

"Anahita, my *yar*," Arash said, kissing me on the head. "We must leave this place."

I clutched my side and gasped in pain as he helped me to my feet. The sound of Tamam's rattled breathing grew weaker. "Will he live?" I asked as we walked to Arash's horse.

"No."

I had never seen a man killed. I numbed, refused to think about it.

"I know of a sanctuary with a hidden seep. It is the most beautiful waterfall in the high desert. We will ride there and rest. No one will find us." Arash touched the welt on my cheek. "Has he..." he hesitated, his jaw line taut. "Has he hurt you otherwise?"

I blushed with shame. Did he mean, "Have you been raped?" Surely he would not be so insensitive. His eyes reached into my soul for an answer. But to acknowledge my tainted honor for traveling with such men would bring a flood of tears. "It no longer hurts," was all I could answer. Talking about this would invade the part of me that I'd fought for *days* to build armor around. Every muscle in my body constricted. No one would disarm me.

Arash looked down. Perhaps he understood. "I found a remnant of your head scarf on the mountain. I feared for your life."

I clutched my rib as I took a deep breath.

Arash unwound his turban and slipped the cloth around the small of my back. "Let me make a brace for you. It will support your ribs, and you will feel less pain." When I tried to lift my arms for him to work the fabric around my chest, he noticed the bruises on my right forearm. "Is it broken as well?" he asked.

"I don't think so. It has not swelled much."

Arash gently smoothed the bandage around my bodice. With his hands on me, I could feel my slightness. "When did you last eat?" he said.

Cradling me in his arms, he carried me to his horse. He kissed my forehead. "Tell me you are well, that he has not crushed your spirit."

After tying Hawk's horse to ours, we mounted Arash's stallion and rode under the light of a three-quarter moon into a warm desert wind. My muscles started to decramp like a camel's might, just after its untoggling from the grinding stone. Eventually, I found the courage—the energy—to tell my story.

"And I dug him up!" Arash exclaimed, realizing that he'd saved Mahan's life. He whistled. "That may be one of the most ironic blunders of my life." We rode in silence for a while before Arash looked over his shoulder at me. "Anahita, I need to know that you are all right."

My lip quavered.

"I can't stand the pain of not knowing whether you were tortured or defiled in any manner whatsoever."

The smell of Tamam engulfed me. I fought back tears as I started to shake all over. Arash let loose of one rein, took my hand, and entwined his fingers with mine, stilling my trembling against his waist. "It's all right. Never again. No one is going to hurt you."

I breathed deeply—in and out. "Other than being forced to ride with them, as I am now with you, my legs straddling their bodies, my hands tied about Tamam's waist, and aside from sleeping with my leg bound to either one of them, I suffered no indecencies other than Tamam's attempted assault tonight."

Arash had squeezed my hand tighter as I spoke. "I am so very sorry," he said.

When we came to the seep and an inviting hot spring, Arash unrolled a saddle blanket on the sand for our bed. We looked at each other and then at the blanket. Arash ran a hand through his hair. "Perhaps I should sleep…" he paused as he looked about, searching for a suitable spot.

"Arash, surely Allah, our families, anyone would understand that you should sleep by my side. Please, I want your protection. I need to be near someone I love."

He curled up beside me. Touched by his breaths, I felt safe in his arms. My own breaths flowed peacefully. Just before falling asleep, I said, "Arash."

"Hmm?" he mumbled, exhausted.

"I know the answer…your riddle."

We awoke to a desert finch at first light, its sweet song reminding me of the miracles of the world.

"Arash," I said. "I knew you would find me. My faith in you kept me—"

He pulled me into his arms. "I want so badly to wipe away your scars."

I looked up at him. His body felt comforting and strong. I hugged him back lightly, as it hurt my ribs to do otherwise. My gaze fell on the natural pool. The weight of my sadness for all that had happened slowed my steps to the water's edge. I stared at my reflection.

"I look abysmal."

"You are beautiful."

I peered at him over my shoulder.

"Soon we will have a proper wedding with all the trappings," he said. He got up to join me by the water, scanning the canyon rim above to be sure we were still alone. "We'll be home in Marv, in the warmth of our own palace."

I broke a smile, it felt good. I splashed Arash. Laughing, I splashed him again. Arash splashed back. Before long, he picked me up, spun around, and we fell back into the warm water.

"Let this bath wash away everything that has happened in the past several days, Anahita." He held my shoulders and captured my eyes. "Everything."

I looked down. "People will talk. They will say that I have lost my…my honor. That I am worthy of no husband."

"Isn't that for me to decide?" Arash held my chin in his hand. "Do you think that your family and tribesmen will think any differently about you? I have met these people, and I think not."

I got up and began to walk out of the pool, my wet skirts challenging me. "No one will believe that I have not been touched. I fear to see the pity in their eyes, Arash. It will be hard to bear."

Arash followed me. "In their gaze you will find only concern and love, Anahita."

Turning to him, I asked, "Do you still wish to marry me?"

He pulled me into his arms. His eyes took on the soft manner of a deer's. He leaned in as if to…to kiss my mouth…but held back. Cupping my face with his hand, he traced my lower lip with his thumb.

The thin scar on his cheek accented the lovely contour of his cheekbone.

Then, pressing my head to his chest, he buried his fingers in my hair. As he caressed my scalp, my body relaxed in his arms. While I had dreamed about our first kiss—and our wedding night—I wanted to feel myself again. I wanted to give my whole body and spirit to him, not just these broken bits.

We sat in the sand as he told me about my family and tribe. After learning that Maman Bozorg was safe, I asked about Dariyoush. "Is he all right? Hawk—I mean, Tamam—knifed him badly."

"He's healing and seems to be getting on well enough. I asked him to look for you on the Bukhara road, and I sent my scout with him."

"That was thoughtful of you." I peeled my tunic from my body to air it dry. The letter I'd written to Arash was soaked. Now my good luck charm, I kept it tucked in my bodice.

"He seemed upset about taking the Bukhara road because he didn't think your captors were taking you to the slave markets."

I leaned away, my body stiffening. "Tamam wanted to sell me to the emir of Bukhara for sigheh. He told me he'd kill me if I told Mahan. I'm not certain what Mahan had in mind for me."

Arash furrowed his brow. "The emir of Bukhara! Sounds far-fetched." After a minute he said, "You know, Dariyoush suffers greatly. He is very much in love with you, Anahita."

I didn't want to hear this. My heart already felt heavy, burdened by homesickness for my mother, father, and grandmother. For my cousin, Shirin. For my tribe.

Arash scanned the canyon rim again as he leaned back on both elbows to enjoy the warmth of the sun. "Dariyoush found your message scratched onto the cave wall, though he couldn't read it. He has better eyes than me. I, however, found that bloodied rag." He looked at me.

I explained what I had done. "I wish we knew the news of the rest of my tribe."

"I'm certain they have reached Marv by now. I left Ismail, my advisor, whom I think you will like, with orders to follow your father's every request upon his arrival—all resources shall be at Kadkhuda Farhad's disposal. He and Ismail are likely en route to the slave markets in Bukhara. I gave my advisor orders to travel with enough money to buy you back at any cost."

I drew my legs up and placed my elbows on my knees.

"Schoolmaster Reza and my young servant Pirouz took the train to Isqhabad to scout out the slave market there. If they received no clues of your whereabouts, they were to go on to Bukhara and join forces with your father." Hearing about the plans for my rescue overwhelmed me.

I cupped my chin in my hands. "I suspect my mother has yet to raise her head from her prayer carpet."

Arash nodded. "I can understand that."

I began to cry.

He sat up, took one of my hands, and wiped the tears off my face. "We'll soon be to Marv, and all of this will be a memory."

My breaths came ragged.

"I was going to save this news as a surprise, but I think it will cheer you up. Want to hear it?"

I nodded.

He caressed my hands inside his. "I have refurbished one of the rooms with a fireplace in the governor's palace for your weaving atelier. It's trimmed with rosewood, and the hearth stone is made of your favorite—"

"Redrock from Abadi-e-Golaub?"

"The very same." He smiled.

I covered my mouth. "You didn't."

"Between its soft color and the wood, I'd say it's the coziest nook in the palace. You might find me intruding—catching repose on your daybed—more often than you would wish." He leaned back, crossing his arms behind his head as he would on my bed.

I laid my hand on his stomach. "I will always welcome your company."

"This fills me with joy. But mind you, I would expect that a marriage can benefit from space in the togetherness." Arash rose slowly, perhaps reluctantly. He offered me his hand and gently pulled me up. "It's time we go."

"Arash, would you mind if I hired a tutor in Marv? I want to continue my studies."

Walking to the horses, he said, "I have already found you one. I hope he proves to be as suitable as Master Reza."

"I trust your judgment."

Arash grinned. His expression reminded me of a boy caught with the white foam of fermented mare's milk about his lips. "Maybe you shouldn't."

I tilted my head sideways, suggesting he explain.

"It was a difficult decision. Quite truthfully, Ismail would tell you that I hired the second-best teacher."

"I don't understand."

"Because the best qualified is too…too exceedingly attractive." Arash winked at me, and my face warmed. "I would be jealous of the time he spent with you."

I smoothed my skirts and laughed. I'd never seen this rather playful side of Arash. I liked it.

But this light mood of his soon fled. Before leaving the hidden seep, Arash gave me a jeweled dagger. I ran my fingers over the sapphire and the beaded floral design. "It's too pretty to be a weapon."

"The road ahead isn't safe."

We climbed out of the hidden pool together on Arash's horse, with Tamam's in tow. Arash studied the horizon and spurred his stallion toward the Bukhara road. Sunlight shining through mulberry leaves threw mottled shadows on the ground. I wrapped my arms around him, feeling calm and content for the first time since my kidnapping. My bandages helped keep my ribs more comfortable. I was utterly drained of energy. The rhythm of the horse and the sun's warmth made me sleepy.

I awakened to the *thwish* of something rushing through the air, like that of a huge bird on wing, followed by a thud. My body crashed against Arash's and someone else's. Our assailant must have jumped from the mulberry trees. Pain seared my chest as the three of us hit the ground. The smell of blood mixed with the odor of sweat. The dappled light merged with darkness. I fell unconscious.

Dust

I lay knotted like a babe in the womb on a blanket watching Mahan as he practiced his martial arts. He no longer wore his mask. His nose, ears and lips were different than I imagined, smaller. Arash was nowhere in sight. As I lay there, the sura in the Qur'an on women came to mind: *Men are their protectors and maintainers.* In whose world? I wondered. Apparently, this didn't apply to me anymore. A laugh burst from my throat. Guttural. It didn't sound like me. I rarely resorted to sarcasm, but it seemed that's all I had left.

When Mahan turned his head in my direction, our eyes met. I didn't look away. In this pit of despair, upholding social codes between men and women, between kidnapper and kidnapped, seemed *tazahor*, superficial. "Where is Arash?" I croaked.

I don't think he heard me. My throat was so dry and my voice so brittle, I hardly heard myself. Walking toward me, he said, "Please get up."

91

"I can't."

"Must I pick you up?"

I felt dizzy and filled with new pain. "Just leave me alone." Curling up was my only defense. If Arash couldn't save me, who could? Would Allah? Perhaps the Merciful One couldn't bother.

We come and go, but for the gain, where is it?
And spin life's woof, but for the warp, where is it?
And many a righteous man has burned to dust
In heaven's blue rondure, but their smoke, where is it?

Surely Arash was injured or dead. May I, too, turn to dust.

Mahan extended his hand, but I lay there, a wanderer with no face, whimpering. "Why, why have I been put through all this?" I sobbed. The aridity sucked the moisture from my mouth. I think Mahan walked away. I rolled onto my back, drew my knees up, and placed the crook of my elbow over my face. Rocking my legs side to side comforted me. The motion reminded me of when my mother used to cradle me on her outstretched legs.

Eventually, an inner voice broke through my misery: "You've still enough gumption to talk back to him. Use this energy."

Again, Mahan loomed over me. I pushed myself to sitting and staggered to my feet. My legs felt heavy, stiff as roof beams. It proved difficult to hold up my head. Hair hung in my face.

"Sweet *gul*, you don't have any weapons concealed in the folds of your skirts, do you?"

"What have you done with Arash?" I asked.

"Don't make me frisk you," Mahan said.

Inches apart, we stared at one another. "Your weapon, or I will find it myself."

I clutched the folds of my skirts and raised my hems. "I have no concealed weapons."

"Please don't make this uncomfortable for the both of us."

Heat flushed my cheeks. I wasn't going to fool him. I sighed. Reaching into my tunic, I pulled out the knife.

"Thank you," he said, grabbing it.

"Draw the keenest blade and strike," I said, trudging away, half wishing he might put an end to this nightmare. An end to me.

"Climb on Arash's horse." Mahan put my knife in his saddlebag and then tied my hands to the saddle horn. As he tethered my horse to his, I squinted at every rock and dip in the sand for Arash. Praying for him seemed of no use. I'd fallen from Allah's view. Surely rust had encrusted any polish that once glistened on my heart.

"We'll arrive in Bukhara in no time," Mahan said.

"And that's supposed to make me feel better?" I growled. "You cannot sell a Persian chieftain's daughter—a prince of Iran's bride—to a slave trader!"

Mahan mounted his stallion. "Anahita, Bukhara is not Persia. It is an unruly principality beyond unnoticed desert passes. Even if a slave auctioneer were to believe your unfortunate story—you can't expect that your credentials will hold sway there. Only friends or relatives of the local emir could be so lucky."

"Oh, you mean we haven't left Khurasan Province?" My homeland. I sounded ugly, even to myself.

Arash's horse seemed to know my scent. He responded well to my weight and how I sat, without pawing the ground or trying to throw me.

Mahan looked at me, but didn't smile. He clucked and his horse began walking. Mine followed on cue. I could not discern malice from his expression nor in the tone of his voice. In this respect he was unlike Tamam. It bothered me that I actually felt grateful to Mahan for the manner in which he had treated me before the avalanche, when Tamam was alive.

"Mahan, what did you do with my fiancé? Is he…is he alive?"

"What do you mean, *fiancé?*" he asked.

"The man I was with when you abducted me *this time* is my betrothed, the governor of Marv. You attacked a Qajar prince in your haste to recapture me." Mahan didn't answer. But his face paled.

"Is he alive? I insist that you tell me."

"Yes, yes, he's alive. I did not know that he was your fiancé. Had I known…"

"What?"

Mahan said nothing.

We rode in silence. I held no fear of Mahan, no fear of slave traders, no fear of predators in any form. I felt nothing.

Were I at home at that moment and seated at my loom, the only color of thread that I would have chosen in order to weave my world—my state of mind—would have been a muddy gray-brown, the wool of a karakul sheep.

Like Wheat Fields

Days forgot themselves as I plodded in my saddle. Mahan said little, and I responded less. Words, like bottled jinns, found no neck through which to escape. No longer were my thoughts festooned with dreaming. Too tired to care, my eyelashes collected sand.

But the days in the quiet of the desert began to still my mind. The soft blue sage and prickly camel thorn reminded me of the infinite possibilities of beauty and danger in life from which no one is spared. I gazed at a mirage in the west. There, I witnessed myself dressed in clouds—diaphanous cocoons of silk or perhaps great billows of steam—and I walked without fear among innumerable stricken faces. The longer I contemplated this vision, the more it strengthened me.

The high desert air at my back swept me along. Iranians, I reminded myself, are like wheat fields—when the storm comes, they bend; when the storm passes, they stand up again. I was no exception. The way home, whether I liked it or not, was through Bukhara. *I would save myself. I would need nobody's help. Not even Allah's.*

Before entering a village, Mahan untied my hands and told me to behave as though nothing were amiss. "May we rest at their well?" I asked. "My ribs hurt from all this jostling on the horse." But more so, the tightness in the muscles of my back and chest caused a shortness of breath.

"Drink some water. We will ride on through."

Children skipped from their mud homes to greet us, followed by a handful of men. Mahan nodded politely, exchanging a few words with the locals as he led the way. Barking dogs nipped at our heels.

I leaned over the side of the horse so that I would fall. Landing hard, I cried out in pain. The children gasped. Two men rushed to my side. In a flash, Mahan was on the ground, striding toward me.

"I am kidnapped," I whispered to the two men kneeling beside me. They drew their eyebrows together and studied Mahan. But with his decent clothing and expensive lapis buckle, he looked respectable. They stood up when Mahan pushed his way through the small gathering to me.

"Are you hurt?" he asked.

I tilted my head back, no. "I must have fainted, I..."

Mahan thanked the men and helped me up. A villager offered me a skin of water. Holding me tightly by the arm as he pulled me away, Mahan said under his breath, "You're wasting your time, Anahita. Even if these men believe I am a slave runner, they will not mention this incident to anyone. They fear that other slave runners will punish them by taking their own women. You are only hurting yourself with such antics."

I yanked my arm from Mahan's, wincing as I climbed back on the horse. Leaving the village, I looked over my shoulder. The children had gone back to playing, the men had dispersed. Mahan followed my gaze.

"I am right, am I not? No one is giving you a lingering thought," he said. When out of sight of the village, Mahan tethered my horse to his.

A long row of poplar trees lined our route, hinting that perhaps the village had a custom similar to my own tribe's of planting ten trees for each newborn son, so that when the boys became men and married, they could cut down these trees to build the roofs for their new homes. The trees reminded me of the poplars by the stream in Hasanabad, where Dariyoush liked to sit and whittle. I missed home. I missed my mother. "Orion, Sagittarius, Scorpio...." I whispered. Even though I recited the names of the constellations my throat tightened with yearning for my family.

Leaving the poplars behind, we rode through steppes of sparse grass and tumbleweed for what seemed like days on end. A film of perspiration covered me. While it appeared that nothing could live in these parts, I saw an occasional stone grouse or a *markhur* with long, spiral horns.

"This land is so dangerously dry that even one's own mother would not offer a drink of water here," Mahan said.

The hoof of his horse nicked the bleached skeleton of a camel. Not the first we had stumbled upon. Ahead, a small party traveled northwest. Mahan kept his distance from them. Men and women trudged through the sand, their necks shackled together with metal chains. While the sun bore down on them, it seemed a wisp of cloud shaded Mahan's and my steps. If we paused, so did the cloud.

"Khiva bound," Mahan said.

I almost asked him where that was, but caught myself. In the past few days, I had stopped pestering him with questions of how far, where, and when, and plying him with suggestions of we should and you should. I showed him that I had the courage to deal with circumstances as they arose. While I acknowledged that I was the supplicant, I acted with dignity. He now seemed more willing to give me bits of information, such as "Khiva bound." I sometimes got the impression that he offered this information simply to break all the silence, the monotony of the wind.

How I longed for my cousin Shirin and our endless conversations, for those safe days as girls when we used to giggle as we spied on our village widow.

I looked away from the wretched travelers. The women looked bent and weather beaten. A sense of gratitude that I was not with them crept over me. Gratitude, too, that my captors had let my grandmother free, that she was not made to endure this.

Pondering what drove my kidnappers to such business, I found myself thinking about their names. I'd always liked the name Mahan, which meant: like moonlight.

"Do you know if it was your mother or father who chose your name?"

He glanced at me, but didn't answer right away. "I do not know who my father is."

The desolation we rode through deepened the gravity of his words.

"I am sorry."

"I don't want your pity."

"I only meant that I am sorry. I have been blessed with the most wonderful father in the world. He loves me and protects me, and all the women in our tribe. He would never dream of *abducting* a woman. Such an act is a failure of a male's duties, a sign of unmanliness—"

"Keep talking like that and I'll have to gag you."

My horse snorted. I pulled my scarf over my face to keep the dust out of my nose and throat. I nudged Arash's stallion to step beside Mahan's. "What do you intend to do with me?" This was one bit of information that I refused to wait for any longer.

He adjusted his reins and his saddle girth and then drank from his goatskin. Handing me the water, he said, "You've heard the saying, 'If she's pretty, her friends may be able to ransom her. If beautiful, her captor will probably not part with her.'" He looked over and smiled with a playful look in his eye. It held not the least trace of leering, like Tamam's gazes.

"So you will ransom me?"

"I have no intention of bringing dishonor to you and your family. But I need money." He spat, and then added, "I would think that your fiancé—a Qajar prince—would offer a tidy sum to buy you back from me."

"You could have asked him that yesterday had you not knocked us both out. I insist we go and find him."

"I am afraid that is not possible."

"Tell me. Why did you spare him?"

"Because he did not end my life when he had the chance."

Swaying with the horse, I closed my eyes. He will ransom me to Arash. The muscles around my eyes relaxed. When I reopened them, he was watching me. I didn't want him to enter this private moment in which I distilled this news.

The sun set in shades of peach and green. The air cooled. "It's time we pick up the pace, Anahita."

"Before we gallop off, I need to ask a question." It would be a long while before we spoke again. "Do you know if Tamam is still alive?"

"I've seen that man survive multiple wounds. He isn't easy to kill."

I studied Mahan's face, waiting for more words.

"I buried him."

Naghal, Storyteller

One night we stopped to buy a meal at a teahouse. The sign on the door read, "All welcome, bonded and free." I would find no sympathy here. It reminded me I was no longer in Persia.

A *naghal*, a storyteller, had been partway through his tale when we entered the inner courtyard. Mahan and I sat on one of the carpeted and cushioned platforms in a dark corner beneath a blanket of stars, only two strides from where we tied our horses. Here and there, little clumps of tobacco burning on the tops of water pipes lit the dim space, while smoke tinged the air with the scent of cherry. Quails perched in reed cages that hung from the branches of hazelnut trees. A young boy brought us *chai* in tiny glass cups. Mahan ordered naan, stewed tomato and eggplant, and lamb kabobs. "I've got to fatten you up before we reach Bukhara," he said, followed by a few terse words warning me not to attract attention.

I reached for a sugar lump for my tea and noticed a sketch on the easel beside the barefooted storyteller. He had drawn on his *pardah* a man with a peacock feather in his turban. The khan of my tribe dressed equally garishly. Despite my present circumstances, I couldn't get over my luck that our khan did not guess my wedding riddle and win my hand.

The boy servant placed circles of bread as plates in front of us. The naghal, whose eyes held an unusual glow, told a story about a locust plague that struck the village of Quchan and how the peasants made no profits from their stricken crops. *Quchan.* It sounded familiar. He spoke of fathers who were forced to sell their wives and daughters to slave traders for cash, in order to pay taxes to the governor—whom the storyteller drew with a feather in his turban. "It is a soul-burning tale," the storyteller's gaze swept his audience, "which I know sounds too awful to be true."

Those women's lives indeed sounded too awful to be true. My prospects, once I freed myself, were filled with love and stability, and relative wealth.

A man in the crowd asked the naghal, "Why is the figure you drew of the official in Quchan wearing a peacock feather in his turban? Why not a usual governor's hat, with a lion and sun?"

My throat caught. He was talking about those same women I saw in that cartoon. I felt again that damp paper wrapped around my leg.

"To save my hide," the storyteller said, patting his backside. "I did not want to tell such an ugly tale—I'll admit I embellished it a little—and then suggest it was a Qajar governor who demanded the high taxes and allowed the women to be sold."

Someone else called out to the storyteller. "How much of your tale is true? Where did you hear such tellings?"

Bonded and free. I looked around. His story likely fell on indifferent ears.

"You may read it for yourself. It was in last week's *Musavat*, that constitutionalist newspaper. All sorts of stories make their way through here. From Isqhabad to Samarkand, people toss newspapers, leaflets, journals, even personal letters out the train windows when they are finished with them." The storyteller shifted position. "The *Azerbaijan* went so far as to accuse the Iranian government of entering the slave trade. 'His Majesty will attend the new slave market that will be built in Quchan, and he will congratulate the nation in person.' Ha! Their sarcasm claims no boundaries."

"The man risks his life speaking out like this," Mahan said.

"Quite the opposite of you."

The muscles in Mahan's face grew taut.

I regretted having said it. Negativity breeds more of the same and would only sap my strength. I no longer wanted to dwell in that state of mind. *Good behavior, good speech, good thoughts,* my grandmother always said. *If your thought is a rose, you are the rose garden. If your thought is a thorn, you are kindling for the bath stove.* No more would my tongue prick as a thorn.

Mahan fixed his eyes on mine. "Did it ever occur to you, Miss Qajar Princess, that I took this job because…" he stopped short. Looking away, he said, "Be quiet and eat."

I wanted to know. I wanted to know, also, why I couldn't hate him the way I despised Tamam. Things would be simpler if I did. It would make it easier for me to betray him, or even pummel his head with a rock, if it came to that.

Hardly chewing, I began wolfing down the lamb, not sure when I'd see food like this again. I tried to think of a way to signal the storyteller that I was in danger. He didn't tell his tale about the daughters of Quchan as one of intrigue or titillation. His words resounded with the injustice done to these women. After another bite of kabob, I spotted the storyteller's *kalabash*, his alms bowl, tucked under his easel. He was a spiritual seeker, a dervish. I knew I could trust him. Maman Bozorg told me always to listen to my intuition.

The Sufi storyteller glanced around the teahouse, smiling at all of those who had come. When his eyes fell on our table, Mahan's focus was on his bowl of soup, which he held to his lips. In that instant, I leaned back to make sure I was out of his circle of vision and mouthed the word, *Komak!*—Help!—to the naghal. The storyteller looked twice at me, but averted his eyes just as Mahan lowered his bowl.

"We're done here." Mahan stood and pulled me up by the elbow.

"Hoda Hafiz," the naghal said to us as I stood to leave.

Leaving the teahouse, the Sufi began to whisper the beginning of a well-known prayer. "May God protect that much-traveled one, followed by a hundred caravan loads of hearts."

Convergence

Reza's train pulled into the station at Kasr-i Orifan. He wondered if tracks would one day extend all the way into the city of Bukhara and why the engineers suggested that they stop several kilometers short. He stood in the space between the cabins by one of the exits so that he would be able to disembark quickly and investigate the cattle car. When the doors opened, he hurried down the stairs onto the platform and shouldered his way through the cluster of people. By the time he reached the cattle car, it already lay empty. This slave business—which surely defied the teachings of the Prophet—worked like a machine with interchangeable people and parts. A caravan pulled away from the station. Horses and camels accompanied donkey carts overflowing with women. He ran to hire a driver to catch up with them. If Anahita was not among the women, he would follow the entourage to the slave market. Perhaps there he would learn something of her whereabouts.

Arash sat in the sand with Dariyoush alongside the Bukhara road. Dariyoush severed the rope that bound Arash's hands. The scout who had accompanied Dariyoush had ridden ahead.

"You had Anahita in your care but could not manage to protect her?" Dariyoush's question seemed to fill the universe. Arash wondered which would last longer, his feelings of frustration and embarrassment that he hadn't looked up to survey the mulberry trees—something he normally did to check for a possible ambush or leopards—or Dariyoush's envy, blame, and perhaps, rightful indignation.

"We might need this." Arash flung the rope to Dariyoush.

"He took your horse and rifle as well?" Dariyoush placed his hands on his hips.

"Correct me if I am mistaken, but wasn't Anahita abducted *first* when under your watch?" Silence, deep as an underground *qanat* opened between them.

After a while Arash said, "I'm sorry. This is not helpful. Yes, he stole my horse. We should be on our way. I am sure he is taking Anahita to Bukhara."

"We better tend to your wound before we go. Your bandage is saturated. That's probably what attracted these bearded vultures." Dariyoush squinted into the white sky.

Arash peeled off the bandage.

"Don't you think it is odd that whoever struck me down allowed Anahita to care for me before he left with her?"

"None of this makes sense."

The scout, who had ridden ahead, now came trotting back.

"A khan from Mashhad hired someone to track Anahita," Arash said, explaining what had occurred on the summit. "The tracker said that he was trailing her…just as I am." Looking at Dariyoush, he added, "Just as *we* are."

Arash traded off between riding with his scout and Dariyoush, stopping at every teahouse and worn-lipped well to inquire about Anahita.

Hours beyond the twin teahouses on the Bukhara road, where Arash's other scout had met up with them, Dariyoush shouted over his shoulder to Arash, now seated behind him on his Arabian. "The proprietor gave us half his attention at that last teahouse. He seemed more interested in entertaining the children with his silly spider."

Arash felt a pang of jealousy. *Thoughts of Anahita are as ever present on his mind as on my own.* "It is unfortunate," Arash said. "We can only hope that he will keep watch for her." Arash wished that the naghal at the other teahouse had been in. Perhaps he had news about Anahita.

"Her captors will never break her mettle," Dariyoush said. He squeezed his calves against his horse's belly and let out the reins, urging their horse to run faster.

Dariyoush, Arash, and the two scouts rode into the village of Kasr-i Orifan, a town just an hour ride from Bukhara, whose name meant "the castle of those who reached divine truth." The vast, dry stretches of the steppes were now behind them. While Dariyoush wanted to continue, Arash convinced him of the importance of this brief stop. "We must water the horses, get the local news, and make a plan for entering and leaving Bukhara." Turning to his scouts Arash said, "Please check the train timetables for the Bukhara-Marv-Isqhabad line."

Dariyoush knew that Arash also wanted to visit the birthplace and tomb of Baha ad-Din Naqshband, the founder of what was said to be the most influential Sufi order in Central Asia. Paying homage could bring blessings.

"Passing by this holy place without making pilgrimage is unthinkable to me," Arash said. "And Inshallah, they might have news of Anahita." He walked toward the Naqshbandi shrine.

Dariyoush squinted into the sun, inspecting the small minaret leaning over a nearby plaza. He found shade under a tarp someone slung between two buildings beside the public water trough. He pulled out the sewing needle container he had been making for Anahita. First, he tidied up the bird he had engraved on it the night before. Then he smoothed a splinter on a flower petal beside the bird. While working, he struggled with the guilt he'd been harboring for making Anahita this gift because she was spoken for. It took away from the pleasure of creating it. Never had he experienced this feeling when carving her figurines or spindles in the past. *Will the moment ever come when I can see her, know that she's all right, and give her this keepsake?*

When he glanced up, Arash had still not come back from the shrine. Dariyoush would never understand Sufi rituals, but the tranquility here soothed him. Almost at peace for the first time in days, he massaged his neck, rolled his shoulders backward and then forward, feeling as limber as the wood he whittled. But he soon imagined himself rescuing Anahita from the auctioneers, and the possible sword fight that might ensue. Stretching his bandaged leg, he worried about his endurance. This thought ruined his restful mood. He wanted to get going. It seemed like forever before Arash strode up to him.

Dariyoush stood, forgetting the little sewing container on the bench where he'd sat. Arash stooped to pick it up. Turning it over in his hands, he looked up at Dariyoush, who wished he could keep his face from reddening. "Are you making this for…" Arash seemed to reconsider what he should say. "It is handsomely crafted. I'm sure whoever receives this will cherish it." Then Arash turned to the horses. Dariyoush followed, feeling touched by a grace he didn't anticipate.

They rode with the scouts through the small town in the direction of Bukhara, passing vineyards and cotton fields cultivated alongside the Rhud Zerafshan, River of Gold. They kept a brisk but unarduous pace for the sake of their tired horses. Arash, seemingly lost in his thoughts, hadn't talked to Dariyoush since they had left the shrine. Finally, Dariyoush asked him, "What do those dervishes do all day, sitting quietly on their carpets?"

Arash looked up. "They practice the art of self-forgetfulness."

How does one forget oneself? Dariyoush wondered, but chose not to ask.

17

Bukhara

For a fortnight, Mahan and I traveled unnoticed over unprotected borders and high passes. I gained strength each day because he fed me well and no longer forced me to walk. Even the pain in my ribs had begun to subside. I trusted Mahan would not hurt me, but still, I could hardly sleep, awakening each morning with a jolt. Most days I fought a shortness of breath. I became more a prisoner of this anxiety than of my kidnapper. Surely, I could find a remedy. An herb. Valerian. Onions, even.

I worried that the glut of slave girls from Quchan would make it much harder for anyone to identify me among so many women moving through this territory. If I concentrated on each single breath, at times my anxiety would subside. I grew up believing that we are given what we need in each moment. If we trust in that, we need not fear what is coming, no matter the circumstances. Breath by breath, I rode on.

We slowed to a halt in front of railroad tracks—the first I had ever seen—which Mahan said belonged to the Isqhabad-Marv-Samarkand line. The train roared toward us, and the wind it created whipped up the sand and tossed my hair. I longed to ride inside a train like this one, which spewed great clouds of charcoal and white steam and was capable of such tremendous speed.

Soon the Zerafshan Mountains receded, the desert thorns turned into irrigated cotton fields, and we rode toward Bukhara—beautiful, blue, and proud. From afar I could see a tower—a minaret perhaps— the tallest I'd ever seen, puncturing the sky.

Nearing this town, I sensed that I was not alone with Mahan. *Someone is here, invisible to the eye, holding on to me.* Rumi's poetry informed my senses. *Someone who does not show himself has seized the front of my robe.*

We walked our horses through the old city gates, down Baha ad-Din Naqshband Street to Lyabi-Hauz, the neighborhood of the pond, to the central courtyard and mosque. Sufis gathered in front of a large, domed *khanegah*, dervish lodge. One of them in a well-worn garment studied me. The blue tiles on the mosque portals threw shades of color upon the adobe walls of the nearby alleys, cast a blue hue on the brows and wrinkled lambskin hats of the men in this northern city, and shadowed the mud-roofed homes, half-buried in the sand.

We rode beneath the branches of an ancient and yet still-leafing mulberry tree in the town square. Its thick trunk and deep roots drew water from the same reservoir that filled the pond. The water in the canal alongside the road rushed at my horse's hooves until it disappeared underground at the arch leading to the moneychangers' bazaar. I scanned the crowds for Arash, my father, anyone from my tribe, but saw no one. Men wearing Jewish yarmulkes and Indians in saffron-colored robes shouted at one another. They exchanged coins and languages with their patrons. I recognized some words of Urdu, Uzbek, Turkish, Tajik, and of course, Farsi. The most unfamiliar to me was likely Russian.

We dismounted and walked through a second small square to the blacksmiths' and shoe makers' rows. I studied the area, looking for possible places for refuge in the event Mahan changed his plans and I would need to escape. I hoped this would not happen because, alone, I would attract the wrong kind of attention and might wind up for sale at the slave market. Mahan offered me the best protection until he turned me over to Arash.

Bells rang. I turned toward this unfamiliar sound, a much fuller and deeper tone than camel or goat bells. There stood an Armenian chapel with a Christian cross on it. Like the *muezzin's* chant, the chiming seemed to signify a call to prayer.

Dodging fragrant fruit stands and water carriers, we came to the goldsmiths' market before entering a neighborhood of twisted alleys. We tethered our horses and waited silently in front of two great wooden doors for someone to open them from inside. My pulse beat faster when I realized we had arrived at a bazaar bardeh furushi, a slave market. I grabbed Mahan's arm. "You said you wouldn't bring me here."

"I'm collecting money owed to me." Mahan easily wrested my hand from his forearm as the door moaned open. He gave me a gentle push inside, but I dug my heels in. Taking my hand, he dragged me behind him.

Two men wearing the dark caps worn by locals ushered us into a side alcove without windows, adjacent to an enclosed courtyard. I shuddered and turned my back to a naked man chained in the corner. Mahan spoke with two large slave traders wearing black boots.

"I know people in high places," the captive shouted. "They will execute you for this."

"What say?" said one of the slave traders. "Do I detect *dissatisfaction* in your voice about your destination?" He snorted. "Dear slave, have you not heard it said, 'Better to be dead than a slave in Khiva?' Keep talking, and we can arrange for your transport there."

Khiva. I silently willed the poor man to keep quiet.

The other slave trader grinned, then said, "In Bukhara, we pamper our prisoners!"

Standing in this old house that served as the slave market seemed so unreal, like a horrible dream. The men smelled like garlic, tobacco, and sweat. I stepped aside to get relief from the odor and peeked under an arch into the courtyard.

Men gathered, some wearing coarse peasant clothing, others in embroidered linens. The auction room overflowed with clusters of women, some of whom were only partially draped in cloth. Their skin looked leathery, like those women trudging in the desert. I squirmed at such shocking indecency—exposed tresses of hair, shoulders, and thighs. *It could be me in there.* Men circled round the women, discussing their qualities as if they were breed mares. "This one has strong legs and ample hips." I could sense the anguish in the room—in the victims' forlorn faces, in the heaviness of my *own* body, even in the vines that shackled the wooden columns of the portico.

A group of armed men with palace insignias on their robes came in through a small door on the other side of the courtyard. One of them asked the auctioneer, "Do you have any Tarter or Uzbek women—those skilled with lance and arrow? The emir would like some to guard his harem."

"Mostly Quchani Persians, today, agha," the auctioneer said.

Those poor women from Quchan were here, the ones I'd heard about from the teahouse storyteller. My legs grew weak. I looked on with renewed curiosity and dread.

The emir's man scratched his chin. "Any Eastern European or Georgian, good concubine stock?"

The auctioneer tilted his head back. "No. Check back in a few days."

"Well I suppose we'll buy the whole lot of them for the emir of Bukhara. We'll match everyone's former bids and offer another thousand for the rest of them."

Several men with drought-stricken eyes who had been walking among the women—as if seeking to find the family members they'd sold—now looked even more crestfallen. Perhaps some had stumbled into money and could buy their wives and daughters back, while others had come because of terrible remorse.

I flinched when a voice came from behind me where I leaned on a portico column. "I have been to Quchan. I saw it with my own eyes, the collective weeping of the men of that village." I turned to look at him. He was speaking to me. My stomach lurched. "Some were tied to trees because they could not pay their taxes. They were whipped each time a passerby did not stop to give them alms to help them raise money for the governor. No one had the means to give his neighbor alms. There was nothing anyone could do but sell these women."

His words squeezed the air from my lungs. I wanted to flee. I turned, ran to the imposing wooden door, and yanked on its latch.

Mahan was busy counting his money. One of the thugs seized me. "How much for the girl?"

"She isn't for sale."

The slave traders laughed.

Mahan finished and led me away.

We walked our horses back through the bazaar. People stared at my full skirts. Most of the women in Bukhara wore baggy pantaloons beneath striped, silk *ikat* dresses—a fabric made by tie-dyeing the warp threads before weaving. Its bold, zigzag pattern demanded much work. Only the settled women wove this material, as nomads wouldn't have time for it.

I followed Mahan behind a synagogue that was once a Zoroastrian shrine. I could tell by the suns cut into its brick tiles. Festive carpets hung beside the entrance. One depicted a menorah, a traditional Hebrew candelabrum with seven branches. Another, a rendering of the prophet Abraham's sacrifice of Isaac. Focusing on my surroundings helped to restore my breath and ease the ache in my stomach. My eyes lingered on a weaving that showed a grey bearded man wearing a yarmulke and a beautiful woman in Persian robes and a veil, kneeling before a king.

"Queen Esther," Mahan said.

I turned and stared at him. I hadn't expected him to notice nor contribute to my musings.

He shrugged. "I have an interest in stories."

My eyes sought the carpet again. I had always liked this tale of a Persian Jewess who saved her people. A story reminding the Jewish people that, even in exile or as slaves, God was ever present. My mother and Maman Bozorg and Shirin would appreciate seeing all these symbols and ancient figures from "The Book" woven into *gelims*.

In exile and in slavery, God is ever present. Then why did I feel so hollow?

Several paces beyond the synagogue, the message of Esther's struggle crystallized in my mind. *Her beauty brought her queenship. Her courage brought her freedom.*

When we came to the Jewish quarter on the southern edge of the bazaar, Mahan stopped to ask a man for directions to Arabon Street. Though I hadn't asked, Mahan told me we were going to a safe house. We plodded down lane after lane, where the walls were punctuated by doors that were not only carved with patterns of six-pointed stars or arabesques and nightingales, but were also covered with paintings and woven images of shrines and grave sites that I believed must be in Jerusalem. The neighborhood smelled of burnt leaves, little piles the locals set on fire to help keep their streets tidy. Children tossed twigs into the *jube*, the water trench lining the streets, chasing them on their journeys downstream. A group of men preparing to slaughter a sheep and standing around a huge, iron cook drum, offered us a bowl of rice *polau.* They appeared to be preparing for a celebration.

It seemed the best of many dreadful possibilities to be in Mahan's hands. But I still didn't feel out of harm's reach. Those Quchan women haunted me.

When we arrived in the alley of the safe house, Mahan walked several paces ahead to the gate and knocked twice. He paused, then rapped three more times in rapid succession. When the old wooden door swung open, we entered a spacious, leafy courtyard with our horses. A man with a singed eyebrow looked at me and launched into what sounded like an argument in Uzbek with Mahan. When the man chewed on his mustache, I realized he was one of the three who raided our camp on the night I was kidnapped. I could understand some of what they said. That Mahan was careless, allowing me to stroll through the city unbound and undisguised. A khan was mentioned, but Mahan interrupted and the conversation changed course. They talked about the emir, who apparently was aware that Mahan was holding out with a "prized" slave girl: Tamam's and Mustache Man's original plan. The emir reserves the right for the last bid in all slave transactions. Heads off to anyone who betrays him, Mustache Man said in so many words as he made a gesture of chopping his neck with the side of his hand. If Mahan betrayed his wishes, the emir would order him tied to a rock and sunk to the bottom of Lyabi-Hauz pond.

"You aren't going to turn me over to the emir!" I said, though I knew Mahan was outnumbered now that the emir and his handlers were expecting me.

"Trust me," Mahan said.

"Trust you!" I laughed aloud.

"I'll respect the emir's rule and negotiate to get you out."

I shouted, "But I am already out! You must ransom me to Arash—" He grabbed my arm as if to shake me into lowering my voice. Before he could speak, I said, "Mahan, you are making the wrong choice! You are educated and talented. Why have you thrown your life away like this?" It stopped him short. It took me by surprise, too, that I actually cared about him.

Mustache Man wrapped a cloth around my mouth to gag me. He tied it too tightly. Same with the cord he used to fasten my hands behind my back. Then he stuffed me into a stiff cloak that local women wore, which included a hood and a mesh horsehair veil, so no one would recognize me.

I could hardly see or catch my breath as the three of us walked back through the neighborhood, back through the markets, past the Armenian church. I swore I caught glimpse of a turban with a peacock feather in it. Could that be my khan? I stepped lighter, thinking that someone from my tribe might be here.

As I walked through the square where the dervishes gathered, I experienced a similar sensation as when nearing this town: that someone besides Mahan was "with" me. *Someone is here, invisible to the eye, like life sweeter than life; He has shown me a garden and taken away my house.* I tried to hold on to the sudden comfort.

The Ark and the Harem

The sun sucked the moisture from my lips. I walked in the sandy square, only steps away from the long rampart that led to the entrance of The Ark—the ancient citadel where the emir of Bukhara made his quarters. Great sand walls extended from either side of the entry, stretching toward the horizon in four directions. A wood-columned gallery was perched between two brick turrets above the massive fortress doors. I shivered knowing that the emir and his royal subjects likely sat in that gallery to watch the executions that took place in the square.

A tremendous horsewhip hung over the entrance to the citadel, bringing to mind the tales I'd heard in the teahouse back home in Hasanabad, tales about the grandson of a Bukharan emir to whom Fatima, the owner, had been betrothed. A man who had killed twenty-eight of his relatives.

Outside the fortress, among all the caravan travelers and rag tag merchants, a troupe of musicians, acrobats, and magicians practiced. A young boy with large round eyes juggled several oranges. A small crowd clapped for him. His wide smile showed that he seemed surprised by his own feat.

Guards instructed Mahan to leave me among a group of women. He went ahead with Mustache Man to "negotiate." In other words, to collect his share of the money for me. I wondered how much I would sell for. Before he left, he turned to me, but didn't say anything, his eyes darkened and confused. I intuited his distress, an apology. His expression puzzled me.

The palace guards escorted me through the threshold of the citadel, where I inched along a cobblestone ramp with the frightened group of women from the slave market. Many were likely from Quchan. I had been destined to meet them all along. I marveled that my mind had refused to see this.

The girls appeared thin, sallow-eyed, and tired. I believed that I looked the least for wear among us. I wished I looked worse. Then maybe the emir would have little interest in me. None of the women around me were crying. Perhaps they had no tears left to shed.

Guards' niches and other small chambers lined the corridor, and their wooden shutters lay open for passersby to view inside. It appeared that people were imprisoned in these bare spaces, their ceilings too low for standing. But unlike a prison, the inhabitants sat on soft carpets and chatted with their cellmates. Two men shared a pot of tea. I overheard one fellow wearing a tattered striped *chupan* grumble to his friend, "May the emir be damned in this and his future life, his kin plagued with festering sores! I don't owe him any more money!" I wondered if the emir put these people on display to embarrass them into paying their debts.

A mosque graced the top of the entryway. Crimson carpets covered its floor. A pale-skinned and well-oiled eunuch greeted me and the other women with a bow. "I am Salar. I will accompany you to the harem." He turned, gesturing for us to follow. I winced at the sight of his bare back streaked with scars.

We walked down a narrow hall with several alleys leading away from it. The eunuch pointed to the emir's quarters at the other end of the lane. I could only see half of his gilded chair with red velvet cushions, which sat outside the royal offices. "This is where His Excellency receives people to hear their grievances," Salar said. Sheer drapes hung on the large windows of the emir's quarters. I glimpsed cut glass chandeliers.

Beside this residence was the reception and coronation court. The area held three spacious galleries, including one where the emir's throne stood beneath four marble columns. The galleries provided shade for the lucky individuals who attended public events at the citadel. Directly across from the coronation hall were stables. They led to the parapet that overlooked the fortress's front gate. The sheer size of only this portion of The Ark overwhelmed me. There would be little chance of escape. But I paid attention to the layout, as my life depended on it.

We passed through an archway with two shoulder-high urns on either side of us. The women and I glanced at the half-submerged door to our right. "That leads to the treasury," the eunuch said. Opposite this was a room filled with drums and other musical instruments.

"Behind it lies the artisans' workshops, the market, and the harem—another kind of treasure." I didn't like the sarcasm in his voice. My legs started to tremble. Once I entered the harem, they'd never let me out.

A lattice screen provided a partition between the new arrivals, such as myself, and the current harem dwellers. Satin bedrolls were stacked beneath a domed niche. Several women and girls embroidered suzani, cotton pillowcases, and dinner cloths. The girls' silk threads shimmered on the cotton weave, adding a strangely cheerful glow to the room. I noted the sound of crying infants, the smell of diapers. Toddlers ran about, one bumping into my legs. This place did not conjure the exotic image of a harem—such as the kind in *Arabian Nights*—of half-clad maidens lounging on cushions and smoking hookah pipes, awaiting their turn with their shah. It seemed more like a gathering of women and children from my own tribe. However, a few appeared preoccupied with soaps, perfumes, hair removals. Perhaps each of them wanted to be the one who gave the emir a male heir.

Hidden in the folds of the curtains there was a sense of overflowing rivalry. A girl with red hair and pale skin brushed by me, smacking against my hip without apologizing. The girl then joined a huddle of others who had been watching and whispering.

I was glad to leave them to their gossiping when Salar led us newcomers down a narrow flight of stone stairs to the bathhouse.

Silver candlesticks, as tall as me, glowed in each steamy alcove. The soaps smelled like perfume. In the dressing area, I removed my clothing, hiding my letter to Arash beneath the wooly *gabbeh* under my feet. My ribs hardly hurt when I bent over. I rinsed myself with the warm water from an ewer and inspected the bruises on my arm that had shielded my face from the tree during the avalanche. They had lightened significantly. Someone took my dirty clothes and exchanged them for a clean robe.

I slipped into one of the octagonal pools. As the hot water hugged my skin, I believed this to be paradise. Skimming my arms across the surface, the rushing water massaged them. I pushed my legs through the water, spread my toes, and delighted in my buoyancy. My calloused feet, after all the trudging, softened. For a moment, my troubles receded. As I reclined with my arms resting on the lip of the pool, I studied the domed ceiling. Its honeycombed vaults resembled stalactites inside a cave. The geometric and curvilinear lines expressed duplicity within unity. They hinted at shapes in the natural world imbued with the stamp of Allah.

Allah. I had not prostrated since Mahan took me from Arash. But I could not see myself in The Merciful One's hands, could not find The Compassionate One in my heart.

Two girls at the other end of the bath introduced themselves. They were talking about the new schools in Bukhara that were offering subjects like mathematics and history to girls and boys alike. They wondered what it would be like to attend them. After, they talked about the outdoor pool at the emir's summer palace, a daylong ride from Bukhara. The older of the two, Shahnaz, said, "The emir climbed the many stairs to his parapet, where he sat in the shade overlooking the palace pool, fanned by billowing draperies. When he snapped his fingers, the women he kept in his harem were sent to swim for him."

The younger one's eyes grew wide. "They swam outside where *anyone* could see them?"

"An outdoor pool *for women?*" I asked, marveling. I wondered if the harem women had asked for this. I had once petitioned that the use of the deep pool in our bathhouse in Hasanabad, which the men in our village enjoyed, be available to the women of our tribe. But the idea was spurned due to most everyone's shock and disapproval.

The pool at the emir's summer quarters sounded wonderful. Though, my opinion changed when Shahnaz said, "That's how he would choose his favorites."

My stomach turned. I changed the subject by asking the bathers where they were from. Several had lived in Bukhara and planned to enter into sigheh with the emir. "I have no family. I lost them in an earthquake. There is no one to support me," a local girl said.

Most of the women who had arrived at The Ark with me were from Quchan. One young woman my age, Parisa, confided that she had volunteered to be sold to the slave traders. "I could not bear to see my aged father tied to a tree and lashed." Hearing their stories, I became acutely aware of how lucky I had fared.

"You are like my kin," I said to Parisa and my Quchan harem mates. "I am an Afshar, and migrate very near your homeland. I am betrothed to the governor of Marv, a Qajar prince."

"You are?" Parisa exclaimed. I was touched by how she took my arm, held me like a sister. Several others swam closer, forming a semi-circle around me.

"Truly, and when I am rescued…" I paused when my eyes fell on an Ottoman carpet on the wall where I saw a motif that depicted the powerful image of a goddess, the same one that was etched in the cave so many nights ago. "When I *escape,*" I corrected myself, "I will tell the shah himself your story and will do whatever I can to help you return to your homeland." The sadness in the young women's eyes made me ache inside. This new conviction to help the girls from Quchan kept me from fretting about my own circumstances or feeling sorry for myself.

Settled back in the harem, servants gave us tea, dates, and goat's cheese. I ate my fill. It seemed like years since I had been treated this well. Parisa shared her dates with me after I'd eaten all of mine. By the time we finished our meal, my washed clothes had already dried in the afternoon sun. Although torn in some places, my skirts looked nearly as new as they did on the night I was kidnapped. The blood stains were hardly noticeable. Some of the women crowded around me to feel the madder-colored tunic I had woven and dyed myself. They talked about its rich tone, and one of the servants suggested that I ask to work in the weaving workshop.

"It's better than cleaning dishes or laundry," Parisa said.

One of the younger girls said to me, "If the emir sees *you*, he will give up wanting to take so many wives for sigheh." The room quieted. The girl's compliment—or bad omen—shimmered in the air. Someone on the other side of the lattice screen, from the seasoned side of the harem, stopped and listened.

Salar announced himself along with one of the emir's men, the pair filling the archway. "The emir wishes to inspect the next group of women. Please stand side by side."

The women and girls lined up dutifully—moving as quickly as camels unleashed. Their obedience surprised me. How fast the girls who had gossiped about me jumped into place. Their action stirred a terrible sadness. It hurt to see Parisa among them.

When I chose not to fall in line with the others, a few of the girls looked at me and nudged each other. I even brought a slight smile to one woman's face, who had previously appeared despondent.

"Is that all of you?" Salar asked, standing on tiptoe to see beyond the row of women and girls. "Come now, I see others in the back. Move on around to the side of the wall, where we can see you." Still I did not get up, not ready to give in so easily. Instead, I gazed over the balcony to the courtyard below. The sight of a young boy's face caught my attention. He peered up at me with large brown eyes. I'd seen him somewhere before.

The emir's assistant moved down the line inspecting the women. Asking to see their teeth, he selected both the healthiest and prettiest, and formed a new line with them. Several women turned to me, their faces full of worry. Parisa waved her hands behind her back, urging me to get up. When the emir's man saw me sitting, he growled, "*Never have I seen such blatant insolence!*" as if by speaking louder he might incite the emir's wrath or somehow bring curses upon The Ark.

Encouraged by the fact that he didn't advance toward me—strike me as Tamam did—I would fight to gain more ground, just as I had done with Tamam in the pictograph cave.

"Get up!" the emir's assistant demanded. All eyes turned to me.

Rather than cower, I slipped into the fold of something much larger than myself, which assured me that what I was about to say next was the right action despite the possible consequences. *If you worry about the future, you dwell in the state of destruction.* Arash's words reinforced my courage. The emir would not defeat our love.

"I have no wish to enter into sigheh with the emir: therefore, I see no reason to join the line."

The emir's assistant's face flushed. I glanced at Parisa. "Anahita!"

she mouthed, but I kept on. "It is my understanding that sigheh is most often initiated by a woman. She decides the length and terms of the marriage. I have no such interest in marrying the emir and neither do many among these women. Even so," I shifted on the floor cushion, "contracts are to be signed in the presence of two witnesses and a cleric. Unless your palace mullah is a puppet of your emir, chances are he will *not* be inclined to honor such an arrangement, as the practice is typically frowned upon as a pre-Islamic custom. I suggest that you take this information back to His Eminence. These women will require high payments. They are aware of their rights."

"You are all slaves. You have no rights."

I found it less scary to speak out among strangers than I had in my village. When petitioning for bathhouse rights at home, I had to consider how my actions would affect my family. For a moment, that cold loneliness that my mother, grandmother, and I faced at the height of my village's chastisement for my behavior over the bathhouse chilled me. All those Fridays when the women of Hasanabad left a wide space around the three of us in the women's section of the mosque. But here in The Ark, I only endangered myself. Standing, I said, "I am a freeborn woman, an Afshar. My tribe has lived peacefully for centuries with the Tajiks and Yomuts of this region. The emir's desert hospitality is disgraceful." I glanced at the women as I walked toward the emir's man. "Need I remind you what our Prophet Muhammad, peace be upon him, said about the treatment of slave women?"

At this, the emir's man turned on his heels. I believed that he might go and get someone larger and meaner to deal with me.

Before leaving, he poked his head back through the door and

glared at me. "You will not go unpunished for this." Salar followed behind him.

The women rushed to me. Some knelt at my side and others stroked my hair.

"They will beat you," said the redhead who had been rude to me earlier. "It will be a *pleasure* to watch." Smirking, she strolled away.

Parisa laced her arm through mine, staring down the girls.

"They will strike you with a horse-hair whip that has been soaked in milk," another said, rubbing an old scar on her arm. I winced at the sight of it, imagining the whistle and crack of the strap that had struck the girl.

"They will lock you in the bug pit," said another.

The bug pit? I would hear no more. "For those of you who choose sigheh, speak your minds, negotiate your demands," I said. "Make the mullah understand what you want. He could be your ally."

"Anahita," one girl asked, "where did you learn this?"

"I was blessed with a good family who allowed me to go to school. Make education part of your marriage contracts," I said, my thoughts drifting to my blue-eyed teacher Reza. "Demand that the emir hire you tutors."

A few of the older women cupped my face in their hands and kissed me on both cheeks. "You must be careful," they said.

New capacities come about through necessity: therefore, O man, increase your necessity, Rumi said. I could feel a new capacity opening inside.

19

Imprisoned

Dariyoush paced as Farhad and Ismail sat on threadbare carpets behind bars in the dungeon of The Ark. Beside them a local tinsmith was busy making a lantern. The man's embroidered Bukharan beanie appeared new and intricately woven, as was the *gelim* upon which he worked.

Staring at Dariyoush, Farhad applied pressure to the slash on his forearm that he received from one of the emir's men at the bazaar bardeh furushi. "The next time you decide to start a fight in the middle of a slave market—or anywhere for that matter—on Anahita's behalf, please make sure that it is actually my daughter for whom you are swinging your sword."

"I'm sorry, Kadkhuda Farhad," Dariyoush said again. "I was certain that slave for sale was Anahita."

"The glitter in your eye for another man's betrothed has clouded your vision," Ismail said.

Dariyoush saw the distaste etched into Arash's advisor's face. The tinsmith paused his work to glance at them both.

"Perhaps you should purchase a pair of spectacles first thing when we're released," Ismail continued.

This remark made the tinsmith laugh. "Bah! No one is ever *released* from The Ark."

Dariyoush looked at his Bukharan cellmate as the man continued speaking. "Were any of the women hurt?"

Dariyoush shook his head no. "Thankfully."

"*Alhamdulillah.*"

Farhad looked at each of his cellmates, resting his gaze on the tinsmith. "Since the day Anahita was born, I have grappled with the notion that I cannot always be there to protect her, that I must believe in her capabilities." The tinsmith stilled his hammer. "Yet, I cannot help but feel responsible for her kidnapping and everything that has ensued."

After a moment of silence, the tinsmith said, "As my Naqshbandi brothers would say, 'Blame keeps the sad game going. It keeps stealing all your wealth—giving it to an imbecile with no financial skills.'"

Farhad crossed his arms, nodding.

This man's a dervish, Dariyoush thought. *And he's not merely practicing the art of self-forgetfulness. He has a trade.* "Why is it that you sit on a fine carpet and are given tin and tools with which to practice your craft?"

"The jailors know that I have been wrongfully accused. A few months ago, we made a pact that I would make things that they can sell at the market. We all profit."

Months ago? Dariyoush paced even faster. The tinsmith looked at him. "But not to worry," the craftsman lowered his voice, "you won't be here for months."

"How's that?" Ismail asked.

"My wife is a weaver and very intelligent. She found the man in Bukhara who had made the locks for the cell doors, and copied the design from him. This she wove into the carpet beneath me, at the spot where my head touches in prayer five times a day. I am a metal worker, too, and this design looked to me like the inside of a lock. While imprisoned, I've crafted trinkets according to the materials I needed to make a key."

Dariyoush knelt, ran his fingers over the design in the gelim.

"Get up." The tinsmith nudged him. "Do not let the jailor see you."

"This is extraordinary news," Farhad said. "When do you plan to escape?"

"Tomorrow during whichever prayer time seems auspicious. This is when most of the fortress guards leave their posts, or generally doze off."

"How will you get out of The Ark?" Dariyoush said.

The tinsmith frowned at him, as if he'd asked a ridiculous question. "By the grace of God."

Caravanserai

Arash, Pirouz, Reza, and Shirin sat on cushions inside their small room on the second floor of the caravanserai. From a window high on the camel shelter's wall, dust particles glowed in the shaft of sunlight that rained down on Anahita's grandmother as she approached—a picture of radiance, Arash thought. Maman Bozorg had been harvesting the latest news from Arash's battalion as well as from Shirin's husband, Ali, who had been keeping watch over the camels, horses, and goats that had made the journey from Marv to Bukhara.

"So you have yet to meet the emir?" Reza asked Arash again, as if hearing this twice might help rectify the situation.

Shirin tucked a hair into her headscarf.

"I prefer to enter The Ark before I request to see him. I'd like to get a sense of the place without any diplomatic fanfare. See what I am up against."

"You have little political advantage here?"

"None whatsoever. Bukhara is a Russian protectorate. If I threaten him with the forces of the shah of Iran's army, it is really the czar whom I would provoke." Arash gazed at the letter he held, sent from his palace courier telling him Russian forces advanced from Isqhabad to the Tedjen oasis, only seventy-five miles from Marv. *Our days, too, our numbered*, he thought. He wished the Turkmans in the region weren't so disenfranchised, different clans vying for power. Arash had intended to unite them this spring against the czar, with the help of Dariyoush and Ali. He smacked the letter on the back of his hand. *I must get back to Marv—but not before rescuing Anahita.*

Pirouz jumped to his feet beside Arash, eager to divulge what he'd learned. Arash laid a hand on the small of the boy's back. "What information do you have for me about The Ark, the inside of the citadel?"

"I think I saw Anahita in the harem!"

Arash took him by the shoulders. "Was she all right?"

Pirouz explained what he learned from his hiding place in the potted plant. How Anahita spoke up for the girls. Arash looked at his companions and uttered, "Mashallah." Then he became quiet.

"And, there's a city inside there! An armory with blacksmiths and metalworkers. Shoemakers and saddle makers. There's even a torture chamber—"

"Thank you, Pirouz," Maman Bozorg said, joining them. She took the boy by the arm, signaling for him to sit down.

Reza handed Pirouz a parchment and stylus. "Can you draw the layout of the grounds for us?"

Pirouz smiled and took the pen. He sketched the emir's quarter, the coronation court, the mosques, treasury, and harem. He then sketched the royal apartments, instrument rooms, music pavilion, pottery and glass workshops. Lastly, he drew the stables, armory, jail, and dungeon beneath the fortress towers.

"This is where Farhad and Dariyoush are likely to be." Reza pointed to the jail. "If only Dariyoush weren't quite so—"

"Hot headed?" Arash offered. "He'd do well to learn that patience bestows benefits." He took off his turban and ran a hand through his hair. "I wonder if I should have asked him to lead up a border battalion without knowing about this aspect of his personality?"

"Dariyoush may not have acted so irrationally were his heart not involved," Maman Bozorg said. Perhaps with Arash in mind, she changed the subject. "Reza, I would prefer to hold on to the hope that Farhad and the rest are not in the jail and were given the opportunity to speak with the emir." She lit a flame under the samovar for tea as Shirin placed glass cups before each of the men.

Crossing his legs, Reza said, "I'm not so sure the emir's subjects were in any mood to welcome them into The Ark."

"It's a blessing they agreed to Farhad's truce and that no one was killed," Maman Bozorg said.

"The fact that they agreed to a truce doesn't surprise me," Arash said. "I heard told that many of the emir's men left the fight with nasty wounds. Dariyoush and Ismail are expert swordsmen. And I suspect Dariyoush learned a tip or two from Kadkhuda Farhad's mentoring." He eyed Maman Bozorg. "They would have prevailed in the end. But Farhad likely reasoned that we didn't come here to cause death but to rescue Anahita." Arash watched as someone led two huge elephants past. The dust they kicked up clouded his vision.

Turning to Reza, Arash said, "Have you heard whether the

governor of Quchan was responsible for the sale of those women?" He never trusted this cousin of his.

"The *Musavat* reported that lowly officials actually sold the women, but the governor took two thirds of the cash."

Arash shook his head.

"This is inconceivable," Maman Bozorg said.

Reza shifted positions. "Apparently the minister of interior in Tehran dispatched an accountant to Quchan to settle the matter, but as the paper said, 'the pen is too ashamed to write about it.'"

"An accountant! What will that settle? My father needs to replace that governor, throw him in jail."

After a moment's silence, Shirin spoke up. "My prince, may I report on what we women learned today?"

"Of course," Arash said, fingering the stiches on his head wound that Shirin had sewn. "And despite Kadkhuda Farhad's objections, I want to thank you again for coming here to help find Anahita. Your courage, caring, and ideas are invaluable to me."

Shirin hesitated, her face pinkened. "The Ark has a carpet weaving workshop and a dye house. They are situated right about...here." She pointed to the place on Pirouz's sketch. "Apparently, there is a back gate leading into The Ark, which the artisans and merchants use to roll their wares in and out of the fortress. It is well guarded, but not as fortified as the main gate." Before continuing, she looked at Maman Bozorg for support. "And we have a plan."

"Let's hear it," Arash said.

"An aunt of our dear friend Fatima, who owns the teahouse in Hasanabad, works in the royal workshop. Perhaps she can help us find Anahita."

Arash looked twice at Shirin and Maman Bozorg. "I do not think Farhad would approve of your helping find Anahita. It is too dangerous."

Maman Bozorg waived a hand. "He did not approve of us coming to Bukhara either. But as you can see by the fact that we are here, Shirin and I occasionally think for ourselves." She winked at Arash as she poured him some chai.

Arash smiled. Turning to Shirin, he said, "And what does your husband think about this idea?"

"He has agreed."

A question shone in Reza's eyes as he glanced at Maman Bozorg.

Arash exhaled. "So be it." Turning to Pirouz, he asked, "My boy, any chance of you getting back inside the citadel this evening? We must find out what plans the emir has for Anahita. Is she kept in the harem or—Allah forbid—in the jail, or is she suffering from other hideous conditions? See if you can get news of Farhad's and the others' whereabouts, as well."

"I saw jugglers and acrobats practicing in the main square today. I know they are performing tonight for the emir. Their troupe is huge. Surely no one will notice if I slip in with them."

"How fortunate," Arash said. "Go with God."

Pirouz sprang to his feet and left. Watching him skip away, Arash wished he could be as detached as the boy about this mission, that he could think of this as some great game of espionage.

"Master Reza," Arash said. "I understand you have old maps. May I see them?"

Reza's face lit up. Reaching behind him, he pulled out a handful of scrolls, pushed up his sleeves, and unrolled them.

The Emir's Covenant

Early that evening, Salar took me by the arm to escort me to the emir. Women touched my skirts as I walked by. Before leaving, someone hissed through the lattice screen from the other side of the harem. "May your womb shrivel up." I flushed, then crimsoned with anger. The woman must have been the emir's barren wife.

When I arrived at the emir's quarters, I felt what a *pahlevan* must feel when he finally enters the arena after weeks of training, tense but focused on the fight. My first glimpse of the emir helped me to remain relatively calm. His pink and gold embroidered turban, piled high on his head, had to be the largest I'd ever seen. Perhaps he thought it enhanced his tiny stature or helped increase the awe that his position afforded. Bent over a small canvas, he was busy painting a miniature depicting a falcon hunt. His artistry seemed quite accomplished. The contrasting colors, rigid postures, and crooked trees captured the dramatic feel of the game. With his finest brush, the emir stroked his parchment to make a slanted dash, a horseman's eye. Holding it up to admire it, he said, "Painting keeps me from killing people."

The emir set down his brush, pressed his fingers on the table as he pushed to standing. He circled around, inspecting me. I sensed his eyes resting on the curve of my hip, my forearms. He tilted my face to his, though I refused to look at him. "You are beautiful. We shall marry. A mullah and two witnesses will arrive shortly, and we shall draw up a contract for sigheh."

His harsh tone rattled me more than I anticipated. *Be strong.* I took a deep breath. "I do not wish to marry you," I said, and turned my back, the rudest and most dangerous of gestures. Emirs had been known to throw daggers at such impudence. But I believed that he wouldn't hurt me, especially since he seemed so keen to wed me. And, I could still see him in the mirrored wall paneling. I'd keep my back to him until I lost my nerve. "And, is it not true that a girl must seek her father's permission before seeking sigheh?"

"Since when does a slave speak her wishes?" His voice had raised, as if straining to keep his anger in check. "And you will address me as Your Illustriousness."

"Your *Illustriousness,* I am not a slave. I am the daughter of the kadkhuda of the Afshar tribe—"

"And I am the son of Tamerlane. You are no longer in Persia, thus your lineage no longer serves you. I bought you. Appreciate that my scruples are such that I am offering you a temporary marriage rather than relegating you to the status of my concubines." He laid his sword on my shoulder. "Were you not the perfect antidote for my desire, I would have run this blade through your pretty neck."

My whole body flinched.

"By the way, my feisty one, I believe it is your father and his comrades-in-arms who are presently locked inside my dungeon."

I spun around, my hand flying to my mouth.

"It seems they tried to kill some of my men. I don't take kindly to that sort of behavior. But perhaps you can help your father and friends by…" the emir allowed his voice to trail off while lifting the edge of my veil with the tip of his sword.

Never. Something within fanned my courage—that same feeling I'd experienced when passing the dervish lodge. *I'm not alone.* I looked the emir in the eye. "I am betrothed to the Governor of Marv, a Qajar prince." The emir cocked his head as if wishing for clarification.

"With the czar's army breathing down your neck, you would be wise to consider my pleas. Perhaps Persia's tribes could be of use to you in defending your city one day."

"Your idea is ridiculous. You are less educated than I have been told. Bukhara has been a protectorate of Russia for decades. This will not change." He let go of my veil and stepped away.

I lifted my chin, though I flushed with embarrassment. Someone knocked on the door. The emir opened it and ushered in his treasurer, the mullah, and a scribe who carried an ebony quill box made of *khatam.* The gold flecks inlaid in the wood caught the light of the setting sun through the windows. Greeting the cleric, the emir touched his palm to his chest and bowed.

When these men entered the room, that inexplicable feeling I had—of an invisible friend watching over me—surged.

"Splendid. We are all here." The emir crossed his arms behind his back and strolled among them. "Let us begin. Shamsiddin, my scribe, please copy down the terms of this *qabaleh-ye nekah*, my covenant with Anahita. Note that this marriage will last for three months, any offspring will be considered a legitimate heir of mine…"

I didn't hear the rest. My head began to swirl with a feverish ring. *Don't pass out.* Through the window plumes of grass moved in one of the large porcelain jars in the courtyard. A set of round eyes peered at me. The same brown eyes of the boy who had watched me before. He put one finger to his lips and sunk out of sight. Someone *was* near, and on my side.

As the emir stated all of his demands with respect to our marriage agreement, the scribe drew his brows together, hurrying to write down what was said. His exquisite lettering rolled across the scroll like a carpet unfurling. Shamsiddin paused, turning his hands over and back as if the lines on his palms were at this very moment being inked with a thousand lies.

My mullah in Hasanabad had once said, "Calligraphy is a prayer spoken by the hand's tongue. If Allah dictates to the scribe, he can write anything away—doubt, despair, even death." Would that this calligrapher could write away the emir.

When my eyes met the scribe's, the words of the Prophet Muhammad filled my mind. Facing the emir, not addressing the cleric, I said, "Your Illustriousness, have you never read the *sura* in the Qur'an that says, 'Not even a slave shall a Muslim man ravage if she wishes to preserve her chastity'?"

The emir's face flinched, just barely. The tiny mirrors on the wall paneling caught his slight faintness of heart, reflecting his gesture over and over.

The mullah gently closed his holy book and rolled up his scroll.

"This sigheh will not be sanctioned." He padded away in his curly-toed slippers.

I exchanged glances with the scribe. Perhaps this man of fine reeds and parchment—who had appeared to examine his hands with repulsion—had sensed that he might be forging a false agreement, one that represented the wishes of only one of the parties involved.

When I looked at Shamsiddin again, I saw not his face, but the serene countenance of the dervish who had studied me in the town's central courtyard when I had passed through it with Mahan. Perhaps the scribe and that dervish were one and the same person. I felt so calm. Surely this scribe radiated deep peace. In his presence little could fluster me, not even the fit the emir pitched after the mullah left the room.

"I shall find another mullah!" he shouted at his treasurer, striking his sword to a blown glass vase and shattering it. Pointing to Shamsiddin from across the room, he said, "You will come back tomorrow. Now everyone, out. Out!"

Salar appeared in the doorway to escort me back to the harem. Before we left, the emir said to the eunuch, "And see to it that this slave girl is fit for my *company* on Thursday. We shall marry then."

Two days! Falling in behind Salar and the scribe, my first thought was to ask the calligrapher to send a letter to my family and Arash about my imminent sigheh. I could trust the scribe. I also remembered the pair of eyes behind the plant. Perhaps the boy—whoever he was— would bear my news. But Shamsiddin was at hand. "Agha, scribe," I whispered as we left behind a palpable stream of wills and intentions that fluttered about the emir's room like torn promissory notes.

Shabnameh, Night Letter

Shamsiddin, as if expecting me to address him, turned and gave me the slightest nod, an acknowledgment that neither the treasurer nor Salar noticed. I put a finger to my palm and scribbled on it as if it were a parchment. "Caravanserai," I mouthed, the eunuch turning to look at me just as I closed my lips. The group walked a few more steps. "Arash. Sigheh with emir."

Again, the scribe nodded. I tilted my head toward the paper he held in his hands. Paper so fine—it must have been made from cotton—without a single knot that could snag the tip of the calligrapher's pen. "May I have?" I mouthed my words as I pointed to myself.

Shamsiddin's brows furrowed. Tiny beads of sweat formed above his lip. When we entered the open-air corridor with the stables to one side and the coronation court on the other, Salar stopped to call out to a tall, muscular eunuch who apparently watched over the weaving workshop. He hauled a large carpet on his shoulder that smelled as if it had been freshly cut from the loom. Two women trailed him.

"It's my turn now," Salar said. "When a carpet is chewed by a goat, what is to stop the world's order from being rolled up and cast aside forever?"

The rug bearer stood still for a moment. "What kind of a riddle is that, you simpleton? How am I to play this silly game if you don't understand what a riddle is?" He had an accent, perhaps from Arabia or farther south.

The eunuch with the carpet looked at the stack of paper in the scribe's hand. "This is what a riddle is: What without paper is like a fish without water?"

Salar appeared puzzled, his close-set eyebrows touching. The answer was so obvious to everyone standing there that I squirmed for poor Salar's pride. This riddle any five-year-old knew. Then a brilliant idea came to mind. *This may be my way out.* I stepped close to Salar and whispered, "A scribe." Sauntering back to the calligrapher, I saw that he had loosened sheets of paper and had curled them behind his back. Within seconds I wrapped the paper inside the folds of my skirt, along with a fountain pen.

Salar beamed. "A scribe. Now I don't owe you anymore, Kufa."

"We agreed on best out of three. You get one more chance to stump me. If I win, I take all."

The two parted.

I said, "Agha, Salar. I wish to work in the weaving workroom. Might this be possible?"

Over his shoulder he said, "I will see what I can do, but I am not promising anything."

On the way back to the harem we passed the scribe's quarters. The shelving inside was stuffed with different colors and sizes of parchment, ink bottles, and old feather quills. I wished I were back in Reza's classroom, practicing writing on slate with chalk. The priviledge of writing on my own piece of such fine paper brought a sudden spurt of anticipation. I would write a letter to the shah of Iran himself and tell him about the plight of his future daughter-in-law. And, I would tell him about the women of Quchan. But then an image of the sandy execution square on the other side of the fortress walls came to mind. Perhaps the scribe would not be brave enough, or foolhardy enough, to send my letters with a night courier. And if he did, would my message actually reach Arash? There were so many caravanserais in town.

Later that night several women in the harem turned their prayer carpets toward Mecca, knelt, and prayed. Instead, I hid with my pen and parchment beneath a suzani bedspread that Parisa and three others embroidered. With everyone occupied, I would have time enough to choose my words carefully—as Schoolmaster Reza had taught me. But I wondered if I dared write this letter. My hands began to shake. The shah of Iran might not like it if I accuse his governor—who is likely one of Arash's brothers—of injustice. He could execute me for treasonous words. I fumbled with the ink bottle.

Dear Shah of Iran,

I am your humble subject, an Afshar from Hasanabad, who is betrothed to your son, Arash, governor of Marv. Due to unfortunate events, I am presently entrapped in the harem of the emir of Bukhara, who wishes sigheh with me. I trust that the Merciful One will come to my aid and that I will have avoided such a fate by the time you receive this letter. I wish to bring to your attention the fact that my father, a fellow tribesmate, and your son's chief advisor are also imprisoned in The Ark with me. I suspect that Arash has already sent a message to you on our behalf.

I devote the rest of this message to the tragic circumstances of the women and girls of Quchan. Many of them are now enslaved in this harem. I send you this headscarf as a symbol of their stolen futures and the infringement against their rights as Muslims to never be sold into slavery. I beg of you to do whatever is within your diplomatic power to help them. It is a disgrace that our nation is unable to protect women from marauding slave runners, as well as—so I have sadly heard—the onerous demands of its own ill-reputed governors. I will rejoice when I hear the news that the scarf you now have is rightfully reclaimed by its owner, Parisa of Quchan, whom I trust you will personally liberate in the name of national honor.

With due respect,
Daughter of Farhad, Kadkhuda of the Afshar tribe, Anahita of Hasanabad

شاه عزیز ایران

من خدمتگزار حقیر شما، یک افشار از حسن آباد هستم که با پسر شما، آرش، فرماندار
مرو نامزدی باشم. بدلایل تاسف انگیز موجود، من در حال حاضر در حرم
امیر بخارا گیر افتاده ام. و این امیر قصد دارد که مرا صیغه کند. من اعتقاد دارم
آنکه بخشنده است به کمک من خواهد آمد که من بتوانم از عاقبت
تلخ انگیز به موقع نجات پیدا کنم.
من می خواهم به توجه شما برسانم که پدر من که هم تبار شما ست و یکی از مشاوران
ارشد پسر شما هم می باشد. الان در حبس با من می باشد. من مطمئن
هستم که آرش تا الان حتما پیغامی به شما از قول ما فرستاده است.
من می خواهم که بقیه پیغامم را به وضعیت حزن انگیز زندگی زنان و
دختران قوچان بپردازم. بسیاری از آنها الان در اسارت در این
حرم بسر می برند. من این روسری را به عنوان سمبل آینده دزدیده
شده آنها و تخلفهای زیاد علیه حقوق آنها بعنوان مسلمان به
خدمت شمای فرشته باشد که روزی برسد که هیچگاه به بردگی کشیده
نشوند. من از شما درخواست می کنم که هر آنچه که در قدرت سیاسی
شماست را به کار گیرید که به آنها کمک کنید. این باعث شرم بسیاری
هست که کشور ما قادر به دفاع از این زنان نیست. در برابر این بردگیرها
که مناسفانه به گوش من رسیده که بعضی از آنها فرماندار بد نام و
بدنیت خود دولت هستند.
من از خوشحالی در پوست خود نخواهم گنجید وقتی بشنوم که این
روسری که در دست شماست به صاحب اصلی آن پریسا در قوچان
برگردانده شده است.
من اعتقاد دارم که شما شخصا باعث آزادی این شخص خواهید شد. بنام حفظ
افتخار ملی

با تمام احترام دختر فرهاد کدخدای تبار افشار
آناهیتای حسن آباد

23

Weaving Workshop

The next morning Salar directed some of the harem women to the kitchens and laundry. Many, along with me, would be sent to the carding and spinning rooms near the weaving and carpet workshops. I was loathe to spend hours carding wool. I needed to find the eunuch in the carpet workshop to set my plan of escape into motion.

When I left the harem with the others, I held my letters and fountain pen tucked under my tunic. Walking past the scribe's quarters, I saw him with his nose to his parchment, concentrating. A musky fragrance from all the pulp in his atelier flowed from his doorway. I slowed to allow the others to walk ahead. I let one of the letters, which I had concealed inside my harem mate Parisa's head scarf, slip from my fingers onto the calligrapher's floor. Shamsiddin looked up. Luck had flown to me on Simorgh's wings.

Touching my bodice, I checked for the other document I'd written the night before—a deed of request for my emancipation, a practice supported by the Qur'an and the words of the Prophet. I would present it to the emir if my escape that night backfired. Even though my grandmother had always believed that if one carries on with a balanced state of mind, there is no need for backup plans, I decided to follow the old adage, "Trust in God, but tie up your camel." I felt safer for having written the deed.

Following the harem eunuch into the spinning and carding room, I wheezed from all the wool fibers in the air. The place needed better ventilation. "Agha, Salar," I said. "I am a master weaver and dyer and would be of greater use in the carpet workshop."

"I was ordered to bring workers here. I do as I am told."

I leaned close to him so that only he could hear. "Suppose I tell you a riddle that is so clever your friend Kufa will never figure it out."

Salar pulled on his chin with his strong fingers. A smile played across his lips.

"What is this riddle that is *so clever* no one will guess it?"

"Promise that if I tell you it, you will take me to the carpet workshop."

The eunuch looked about. Then he spit on the ground. "All right."

I smiled. "This is the riddle: What is sovereign and ceaselessly moves?"

"Sovereign..." Salar repeated, a trace of unknowing in his voice.

I held my breath.

"Follow me." He led me through the courtyard, under an arch, and past the dye workshop, which abutted the baths. An elaborate system for channeling water for both purposes caught my eye. These lucky dyers worked beneath a balcony, upon which tall looms stood in rows. I spotted a gate to the citadel, a utility door through which supplies came and went from the fortress. Perfect.

Salar brought me to Kufa, who stood at the foot of a winding staircase. "She claims to be a master weaver. I can spare her." Then he turned to leave.

"I am ready for your riddle, any day now." Kufa tapped a foot. His accent was difficult to follow.

"When I see fit," Salar said.

I didn't like Kufa's demeaning manner. I felt sorry for Salar, who wasn't so bright, and felt bad that I would have to betray him.

"But you owe me. If you drag this contest out another day, I might have to steal your purse, whether it's tied around your neck or not." Kufa laughed. A string of coins with holes punched through them hung around Salar's throat. Slaves were not permitted pockets. I wondered if the coins held any value outside The Ark.

Salar said, "All right then. Have it your way. Here's the riddle I pose: What is sovereign and ceaselessly moves?"

Kufa's face paled.

"How did you think of such a riddle? Were you suddenly enlightened by some *jinn*?"

"Sand clock's pouring. Solve it by this time tomorrow or I keep the purse." Salar tossed his head and walked away.

Taking my arm, Kufa half-led, half-dragged me up the stairs to the looms. "You will be on relief duty. If any of the women need to get up, take their seat and continue the work."

The weavers referred to sketches. I recognized many of the patterns and believed I could reproduce them with few or no mistakes. One of the weavers must have overheard Kufa because she got up right away to allow me to take her place. The woman didn't even bother to look at me as she hurried by.

I reached above my head for a madder-colored thread, made a pile knot, and cut it with the curved knife. While I wove, female guards frisked the slaves as they left the room. I suspected they were searched because of all the scissors and knives and dye mordants—potential poisons—that could be used as weapons. With so many ears and eyes about, I worried that my plan might not work. But I had to give it a try. Tonight.

Fresh carpets were washed, set to dry, rolled, and stacked in an alcove in the courtyard below. Male slaves loaded the rugs onto Bukharan merchants' carts, which came and went through the citadel's side gate. I watched them carefully as I wove and wondered how long into the evening they toiled. One of those carpets could lead me out of captivity.

When Kufa swept by on his rounds, I attempted a conversation. "So, Kufa, you seem to like riddles?" The eunuch paused and raised an eyebrow. I didn't imagine many women talked to him.

"Huh," he grunted and strolled on.

I noted how the workers inspected huge sacks of wool coming through the gates to the workshop, occasionally slashing them with a knife. Others carried them into a storeroom near the carding rooms. I also observed that some of the weavers were permitted to enter and leave The Ark. I assumed they must be free women hired by the palace. Perhaps the slaves did not offer a talented enough pool. The quality of the wool and silk yarns was exquisite. I wondered if the emir kept a pampered flock of sheep. Glimpsing such an enterprise excited me because I had plans to start my own carpet workshop in Marv, putting into practice my own methods and designs.

Around again came Kufa, and I said, "It is awful when someone owes you money." He stopped beside my loom. I pretended nanchalance, letting my hands flutter between warp and weft, taking this opportunity to show off my skills. "Excuse me?" he said.

I repeated myself.

"How do you know Salar owes me?"

"I have ears. And I am good with riddles. I will help you win your money back," I said quickly, fearing he was on the verge of losing his patience.

Kufa crossed his arms. "And how will you do this, my newcomer who is so confident of herself, whose words both assault and tantalize the emir's ears."

"How would you know what I have or have not said to the emir?" I looked at the knot I was making.

"Palace carpets have ears...and lips. They whisper stories." He laughed and walked away.

The woman returned to the loom where I had been working, so I got up to seek other weavers who needed a break. An old woman patted the bench beside her. "Please sit. Weave with me for a while. Tell me, dearie, from what star did you fall? Your eyes sparkle with a brightness that most women here lack." The plump woman shook when she laughed. I looked at her twice. I picked up a thread and began to weave the floral pattern indicated on the sketch fastened to the loom frame. A design I'd woven into some of my own carpets.

"You are familiar with this pattern?" the old woman asked, little gray hairs gracing her chin. Catching a glimpse of them reminded me of what was in store for me that afternoon. Part of my preparation for meeting with the emir would involve bathing and hair removal. I shivered as I answered the woman.

"I'm an Afshar. Our tribe often weaves this pattern in our rugs. It is one from Mashhad."

"An Afshar? My niece married into an Afshar clan. Last I heard she was living near Nishapur."

I looked closely at the woman. "That's near my home, Hasanabad."

"You may call me Naheed. Now, tell me your name, azizam."

"Anahita."

Kindness and acceptance radiated in this woman's eyes. She reminded me of someone.

Naheed paused, threads dangling from her fingertips. The old woman glanced over both of her shoulders. "Your grandmother is looking for you. She is sitting five looms behind us."

My mouth fell open. "What is she doing in here? Has she been captured?"

Naheed raised a finger to her lips. "Fatima from Hasanabad is my niece. I'm the head weaver here and a free woman. Your grandmother came in with me as a hired hand and will leave with me at closing time. Go to her."

Fatima. That's who the woman resembled. Upon arriving in Bukhara, Maman Bozorg must have sought her for help. When I got up, Kufa was coming round again. Before making my way to my grandmother, I inquired at each of the looms to ask if I may relieve anyone, just as I had been instructed. "And ceaselessly moves..." the eunuch muttered as he strolled by.

Coming upon the loom at which Maman Bozorg worked, I

recognized the shape, strength, and agility of my grandmother's hands pulling on the warp. I would recognize them anywhere. When she looked up, my grief of missing her lodged in my throat and crushed my chest. Pent-up tears rolled down my cheeks. I quickly wiped them away and took a seat beside her.

"My Anahita, I have found you and you look…fairly well," she whispered, touching my scabbed cheek. "I will sleep better knowing this."

I could hardly speak, as if a spindle were stuck in my windpipe. "Oh, Maman Bozorg, if only I could hold you!"

"There have been many 'if only's' since you've been gone. But let us pray that we will get you out of here—now that we know the weaving workshop is where you will be spending your days."

"Baba allowed you to travel here?" I said, astonished.

Maman Bozorg smiled. "Shirin and I stole away among the textile litter in the caravan."

I looked for eavesdroppers before telling my grandmother my plan for escape. Naheed had gotten up from her loom and begun walking up and down the rows, correcting others' mistakes. She sang a weaving song, and some of the women joined in. Her voice sounded tender and melodious.

"We heard from Arash's servant boy Pirouz that you—"

"I think I saw this boy spying on me in the emir's quarters."

"He will try and contact you in the harem tonight. He came in with a company that performs for the palace. He does magic tricks. Let him be of help. He is very good at sneaking about, as you can see."

"Seems you are, too."

"I will come every day until you are free." She placed her hand on mine. "Anahita, do not let your circumstances make you bitter. Embrace this turn in life." She paused. Gently squeezing my fingers, she continued. "Find that hidden treasure inside from which all possibilities come. Bring your fire to God's light so that yours dissolves in Allah's."

I dropped my head. I could not tell her that I felt no compulsion to kneel, pray.

Kufa circled again, stopping at the loom in front of us to wake up a weaver who was ill. Maman Bozorg and I stopped talking. He stepped back and told me to take the woman's place. I nodded to my grandmother, hoping Kufa could not see the tears still shining in my eyes. But he didn't notice as he took the tired woman away.

From this other loom, I leaned back on the bench seat and spoke to my grandmother through the wall of warp threads between us. "I must escape tonight, or tomorrow the emir will—"

Maman Bozorg nodded as if she knew and hurried on with clipped sentences. "I am not certain what Arash's plans are to rescue you. Should you escape, avoid the caravanserais."

"Maman Bozorg, please tell him and Baba and Maman and Shirin that I love them and miss them."

"Shirin has come inside the fortress, too. Naheed's husband hid her in his olive oil urns. They are long and trusted workers here. They have taken a great risk on our behalf."

"Shirin could be enslaved!" I remembered with downcast eyes the grudge I had held against her because she spoke critically about my wedding riddle contest. And yet, here she was endangering herself for me.

"She could not sit idle. Two sets of eyes would find you faster than one. Several good minds will work to get you out of here."

"Naheed's husband should not risk this again. Maman Bozorg, since you are permitted in here as a hired hand, please come tomorrow to see whether I come to work. If my plan goes well, I will have escaped by the light of dawn." I quieted as I heard Kufa's voice came up the line.

"Anahita," my grandmother whispered. "Remember that patience can be an action, a form of receptivity." I leaned forward and resumed weaving. I had always thought of patience as something I either had or didn't have. "Patience for what?" I wanted to ask her, but the mid-day meal would soon come, and I didn't know if I would get a chance later this afternoon to make Kufa an offer—one he couldn't refuse. As the eunuch passed by my loom I said, "I know the answer to Salar's riddle."

He stopped and turned around.

"I will tell it to you for a favor."

Placing his hands on his hips, Kufa said, "A slave is bargaining with me—a *woman* slave?"

"Are you not a slave, too?" I pounded the weft with a heavy metal comb.

Kufa laughed and began to walk away.

"But of course, if it isn't much money that you are going to lose… then I suppose—"

He took a step back. Beneath his breath, he said, "What's your price?"

"I wish for you to open this weaving room tonight for me to work. I do not sleep well, and weaving calms me."

"Please lower your voice," the eunuch hissed.

"I'm already whispering."

"I thought you were going to request what all the rest of them want, such as more rests or extra cups of chai." He drew his brows together, looked right and left. "But you are asking me in the plain light of day to let you come into this weaving room at night, unattended, where we keep all sorts of sharp instruments?"

"You may search me before I leave."

A female guard walked by, eyeing the two of us.

Kufa squinted. "How am I to be sure your answer to Salar's riddle is the correct answer?"

"When you hear it, you will realize there is no other. If I am wrong, you can deal with me after your contest with Salar is finished."

"What good will that do if Salar has got my money?"

I returned to my weaving. "It seems that it is you who has more to gain from this bargain than me. Perhaps I will withdraw my offer to tell you the riddle's answer."

Behind me, Maman Bozorg cleared her throat, her way of spurring me on. Her love comforted me.

"What makes you think I won't think of the answer to the riddle on my own?"

"One day you will think of the riddle's answer, but you must think of it before midmorning tomorrow. I have bested many at riddles in my day, but this one took me weeks to figure out."

Crossing his arms, Kufa said, "You're a master weaver and dyer and also a master of riddles."

Despite his sarcastic tone, Kufa's expression suggested that I had made an inroad, even though he walked away without answering me.

Before long the eunuch announced the workers' mealtime with the wail of a ram's horn. The women got up from their looms. I fell in with Maman Bozorg among the line of weavers. My grandmother touched my arm ever so lightly before she walked away with Naheed. Kufa gathered the girls who would go back to the harem. Before turning his group of slaves over to Salar, he whispered to me, "I will open the weaving room after sunset."

Bug Pit

hile the others went back to work after the midday rest, Salar escorted me to the baths. Inside, I walked past cabinets crammed with medicine bottles of every size and color, and others stacked with tweezers, scissors, and clippers. A woman held an awful-smelling paste for the removal of body hair and a mud clay mixed with rose petals to wash the hair on my head. I protested the smelly paste, but the bath attendant ignored me and set about smearing it on. While she waited for my skin to absorb the hair remover, she took a dry sponge to my back, exfoliating every flake of dry skin. All the while I meditated on my sweet grandmother's face. After washing and combing my hair, the attendant turned me over to someone else.

With her thick wrists, this woman kneaded and pummeled every one of my muscles, oiling them with perfumed lotions. While she worked on me, I examined a large tapestry on the wall woven with deep purples and indigo blues. The image portrayed a gallantly dressed man offering a beautiful woman, who wore a necklace draped about her ivory throat, a cup of wine.

My attendant pressed too hard on my back, forcing air from my lungs and hurting my rib, still sore from the avalanche. "Gently," I said wincing, and turned back to the tapestry. At first I thought this image depicted vice, like a painting in the emir's office of Timur and Dilshad. But then I realized this tapestry evoked a spiritual theme based on the poetry of Omar Khayyam: *And then the Tulip for her wonted sup of Heavenly Vintage lifts her chalice up.* Seeing this weaving reminded me that Omar Khayyam, the astronomer and poet from Nishapur— very near my home in Iran—once also lived in Bukhara. What a long history of science and art this city holds.

Despite the steady stream of adrenaline coursing through my body, the softer touch of my attendant helped me to receive rather than resist her "pampering." The massage helped rub away my fear.

Later, as I walked to the harem from the baths, words—curses— came from an iron grate at my feet, near the stable entrance. The voice sounded familiar.

"Back!" I heard a swatting sound, followed by, "Take that!" I squatted to listen more closely. The cone of light falling to the floor of the dungeon beneath me lit up a circle of seething insects. The bug pit. My eyes focused on the person standing in the shadows. Dariyoush! I covered my mouth to stifle my gasp and looked in all directions to see if anyone saw me crouched there.

"Dariyoush, is that you?" I whispered, but he didn't hear me above the deafening sound of all the insects. The ground seemed to sway and swirl as the bugs raked the stone floor for food or water. But the only source of water appeared to be my dear tribesman. A battalion of insects marched toward him, clacking and snapping and pinching. Beetle-like bugs gushed over his sandals, under the leather straps, and began crawling up his legs. Shuddering, I tried to wrench the grate free, but it wouldn't budge. "Dariyoush," I said, much louder this time.

He glanced my way as he unraveled his turban, wound it into a fat rope, and whacked at the bugs.

Still no one watched me, so I called to Dariyoush again. "It's me, Anahita."

He looked up. "Anahita? Are you well? Have you been hurt?" He wielded his turban whip against the winged ants, scarabs, cockroaches, and earwigs. I remembered as children how much we detested those the most, how they fell out of apricot trees when we picked fruit together.

"They're working their way under my clothing!" he said.

Poor Dariyoush! Even as an adult, he never did shake off the gruesome stories we'd heard that earwigs like to burrow into people's brains through their ears and nose.

I caught sight of a camel spider. It appeared like an elephant among ants. I convulsed. The news I'd heard from a neighboring village about the baby whose cheek was half-eaten by a camel spider sprang to mind. If Dariyoush disrobed, the hairy camel-colored spider—a species that typically leaps from the sands and clings to the hair beneath camels' bellies—would have nothing to hold on to besides his slippery skin. We both watched it run like wind over the mound of insects.

"Grab that leather boot behind you," I called. If only he could gain hold of it, he could smash the spider that was as large as his foot. But even the boot may not be sturdy enough to kill it. I refused to think of what may have happened to the owner of that boot.

The clopping of hooves on cobblestones startled me. I stood up and peered around the corner. Several mounted guards headed in my direction. I left the bug pit and hurried down the opposite lane, past the treasury toward the harem. *I must get him out! I will demand the emir to…* Stopping, I faced the lane to the stables, thinking I could find the dungeon and… Helpless, I threw my arms up. *I am powerless. Useless!*

Dragging my feet toward the harem, I felt so homesick, so responsible for Dariyoush's misery, so full of fondness for him and remorse that my tribespeople were risking their lives for me.

As I looked back, someone was dumping buckets of bugs through the grate into the pit. My stomach lurched, and I vomited into the jube running along the clay wall through which water and debris trickled. As I heaved repeatedly, my determination to escape increased a thousand-fold. I had to end this nightmare so no one else would try to rescue me. Doubled over, I tried desperately to walk.

In the harem antechamber, tall grasses wavered in a large urn. "Anahita," came the high-pitched whisper of a boy not yet a man. I marveled that he managed to get in here. I stopped beside the plant and pretended to fix my sandal strap.

"Pirouz?" I whispered back, my throat sore.

"Yes—how can I help get you out of here?" he asked.

"Dariyoush is locked in the bug pit!"

"Maybe I can free him."

"Bless you." Salar would be coming for me, so I hurried to answer Pirouz. "Come to the weaving room after sunset." We both glanced about for anyone who might hear. I cupped my hand and told him my plan. "Can you do this?"

Pirouz raised his chin. "I can and I shall."

"Remember to tell the eunuch '*eshq*' is the answer to the riddle."

He turned to leave and then glanced back at me. Pulling a rabbit's foot from his pocket, he beamed. "See? Luck is with us."

His gesture, his childlike certainty, tugged at my heart. I would never forgive myself were something to happen to him. I stood up when Salar appeared from behind a curtain in the women's quarters.

"They released you from the baths earlier than I expected. Perhaps you were not so dirty."

"I bathed just yesterday." I glanced at the potted plant, Pirouz had disappeared like *jadu*, magic. "Salar," I said, shading my face with my veil, "I slept terribly last night and would like to sleep better tonight, for tomorrow I must—"

"Marry the emir!" he said, and laughed deep from his belly.

Stone-faced, I stared as he laughed. "I cannot rest unless I weave for an hour or so before going to sleep."

"You are joking? I thought women loathed to sit at looms."

"Perhaps when they are enslaved they loathe it!" I clutched my skirts. The silence between us filled with the sound of murmurs coming from the harem behind the lattice screen. I softened my tone and reached toward him. "I haven't told you the whole reason." I refined my ploy. "Kufa wishes for me to work tonight in the weaving room. Will you please deliver me there?"

"Why does he want you to work tonight?"

"He needs me to complete a carpet that a sick weaver could not finish today. The batch goes out in the morning and…and he bears the blame when rugs are not finished on time."

"Why should I help Kufa?"

Sigheh loomed nearer and nearer.

I hesitated, fidgeting with my headscarf as if this would help me perfect my answer. "Perhaps one day you'll need a favor from him." I stepped a bit closer to Salar and lowered my voice. "He doesn't know the answer to your riddle or he would have told you by now. Bringing me to Kufa tonight would remind him that he hasn't been smart enough to solve it."

Camel Spiders and Broken Brooms

In the bug pit, Dariyoush watched the camel spider run like wind over the mound of insects. *Dear Allah, don't let that thing launch into the air at me. It's more animal than insect.*

Dariyoush brandished his turban-whip. Different kinds of bites and stings penetrated his skin beneath his clothing. Shivering all over, he spotted more hairy legs emerging from the angry pile—a second camel spider. His eyes darted from one corner of the bug pit to the other, keeping an eye on both arachnids.

Remembering the flint Shirin had sewn into his sash, he paused from his whipping to fumble with his waistband. Bugs now flew at his chest, made their way up his tunic, and soon descended down his neckline. He pulled the garment off, thinking he could use it to trap one of the camel spiders. Suffering a leg laceration for Anahita was one thing, but must he be eaten alive?

Beating back the bugs, he fiddled more with his sash. He pulled out the flint, struck it on the wall. A spark! He lit his turban on fire and laid it on the ground in front of him, burning some of the insects. A million tiny legs retreated from the flame. But while the fire managed to scare away the bugs nearest it, it did not seem to deter the others. The camel spiders had now made their way to within four feet of him. He tried to light his tunic, too, but the cotton wouldn't catch. Dariyoush eyed the spiders as he exposed more of his garment to the flame. The fire surged. But by then, one of the camel spiders had already leapt and cleared it, sailing directly at him. Dariyoush jumped aside just as the heavy door to the bug pit scraped open over the stone flooring. A rush of air fanned the flame even higher.

He heard a woman scream as he thrust his body over the threshold, the door pinning his arm and shoulder against the doorjamb as the person on the other side tried to slam it closed. When Dariyoush burst out, insects poured into the hallway, the iron latch clamping shut behind him.

"Oh!" Shirin gasped, beating the camel spider off Dariyoush's pant leg with her broom. It fell to the ground. Dariyoush grabbed the broom and rammed the handle through the center of the spider's back, injuring it. He sent it flying down the corridor. Then he swiped several earwigs and beetles from his pants and arms onto the floor. "Oh!" Shirin exclaimed again, still shaken.

Dariyoush put a finger to his lips. He took her by the arm, and they ducked behind a pillar.

Shirin, disguised in the baggy peasant pants of a fortress work maid, turned so as not to look at Dariyoush's bare chest.

"What are you doing here?" Dariyoush asked.

"It's a long story."

"Aren't there guards around?"

Shirin clutched her broom and feather duster. "There are soldiers in the armory." She pointed down the hall.

"Have you found Anahita?" Dariyoush asked.

"I've been to the harem, but could not see her, though I heard her name mentioned. I came to find you and Kadkhuda Farhad. Why were you locked in the bug pit?"

"I complained about insects in my rice to the jailor."

Shirin's eyes widened.

"Do you know if the armory is locked?" Dariyoush asked.

"You can walk right into it from here. The bug pit, jail, and armory are each different corridors of this same dungeon section of the palace. But it is well guarded on the outside. You will have to fight your way out." Shirin thought for a moment. "A few minutes ago, there were only a few men sitting on carpets drinking tea in an alcove beside the stocks of bayonets. Another room is filled with pyramids of canon balls. Beyond that is a storage room, a cloakroom with soldiers' uniforms hanging on pegs. Maybe you could dress—"

"Good idea. Shirin, do you think you could distract the jailor long enough for me to slip by?"

She nodded.

Dariyoush took her broom and tore the twine that held the bristles to the broomstick. "Bat your pretty eyelashes at the jailor and ask him to fix this for you. He won't be able to resist."

Shirin's knuckles turned white from the force of her grip on the broomstick.

"Are you all right? If you don't think you can do this, just tell me. I might be able to steal past him on my own."

"I'm fine."

"Shirin, if Farhad, Ismail, and I do not manage to escape from here, promise me you won't come back tomorrow."

"I won't, Dariyoush. Ali won't let me, anyway. He said only this once. But he wants Anahita to be rescued as badly as any of us, and for all of us to be together in Marv." Her voice cracked as if she were about to cry. "Anahita and I had the whole summer planned. While you and Ali are gone recruiting fighters for the border battalions, we were going to set up a palace carpet workshop, hire tutors for the women and..." She let her voice trail off.

"I understand," Dariyoush said.

Shirin sauntered over to the jail keeper as Dariyoush waited behind a colonnade. She saw Farhad and Ismail behind bars in the cell, along with another man she did not recognize wearing a Bukharan beanie. They looked astonished to see her. Farhad stood up. She tilted her head toward Dariyoush to indicate to the kadkhuda that she wasn't alone. Then she said to the jailor, "Excuse me, agha, but I seem to have broken my broom."

He momentarily glanced up from his newspaper.

Shirin sashayed closer to him, knowing Dariyoush couldn't creep by unless the man got up from where he sat on the floor with his back to the wall. The jailor looked up and eyed her hips as she walked. He folded his paper and said, "Now, what is the problem? Come here with that broom."

Shirin hesitated.

"Come on. Don't be a shy thing," he said, leering.

"I'd rather not get so close to the prisoners. They… they scare me."

The jailor got up and walked over to Shirin. Before taking hold of her broom and examining it, he slid his hand around her waist and pulled her next to him. She gritted her teeth but stayed still. Never had she felt so nervous. Dariyoush crept from behind the arch and ducked behind another one closer to Shirin and the jailor. She eyed the cell. Now Ismail was up and pacing. Farhad wiped his brow.

Dariyoush slunk nearer.

The man in the cell wearing the beanie took off his cap and pointed to it. Then he held up two fingers. He also tugged the lapels of his *chupan*. After, he gestured with his hand, as if to say, "Bring me two of these caps and robes." She looked at Farhad for affirmation. He mouthed the word *azan*. Prayer time. This would mean that she must con some of the hired hands into selling her the clothes off of their backs before sunset.

Shirin slipped from the jailor's grip, pulling her broom between them. The man frowned, but began fiddling with the twine that held the bristles together. "You must have been sweeping very hard to cause this damage," he said. Shirin forced a smile. While he worked, Shirin leaned around him and peered down the hall. Dariyoush, now wearing a soldier's uniform, strode toward the dungeon gate. *Oh my,* she thought. *His trousers are too short and the jacket looks child-sized on him. Surely, someone will notice!*

26

A Scribe's Pen and
a Brand New Key

"I have business with the emir's scribe," Arash said to the official standing guard at the front entrance to The Ark. The sheer size of the fortress before him felt daunting. Its mass defied imagination. He held up the document the scribe had sent on Anahita's behalf, which contained an invitation to visit. Arash hoped that this time he would be granted entry, as it was a different guard than the one he had argued with earlier that morning. He smiled to himself again that Anahita had convinced the scribe to mail the letter. The official took the parchment and turned it over to inspect its wax seal. Recognizing it, he waved Arash through. Arash was surprised the guard didn't read the note. He'd make sure his own palace guards in Marv wouldn't be so negligent.

When he came to the scribe's atelier, Arash found the door open. He hesitated before knocking because the calligrapher looked busy blending colors of ink. But the man looked up promptly and said, "Yes?"

"I am Arash, governor of Marv, and the recipient of the letter my fiancé asked you to send me at the caravanserai."

"The enslaved girl, Anahita?"

Arash nodded.

"Please come in."

Arash noticed the musky aroma from all the pulp in the room and the fresh sheet on which Shamsiddin wrote. It shone like silk. Arash said, "What can you tell me about this emir, other than he has a penchant for buying female slaves?"

The scribe drew his eyebrows together. "I sent that letter to you with some risk. Anahita also asked me to send a *shabnameh* for her to the shah of Iran." He cleared his throat before asking, "Your father, I gather?"

Arash nodded. "What news did she tell him?"

"She told him about her captivity and her father's, but mainly she implored the shah to investigate and rescue the women and girls of Quchan, who are now part of the emir's harem."

Arash removed his turban.

"Not only did she ask *not* to remain anonymous, as do most authors of night letters, she even sent a scarf to the shah that belonged to one of her harem mates and suggested that he return it to this young woman *in person*." Arash wished he could be at his father's court when her letter arrived. He doubted anyone had ever sent the shah such a request.

The yellow light streaming through the window painted all the parchment in the room gold. Arash admired that Anahita could stand up for herself. But this glimpse of his fiancé's personality he had not yet seen. Her willingness to act for the sake of others took him pleasantly by surprise. There, in the warm corner of the scribe's atelier, Arash's heart filled with love.

Putting his turban back on, he paced the scribe's office. "I am indebted to you for obliging Anahita's requests."

The calligrapher tilted his head as if to say that it was nothing. "Let's just hope that her letter—a whisper sent from the Persian border—will cause the Qajar Court to listen. To wince in shame."

Arash studied Shamsiddin. Perhaps this fellow was sympathetic with the *Jadid,* the reformist movement in town that called for women's education. He wondered if the scribe wrote for the underground newspaper *Tardjuman,* The Interpreter, which Arash had read in the caravanserai. "I am happy that she was able to express herself so eloquently." He placed his hands on the scribe's desk. "May I ask why you agreed to help her?"

The calligrapher looked into the courtyard. "There is an old saying among scribes. 'Beautiful calligraphy tells the truth.' I helped her because she chose *and dared* to tell the truth."

Arash held the man's gaze.

"How do you intend to persuade the emir to give her up? He seemed quite taken by her. He demanded that I come back tomorrow to document the sigheh with her, though he must find a sympathetic mullah."

"And you will honor his wishes?" Arash asked. He couldn't imagine this man complying, but understood that noncompliance would bring him undeserved risk. He wondered how many other sighehs he had put his seal upon?

"I have penned only those who have entered into sigheh freely. It is not so hard to distinguish between those who do and those who don't. In fact, Anahita's refusal is quite unusual. Most of the other women have nothing to lose and everything to gain."

"Will you jeopardize your position as palace scribe should you refuse to write the qabaleh-ye nekah?"

"Perhaps. But I am not the only scribe in Bukhara, so whether or not I agree to draft the marriage agreement will not affect the outcome."

Arash felt a flash of dislike toward him, though he fought his possible misjudgment of the scribe's intentions. The words of his dervish friend came to mind: "If you are living in the past or the future, you are living in the state of destruction." Arash willed himself to stop speculating about what the calligrapher might or might not do.

"I will not transcribe the qabaleh-ye nekah. This will force the emir to take the time to find another scribe. I've already explained the situation to my colleagues in Bukhara. They, too, will likely decline. So, at best, it may stall things by another day. There are second-rate copyists in the bazaar who can be hired for little money."

Arash smiled. "Please accept my deepest thanks."

"Allow me to disclose something about the emir, which may give you an edge. He is childish. Sometimes he can be bought off with a new idea, which can make him forget about a former one quite readily."

Arash nodded.

Shamsiddin continued, "Often several guards stand duty outside his offices. They respond to bribes, so I hear. But you cannot be armed when you approach them."

Arash fingered his janbiya, and the sword at his hip. He decided to see how far he would get wearing his weapons.

Arash thanked the scribe and left. He walked past thick doors that presumably led to the treasury, knowing from Pirouz's description that the harem lay behind it. He wished to break in, sweep Anahita into his arms, and battle his way out of the palace. Perhaps five or six years ago he might have done such a thing, much as Dariyoush tried to do at the slave market. However, experience told him that such behavior often leads to deeper trouble.

Just before the call to prayer, Shirin, as requested, returned to the jail with two Bukharan caps and only one chupan. "You again?" The jailor said, though he paid her little attention this time as he rolled up his newspaper.

"The armory needs much cleaning. I must beat every carpet," Shirin said as the call to prayer sounded, "*La ilaha il Allah.*" The jailor gathered his prayer beads and carpet and left the premises.

Shirin hurried to Farhad and Ismail's cell. Wasting no time, the tinsmith pulled a key from under his carpet and unlocked the door to their cell.

"You made a key?" Shirin exclaimed, looking first at the tinsmith, then at Farhad and Ismail.

"We Naqshbandi are grand designers," the tinsmith said, rolling up his carpet.

"It was a matter of a design within a design," Ismail said.

This made no sense to Shirin.

"Let us not delay." Farhad placed his Bukharan beanie on his head and donned the chupan that Shirin gave him so that he would resemble a local. Ismail followed suit. The men grabbed their belongings— swords, daggers, and pouches that had been taken from them when they were imprisoned.

"Leave the swords. Palace workers don't carry weapons," the tinsmith said. The men hid their daggers in the folds of their clothing.

When they reached the guards, who instead of praying were sipping chai and playing dice, Shirin swept into their alcove and began to clean the rifle stacks along the wall with her feather duster. The room smelled of rose tea and boredom. She cleaned the bayonets until they shone. Dust stung her eyes. The militiamen's gazes rested on Shirin when they were not calculating the numbers rolling across the carpet. Unobserved, Farhad, Ismail, and the tinsmith hurried down the corridor, under arches, and past alcoves until they came to the iron gate that led out of the jail, armory, and dungeon. Shirin soon caught up with them. She walked to the wrought gate while the others stood out of sight, and she requested permission to leave. As the guards opened the gate for her, Farhad and the others rushed on through. The guards exchanged glances and shrugged. The three men in disguise followed Shirin down the hall a few paces behind her. She stopped now and then to sweep the corners whenever someone passed by.

The foursome climbed a circular staircase inside one of the two citadel towers and emerged in the outdoor stables. Shirin picked her way across the manure-strewn cobblestones, giving a wide berth to the man splashing water across the sloped flooring in an effort to clean it. Making a wrong turn, she led Farhad and the others away from the mosque near the entrance of the fortress. They found themselves in the courtyard outside the emir's quarters. When Shirin looked through the lace curtains of one of several windows, she thought she saw Arash gazing back at her. Her adrenaline gushed. "Come quickly," she said, hurrying back down the thin hall from where they had just come, passing the Coronation Court. Hustling onward, she pointed as she whispered, "The harem is just down that lane." When Farhad and Ismail paused to examine the path, Shirin heard boot steps. Lots of them. Militia approached from behind the tinsmith.

"Leave us, Shirin," Farhad said quietly. "Now!"

She ducked down the corridor toward the harem.

Just after the call to prayer, Arash strode into the emir's quarters in full princely attire.

"May I ask who granted you entry?" the emir said to him, pouring water into the glass he used for rinsing paint brushes. Sad colors, like cumin and cinnamon, dotted his palette.

"Who else but your guard?"

"What did you say to him that he allowed you admission?" The emir examined Arash's clothing.

"Let's just say that perhaps you need to hire more reliable men. Now can we discuss what I came here for?" The emir sat on a snow-leopard skin rug, which disgusted Arash.

"So, you claim to be the governor of Marv. Why did you not send word of your arrival ahead of time so that I could welcome you properly? I do not recall having received such a dispatch…nor any gifts."

"The circumstances under which I have come are most unusual, and I do believe that you know the reason I am here."

"Apparently I have purchased your fiancé."

"I'm glad we understand one another. Anahita was not and is not for sale."

"My men purchased her at the slave auction."

"She was kidnapped. She is a free woman, not a slave. Tell me what price you want for her."

He dipped a different brush into brown paint. "Her first born son."

Arash's whole body seized. He couldn't speak. Reaching for his janbiya, he remembered that the emir's guards had stripped him of it and his sword.

"She clearly comes from quality stock. In fact, she's at the baths right now, being plucked and oiled and massaged for our wedding day, tomorrow."

"Don't delude yourself, Emir." Arash willed himself to stay cool, focused.

"Oh, I am not deluding myself. But your plea doesn't fall on deaf ears. Perhaps after she's given me an heir, you may buy her back. But from what I understand, once a woman becomes a mother through sigheh, they usually choose to stay with the father of their child."

Arash turned toward the window, formulating his ultimatum. "I know you don't want the Russian authorities interfering in your illegal slave markets. Release Anahita by sunup and I will not bring news of your recent purchase of women and girls from Quchan to the attention of the czar and the shah of Iran. Surely, the position you enjoy here means more to you than one woman in your harem."

The emir said, "You have overstayed your welcome. It is prayer time."

Arash bowed and turned toward the door. Lifting his gaze, he caught a glimpse of a woman with a broom…was it…*Shirin?* Behind her were three locals. No—behind her were Farhad, Ismail, and another man whose face he could not see. *I must leave and help them.* Four swordsmen would be better than three if it came to battling through the heavily guarded entrance to The Ark.

He had to believe that the scribe was right, that the emir would be forced to wait at least another day before sigheh with Anahita could take place. He kept faith in Anahita's ability to devise her own escape. What mattered in this moment was that Farhad and the others get out of the citadel. He would need them if the emir ignored his ultimatum. "Until tomorrow," Arash said to the emir. The man's face looked a mix of surprise and self-satisfaction, as if he'd won this round with his uninvited guest.

Arash turned and left. The guard was missing from the emir's foyer, perhaps gone for prayers. Arash retrieved his arms and fell into the throng of militia that followed the kadkhuda and others to the mosque near the entry to the The Ark. The four of them squeezed onto a free patch of carpet, joining the workers, artisans, eunuchs, and soldiers who knelt as equals before Allah.

"How do you expect to walk out of here?" Arash whispered to Farhad as they all lowered their foreheads to the carpet.

"The tinsmith's got it figured out."

Ismail whispered from Arash's other side. "I still have some of the slave market money, if we need to bribe our way out. It's sewn into my sash."

When the cleric sang the last of the verses from the Qur'an, Arash, Farhad, Ismail, and the tinsmith followed the stream of people toward the front gate of The Ark. Several prisoners in the cells that lined the walk waved or nodded discreetly to the Bukharan tinsmith.

The foursome waited quietly until a clerk came out of his closet-sized office at the gate. Arash noticed an open book sitting atop a pile of papers on the clerk's desk. An image of Mullah Nasreddin and his donkey filled the cover of this tale about a champion of the downtrodden. The clerk eyed the lot of them, including the Qajar insignia on Arash's sash.

Addressing Farhad, the clerk said, "What was your business in The Ark today?"

Farhad looked to his Bukharan cellmate. If he uttered a word with his Persian accent, he'd blow their cover.

"We are artisans employed by The Ark, on our way home," the Bukharan said.

"Why are you not using the back gate as is customary?"

"We just came from prayers. This was more convenient."

The clerk turned to Arash. "Are you with these men?"

"No." Arash knew it would raise more questions had he told the truth.

"Step this way." The clerk signaled the guards to remove the heavy iron stays on the massive gate. "Go on, go on," the clerk commanded. "I've got to get back to my read—my work."

Arash and the others hurried down the rampart to blend in with the jumble of merchants' carts toting dried apricots and spices across Execution Square. Their former cellmate slipped away alongside a camel piled with textiles heading to the market.

"I know of a safe house," Arash said, and the three soon plunged into the maze of mud brick alleys in one of Bukhara's oldest neighborhoods.

Safe House

Arash left Farhad and Ismail at the caravanserai with his battalion from Marv and continued on to the safe house, where they would eventually all meet. Rounding the alley near his destination, he heard the familiar neigh of his horse. The man holding its reins was the man Arash had dug out of the avalanche. Arash bristled as he walked beside his horse and stroked its neck. The horse was in good form. He said, "What do you want?"

"I've come in peace." Mahan held up the reigns for Arash.

They entered a courtyard enclosed by high mud walls that looked as pitted as bruised apples. A woman brought them tea, where they sat beneath a spindly narenj tree. Arash's horse licked his forelocks.

"I never meant to harm Anahita, only to protect her. I met her long ago, when she was ten or twelve years old." Mahan folded his legs beneath him. "I had agreed to the kidnapping because Anahita's khan blackmailed me. If I didn't accept the job, he would have disgraced my mother's name. I also accepted because I knew he had hired Tamam. He's a man of few scruples. He would have hurt Anahita the first chance he got."

"In a sense, by doing harm, you were also doing good."

"This is a paradox in life, isn't it?"

Arash let the quiet moment unfold as he poured them tea. "Perhaps the more relevant question is, why should I believe this story?"

"When I took Anahita from you, I did not know that you were her fiancé."

Arash touched his head wound. "I don't appreciate this."

"I'm sorry. I accidentally knocked Anahita unconscious when I attacked you. I wasn't sure who you were, but soon realized you were the person who saved my life. So I spared you." Mahan reached for a sugar lump, held it between his teeth, and took a swig of tea. "Had I known you were betrothed to Anahita, I would have left her with you. But I didn't know if you were her friend or foe. You didn't tell me who you were back on the mountain after you dug me out of the snow, as you might recall."

"What do you want from me?" Arash said.

"I was planning to contact you for ransom. All roads lead to Bukhara when looking for lost women, and I knew you would come to this city."

Arash blew on his tea as he listened. Mahan reminded him of someone. He wondered why he had met Anahita only once, and so long ago.

Mahan swatted a fly from the bowl of sugar cubes. "But as you have learned, the emir reserves the right of refusal on all slave transactions in Bukhara."

Mahan was either asking for his forgiveness or hoping not to be thrown in jail for his crimes once they returned to Iran. But he sounded sincere—his tone of voice, the slump of his shoulder, and his obvious fatigue. It seemed that Mahan needed to clear his conscience.

"Oh, I almost forgot..." Mahan said, putting down his tea and unraveling his waist sash. "This is Anahita's."

Arash held out his hand for the jeweled dagger. "I see my precautions have done her a lot of good." Arash contemplated receiving Anahita's weapon back from the very man who had kidnapped her. Studying Mahan, he asked, "Where will you go from here?"

"Maybe back to France."

"Do you have family there? Are there many Persians living in Paris?"

Mahan shifted. He said nothing, appearing ill at ease. Then he waved his hand, a dismissive gesture. "Some are attending universities."

Arash pressed. "Are some of your family members studying there or do you mean Persians in general?"

"Look, I'd rather not talk about my family." Mahan held his chin in a way that reminded Arash of Anahita's khan.

"Withholding information is not your prerogative. I could kill you for what you've done."

"Perhaps." Mahan said. "But I think that's a fight neither of us wants."

Point taken. Arash met Mahan's gaze. Contention doesn't win anyone over and Arash needed a man with Mahan's skills. A flick of his palm could fell an entire squadron. Time was running out.

"You'll work for me." Arash said.

Mahan lifted his head, a startled expression on his face.

"You can start tomorrow by helping me rescue Anahita, should the emir refuse to turn her over to me peacefully."

Mahan didn't answer. He stirred his chai.

"Tell me more about Anahita's other kidnapper. This man, Tamam."

Mahan grimaced before speaking. "Tamam. What is there to say about Tamam Bas?" He thought for a minute. "I'll bet there is something to that old belief having to do with the Sanskrit language, that the vibration of the name when spoken is also the vibration of what is named. That there is a mystical relationship between a name and what is named. Its understandable why compassion is something Tamam neither gives nor reaps, given his name means 'enough, finished.'"

This wasn't the answer Arash expected to hear. He crossed his legs at the ankles, thinking about this man's knowledge of Eastern philosophy, his martial arts, and the like.

Soon the smell of incense streamed over the courtyard wall. Seekers burned the wild rue in celebration that Baha ad-Din Naqshband's spirit would reach them when needed. The smoke reminded Arash of his plans to speak with the local dervishes. He need only follow the scent to find where they gathered.

"When I return, I want more facts on Tamam, his business with Anahita's khan." Getting up, Arash left to the sound of Mahan's spoon tinkling against the glass of his teacup.

Maman Bozorg, Shirin, Reza, Dariyoush, and Farhad stayed in the safe house that night with Arash and Mahan. They gathered round a low table, seated on carpets. Arash introduced Mahan to them all, and told them his story. Maman Bozorg turned to her kidnapper. "Shame on you," she said. "May the Merciful One forgive you."

Mahan palmed his heart and bowed his head to Maman Bozorg.

The woman of the house served them flatbread and a polau while they discussed possible plans and contingency strategies for departing Bukhara with Anahita.

"Anahita hopes to escape by morning," Maman Bozorg said, eyeing Mahan again.

"How?" Arash asked, noting the rather bland taste of the rice, which contained no Persian saffron seasoning.

"To where?" Reza said, unrolling his old map of the city. Looking at Maman Bozorg, he said, "You told her the caravanserais aren't safe, didn't you?"

"Yes. Even if she does get out, what is our plan to leave this city? Will not the emir's men still be looking for those of you who escaped his prison?" Her words came seconds before what initially sounded like a distant beat of a Persian *dafs* drum—soldiers butting their rifles on some poor soul's door.

Arash tore off a piece of bread. "I believe I can back the emir into a diplomatic corner. He will release her, rather than risk international repercussions."

"But perhaps he'll only let her go for a large sum," Farhad said.

"We've still got money." Reza smoothed the map with the heel of his palm and turned it toward himself and Shirin, who sat beside him.

Dariyoush spat in the dirt.

Shirin looked up from the maps, her expression turned thoughtful.

"Kalyan Minaret," she said, softly. "Fatima told Anahita and me about this minaret."

Farhad crossed his arms and turned to Arash. "What if the diplomatic approach doesn't work?"

"That's where Mahan comes in." Looking at the martial artist, he said, "We are in agreement on this, aren't we?"

Mahan gave a slight nod.

Arash continued. "I don't want any of you other men going back inside The Ark. You need to ready the caravan and position to leave as soon as you get word that we've got Anahita out. Now that we know she's working in the weaving room, we have more options in terms of escape."

Dariyoush fidgeted, shot a glance at the kadkhuda.

"But they guard the east gate well," Maman Bozorg said.

"Not as well as the main entrance," Shirin said.

"But you can bet it is guarded heavily now that we've escaped," Farhad said.

Maman Bozorg frowned. "Pray that this doesn't impede Anahita's plans."

Everyone fell quiet.

"Say she does get out on her own. Then what?" Reza said.

"I'll find her, and we'll leave for Marv by train from Kasr–i Orifan." Arash looked at Farhad. "I would like to buy Maman Bozorg and Shirin tickets to Marv on the next train." Glancing at them, he said, "There is no need for you to stay here with us."

The two women began to balk, but Arash raised his hand. "If Mahan's and my plan does not work, the only other option is to take The Ark down by force. The Yomut and Turkman nomads should be here imminently and will join our battalion from Marv. It's an ancient sand citadel—gunpowder will riddle it to smithereens. You women need not be around for that."

"You'll fire upon The Ark with Anahita inside?" Maman Bozorg said.

"Have you any other ideas?" Arash said.

"Surely, Naheed's husband could help us smuggle Anahita out. It worked with me," Shirin offered.

"We don't have that kind of time. She will be married tomorrow." Arash shoved his plate away and drew his knee to his chest.

"Better married to the emir and alive than unwed and dead from your guns," Maman Bozorg said. Her frankness stung. "Arash, I have always thought of you as a man who could catch the scent of a rose when staring into the eyes of a swine. But, all this talk about a show of arms suggests that tonight your mind is muddied, your keenest senses are blunted."

Arash's hand drifted over his bent knee to scratch his temple. Shirin looked sadly at Maman Bozorg, at everyone. "This is so awful," she couldn't help saying. A tear slid down her cheek.

Dariyoush turned to Arash and said quietly, "Perhaps your own wishes to have Anahita for your wife before the emir marries her—and plunders her virtue—are clouding your ability to think this through clearly. Maman Bozorg has a point."

His remark cut Arash like a scythe. "Who are you to talk about whether or not force should be used? Your hotheadedness landed the three of you in jail." He hated that Dariyoush had read his mind and spoken so truthfully.

"Listen," Farhad said, "I believe Arash has stressed that diplomacy is the first option. Stealing Anahita back is second. Only lastly will he consider force. I am certain, mother, that it won't come to that."

"Good," Maman Bozorg said. "As I will not be taking that train to Marv. I intend to sit at a palace loom everyday until I see that Anahita is rescued. It would be quite alarming to have to do so with cannon balls raining down."

Farhad eyed everyone sitting on the carpet. "Have we all forgotten that at this very moment she may have already escaped? I have every reason to believe she will get out on her own."

"Inshallah," Arash said, getting up to fetch a bedroll. Others followed suit. But he wasn't tired. He just wanted time alone. When Dariyoush drew near, Arash almost excused himself. But he saw that the young man held the camel bone vial that he had whittled for Anahita.

"My prince, since you do not need my services tomorrow in rescuing Anahita, I would offer that I return to Marv with Ali and begin recruiting nomads to form the border battalion as we had originally planned."

Arash just looked at Dariyoush.

"When I was locked in the bug pit, I realized that, although I care very deeply for Anahita, I…I wasn't certain that I wanted to die for her." Dariyoush placed the sewing needle vial into Arash's hands and held them. "I am happy for Anahita that she has found a man who is willing to give up his life for her."

Arash's heart ached for Dariyoush.

"No longer will I pitch my tent in her shadow." When Dariyoush turned away, Arash saw the gleam of water in his eyes.

As Arash lay down and stretched out, he wondered if Dariyoush spoke the truth or if his words stemmed from an attempt to soothe his pride. Curling up on his side, he rested his face on his hands. *Both Dariyoush and Maman Bozorg were right. Force isn't the solution, despite my urgency.* Arash remembered his impatience back at the desert pool when he needed to know whether Anahita had been touched by Tamam. His lack of inner mastery, and his unawareness of what Anahita's feelings might have been at the time, had allowed him to dump the rubbish on his mind and in his heart into the space between them. *The Naqshbandi shaikh was right—I had permitted my lower self to rule my tongue.* Arash felt ashamed and saddened that his behavior at the seep, and only minutes ago, had been motivated more by self-interest than by his love and fear for his fiancée.

He came to appreciate Dariyoush's devotion to Anahita, his willingness to risk everything for her, for no personal gain. Arash would tell him this. Looking at the stars, they seemed so very far away. Almost as unreachable as tomorrow.

A Silk Chain

Just after sunset Salar and I met Kufa, who stood with a torch at the weaving workshop door. "The hourglass is still dripping, Kufa," Salar said. "I'm all ears, awaiting your guess." He tossed his head and turned on his heels.

Kufa took Anahita by the arm. "The riddle's answer, or I don't unlock the door."

"My two hours of weaving time, or I won't give you the answer." I yanked my arm from his.

"*Two* hours?"

He was so tall that I had to tilt my head back to look into his eyes. "Two, and I do not want your company inside the room."

"One or none at all."

"Agreed. I'll tell you the answer when you search me for 'weaving weapons' before leaving the room."

Kufa unlocked the door, and I found the loom at which my grand-mother had sat earlier that day. He lit a lamp with his torch and left. Sitting, I placed my palms on either side of the bench. I could feel the oil from Maman Bozorg's fingertips on the wefts she had woven, smell the lingering scent of the rosewater from her clothing. Tears welled behind my eyes. I picked up a thread. As I started weaving, the hypnotic rhythm of my hands seeped through my entire body. I hadn't lied to Kufa and Salar. Weaving *was* my balm. It was at the loom that I always felt the most rooted. Safe. Confident. Weaving would help me find my way home.

I worried if Pirouz would come in time, and if had he been able to help Dariyoush.

Wrapping weft threads around a pair of warps, making a *soumak* knot with a shimmering silk thread, a sequined veil glimmered in my mind. A sequined veil—it seemed like a dream belonging to another Anahita. The wedding celebration meant nothing to me anymore. I just wanted to be with Arash.

After a while, I heard voices in the corridor. Pirouz!

"You look like a man difficult to impress," my young accomplice said to Kufa. "Would you do me the honor of critiquing my magic show before I have to give a solo performance for the emir tomor-row?" His slick talk made him seem much more mature than his voice suggested. I peered down the rows of looms and through the opened door to see Pirouz begin his repertoire with a coin trick. Then I looked over the lattice balcony into the courtyard below to the stack of carpets warehoused in the alcove waiting for morning pick up by the local carpet sellers.

I crept to the door at the top of the spiral stairs that led to the courtyard. I tried the latch. *Locked!* I ran to the balcony again. If I jumped, I would risk spraining an ankle—or worse. Hurrying back to the loom, I glanced at Pirouz. He was building a house of cards. I wove more rows of knots to keep up appearances, lest Kufa came to check on me.

I could make a chain out of the silk skeins of yarn hanging on the loom and lower myself off the balcony. Silk would not break. Three skein lengths would be enough to cover two-thirds of the distance. I could jump the rest. Lowering myself down the balcony pillar would be no more difficult than scaling the rocks to the caves at Abadi-e-Golaub. I grabbed the closest two skeins within reach and tied them together. Just then Kufa said, "Excuse me for a minute," to Pirouz. I hid the yarn beneath my skirts. Kufa came to my side.

"Tell me the answer to the riddle."

"Surely the hour glass has not spilled even half of its sand. It was our bargain that you would leave me be." I looked up at him. "If I give you a hint will you promise to stay away until my time is up?"

Kufa crossed his arms. "That depends on the hint."

"The answer is only one word."

"What kind of a hint is that?"

"Kufa, the answer to this one cannot be reasoned. Use your heart to discern it." I waved him away, and to my surprise, he obeyed.

Before reaching for another skein, I watched as Pirouz made use of large shining props. He enlisted Kufa's help with this act, a brilliant tactic on his part. Kufa now held an armful of batons that he was to toss into the air one by one as Pirouz incorporated them into his marvelous stream of flying instruments. Pirouz even managed to maneuver Kufa's back to the weaving room door.

I reached for the third skein and tied it to the others, securing it to the worn balustrade beside a balcony pillar. Kufa wouldn't see it in the dim of the weaving room. I peeked at Pirouz and Kufa one last time: Pirouz juggling seven batons and Kufa counting.

Tucking a weaving knife into my tunic, I strode to the balcony. I gathered my skirts and slipped over the railing, holding fast to the silk chain. My hands were sweating as I lowered myself step by step. My sandals caused me to slip against the pillar's painted wood, slowing me down. I didn't dare kick them off for fear that they might clatter on the stone flooring below.

The lattice creaked. I looked up at the balcony hoping it wasn't merely ornamental, and that it would hold my weight. But descending a few more steps, the wood did not protest. When I was within a meter or more from the floor, I let go of the silk and jumped. As my feet touched ground, I realized my mistake. Someone will see the silk rope.

There was no turning back. I ran to the stack of large carpets, those wide enough to span an entire room. I climbed to the top and struggled to unravel one. Though it weighed more than a sack of Solomon's gold, I was determined to wrap myself inside. Glancing up at the weaving workshop, the room was aglow. I imagined Pirouz in the hallway, twirling magic into wheels of color—gold, red, blue and charcoal-tinged flames—mesmerizing Kufa. I could not let the boy down. If I were caught, the emir's men would string him up by his ankles. Flog him with that giant whip.

I lay down on a carpet, pulled the knife out of my tunic, and held it in my right hand, which I stretched above my head. With my left hand, I gripped the rug's selvedge at my thighs. Holding tight, I rolled myself up inside its weave. I didn't manage to roll as tightly as I had hoped, but snugly and neatly enough to fit in among the stack of other rugs. No part of my body stuck out of either end. If all went according to plan, I would lie hidden here until dawn, and soon after, unassuming eunuchs and merchants would carry me outside of the palace.

But, even though I lay as still as possible, my carpet slid, then slid some more. *No!* Before I knew it I had unraveled half way. *This will never do! They'd see me.*

As I struggled with my carpet, the sound of Pirouz's fire baton—its flames cutting the air—rushed as loudly as a windstorm. He must have been tiring by now. I was touched that he kept at it for this long, showing such loyalty to Arash. He had been twirling his baton above his head, behind his back, and under his legs for at least half an hour, with Kufa clapping now and again. Lying on my stomach inside my rug with my face forward, my window of vision measured the width of my shoulders. I could see up into the weaving room from my circular vantage. The eunuch dashed into view.

The upstairs darkened as I heard Pirouz smother his flames. He came into the weaving room and stood with his back to the railing beside my silk chain. After unfastening it, he tossed it under the loom among the other loose threads.

"She's gone," Kufa said. He leaned over the balcony and scanned the courtyard, warehouses, and dye workshop below.

"I know she's gone."

Kufa whipped his head toward Pirouz. "What do you mean you know she's gone?"

"She left a while ago."

Kufa screwed up his face.

"Yes, she thanked you, and then said something like *eshq*."

"*Eshq?*"

"Yes. She said the word love."

"How is it that I don't remember this?"

"Well, come to think of it, you didn't acknowledge her. Perhaps you couldn't hear her over the sound of my fire batons."

Kufa knelt below my view. I presumed he was looking beneath the loom benches for me.

"You were quite engrossed in my show—I have been told that my acts have hypnotic effects. And by the way, your enthusiasm makes me feel good about tomorrow when I—"

I admired Pirouz's courage. Perhaps his childhood on the streets made the possibility of prison seem comforting: a relief from fending for himself and a place where he'd be guaranteed shelter and a meal. But I wondered if working for Arash had somehow changed all that— if Pirouz longed to go home to Marv and be with Arash as much as I did.

"Wait. You mean to say that you saw her walk out of the weaving room and say the word love. Was it the answer to the riddle?" Kufa said.

"How would I know if the word was an answer to a riddle? I suppose it sounds like as good an answer as any—"

"I don't believe you."

"I may be good with illusions, but I don't lie. And besides, why would I want to fool you? I don't even kno—"

"Which way did she go?"

"That way." Pirouz pointed toward the harem.

"Come on," Kufa commanded, blowing out the lamp. "Are you sure she said the word love?"

"That's what I heard."

The eunuch stroked his smooth chin with his hand. "Love is sovereign and ceaselessly moves. Of course—this is the *only* answer to Salar's riddle." As he turned and left, Kufa sang, "The money is mine!" Then he whistled a tune as he locked the door behind them.

The weight of the folds of carpet pressed against the back of my head. I wondered was this anything like the feel of wearing one's death shroud, should we continue to sense anything after we've taken our last breath. Feeling claustrophobic, I didn't know if I could last the night.

Lock Down!

$\mathcal{I}$ awoke at dawn to the sound of rustlings, water sloshing, and the strike of flint. The putrid urine smell emanating from the warming indigo dye vats soon penetrated my layers of wool. The slaves had begun a new day's work. Soon merchants and hired hands from the city of Bukhara would burst through the workshop gate and add to the bustle.

Within minutes the great fortress doors rumbled open, followed by the clop of donkeys' hooves and wagon wheels on the flagstone. People talked as they waited for permission to enter.

"I covet these Akhaltekin horses—their great height, endurance, proud tempers." The voice was unmistakably Arash's. My adrenaline surged. I wanted to run to him.

Papers rustled. "This is dated yesterday," a guard said.

"You look like a smart fellow, someone who can…" another voice paused. "Someone who knows how to read between the lines. Surely you understand that the duration of the invitation extends for any day after the date it was signed. The palace scribe will be upset if you do not let us pass."

The voice sounded like Mahan. It couldn't be Mahan. With Arash?

"Scribe Shamsiddin is waiting for us," Arash said.

I pictured the guard squinting at them as he tucked the note into his uniform. I crossed my fingers, hoping they'd win their entry.

"May I have the invitation back?" Arash asked.

"I am granting you passage today. Take it or leave it."

Arash and Mahan strode through the gate as an elderly carpet merchant drove his cart into my view. The pink light of dawn made the madder-dyed skeins of wool hanging to dry behind him look even rosier. Several workers lifted carpets onto the merchant's cart. As Arash and Mahan walked beside my carpet, Arash said, "Perhaps you should wait here a while and see if Anahita comes to work this morning. And if she doesn't, go to the harem as planned."

I wanted so badly to tell them I was here, safe and almost out. I wanted to tell them to free Dariyoush. But I didn't dare. It could put us all in danger.

Pausing, Mahan said, "Don't let the emir's plans for sigheh distract you."

"That's not helpful," Arash said.

"Just don't do anything to bring the house down. I want to live to see another Nurooz."

Stepping into view, Arash pointed to the looms on the balcony. They made for the spiral stairs, taking them two at a time to the weaving workshop.

I held my breath when palace workers strolled toward my stack of carpets. As the men took hold of a rug beside me, the pile shifted. Removing it, they walked out of my line of sight. The workers picked up another from my stack. My breaths came fast and shallow as I waited my turn. If they removed the one directly beside mine, I might unravel and give myself away.

Another and another carpet.

Before they lifted mine, the merchant said, "Enough! I can carry no more. My donkey is limping today."

I closed my eyes. "Pick me up. Pick me up," I silently chanted. But knowing I could do nothing, *nothing* to save myself, I lay limp, lifeless—a sack of skin melted into a plush wool tomb. I could only be patient. Leave my fate in the care of an old man, two neutered slaves, and…and…maybe God, were Allah to notice.

The eunuchs ignored the carpet merchant. "They will cut off our heads if we don't send this whole batch of carpets today." My eyes flew open when the slaves lifted and swung the rug in which I hid. My stomach dropped, the movement almost ticklish. They loaded me onto the merchant's cart, feet first. I could see out the rear of the wagon.

"That is enough, I say!" the merchant yelled. "Are your ears broken? My donkey's leg is lame." This time the eunuchs heeded the old man. Just as the slaves loaded the last of the carpets onto a different rug merchant's cart, horns sounded. Loud, urgent blows. One after another,

"Missing slave! Lock down!" Guards yelled.

People scurried here and there. The great doors to The Ark groaning shut. *Oh no!* I kicked the inside of the carpet. *No!* I kicked again, making a fist of the hand pinned to my side.

When Arash came to the emir's quarters, the Bukharan was eating breakfast. "You again," he said. "How did you get past my guard this time?"

"He wasn't there. You run a rather loose operation here, Emir. What with four prisoners escaping yesterday? Seems your dungeons are not made of iron and rock, but dice and chai."

"They escaped just about the time you left here. Quite the coincidence."

"Quite."

The emir did not ask Arash to sit with him on the carpet. He salted his egg and took a bite, followed by a sip of tea. The many portraits on the wall of the emir and his predecessors caught Arash's eye as he crossed the room to where the turban-heavy man sat on his snow-leopard skin.

The emir looked up at Arash, who now loomed over him. "Why is it that you insist on coming here day after day right to the point of my knife—uninvited?"

"Love."

"Ah—this can be the *only* explanation."

"Bring me Anahita, and I will leave this city peacefully."

"Why should I believe the threats of a governor who is so low among the tier of Qajar princes that his father sent him to rule a principality on the most remote fringe of his kingdom? One that will surely fall to Russia."

"Yomut and Turkman battalions, under the auspices of the Qajar Dynasty, await just beyond your watchmen's binoculars." Arash bluffed, not certain they'd arrived. He looked up to the sudden sound of horns ringing throughout the fortress. The emir stopped eating and slowly stood. Arash assumed the horns were an alarm. He worried that Mahan had slipped up. Or perhaps he found Anahita and was fighting their way out of The Ark.

No! This cannot be happening! Not when I am so close to escaping. My mind grasped for solace, training on a memory of my grandmother in evening's soft light, prostrating on her prayer rug. *Patience. Receptivity.*

I could not fail. My errors since Mahan abducted me at the seep flipped before my eyes, one by one, like pages filled with Qur'anic *surahs* I had forsaken since that moment I had declared that I needed no help from Allah to survive this journey.

Men shouted all around me.

What could I have expected from that lack of need? Allah guides those who will to be guided.

Even the marrow in my bones could not bear the weight of my shame. *Come, lover of leaving, it does not matter that you have broken your vow a thousand times, still come.*

I stilled my kicking. I unclenched my fist. "Allah, for my people's sake, shepherd us all out of here."

"Please."

God's name lay thick on my tongue, so difficult to invoke. I repeated my prayer—not merely with my lips, but from a place that ached in my inmost being.

A needlepoint of light came to rest in a dim corner of my heart.

My cart lurched.

A space opened in my chest. I breathed more easily smothered there in that carpet than I had during those long days that I parched in isolation under the vast blue skies with Mahan. To think that I had sought valerian and onions to cure my suffocation. No, those painful weeks of separation were caused by my constricted heart, my arrogance.

Coming to mind was the image of the cloud that seemed to shade Mahan and me as we traveled through the desert. *Allah, how many favors of yours have I denied? You have never left me.*

A guard came to the emir's door and asked for entry. "It is the new slave in the harem. She did not show up for work at the weaving workshop."

Arash held a straight face as the emir studied him. Without taking his eyes off Arash, the emir said to his guard, "Thank you. Send Hassan to me, please."

"*Another* escapee, Emir?" Arash said.

"I am growing tired of your company. Either take your leave or I will see to it that you are locked in my dungeon."

Arash laughed. He strode toward the door, and the emir said, "You won't be laughing when it is my men who find her first."

The merchant who drove my cart cracked his whip and set his poor old donkey trotting. His cart converged with others—ramming, pushing, and bullying their way to make it through the gate as the guards struggled to close them. "Let me pass! I have work to do today.

Let me pass!" he shouted. Only a handful of impatient merchants slipped through the barricade with us.

Nearly blue from holding my breath, I rejoiced in Allah. *I am out!* I kissed the inside of the rug. I waved my feet like two nursing lambs' tails wiggling with ultimate glee. The cart rattled and jounced over the gravel. I had escaped!

We rolled across Execution Square, where the emir's militia had gathered. I could hear someone in charge calling out the various sectors of the city for each soldier to search: "The carpet bazaars, Lyabi-Hauz Courtyard, the railroad station." The cart driver rolled by a caravanserai, and as Maman Bozorg had warned, militia crawled everywhere.

The rug surrounding me made for a smooth ride. The merchant stopped near an alcove in an alley, climbed off the cart and disappeared. Now was my chance. I began to inch my way out of the rug. If I rolled from side to side, the carpet unraveled a little with each of my movements, allowing me wiggle room. The man didn't seem to be coming back.

I thrust my right arm, which had been pinned straight above my head, out the end of the rug and was able to push against the stack of carpets beneath me. Meanwhile, I shimmied with my toes and managed to free my shoulders. But, my left arm was still pinned against my thigh. I rolled side to side again, this time with more vigor, trying to shake loose the heavy layers of rug around me. Grunting, I freed my left arm, then hips and legs. Finally, like a babe in birth, I slipped out from my wooly womb onto the ground.

My nerves fired like a repeating rifle. I scrambled under the cart to collect my thoughts. Surveying my whereabouts, I recognized the ancient minaret that was near a mosque and madrasa. The Kalyan Minaret.

The merchant came out of his house carrying a newspaper. "Tssk. Tssk. Tssk." He shook his head. "What will that emir do next? Buying women and children who belong in Quchan!" I felt safer knowing this man did not sympathize with the emir, but I wanted to remain hidden, so I held onto the underside of the cart when it resumed its journey. I scurried close to the ground, like a scorpion, at the clip of the donkey's pace until we came to the lane leading to the minaret. Then I ducked and allowed the merchant to continue on without me. After crouching momentarily in place in the middle of the street, I stood and walked on—as if I were in no hurry at all—toward Kalyan Minaret. My body felt stiff from my night in the carpet.

When I came to the edge of the neighborhood, I saw that the base of the minaret stood beside the mosque in the same plaza as the madrasa. A wide brick staircase led down to the square between them. No trees would seclude me from anyone's view. I took a deep breath and left the protection of the enclosed alleyways. The largest minaret in Asia loomed above. Eight of many arched windows in its cupola faced me. When I reached the mosque, I peered around the corner and froze. My spirit sank when I discovered that the door to the minaret was two stories above the ground. I could only reach it by the mosque roof.

Across the square, militiamen talked beside the madrasa. Soon, several more soldiers joined them. Behind me a row of doors led into the side gallery of the mosque. I backed my way into the first and closed it slowly, keeping an eye on the movement of the militia outside. When I turned around, I covered my mouth and gasped.

After leaving the emir's quarters, Arash made his way down the corridor alongside the harem and treasury. Passing the scribe's atelier, he looked in. The calligrapher stilled his pen, nodded.

Mahan fell in step with Arash, giving him a start. "You have a knack for dropping in on people, don't you?" Arash said.

"Word from the harem is that it was Anahita who escaped. Apparently, she was quite a spokesperson for the women."

"How did you get in the harem?"

"I didn't. Pirouz told me," Mahan said.

"How did he know you were with me?"

"Who knows? Pirouz will leave The Ark this afternoon with the entertainment troupe," Mahan said. "He says he is counting the seconds until that time."

Arash thought perhaps he should not have allowed Pirouz to take such a risk. But the boy seemed so eager. Arash and Mahan walked toward two eunuchs who appeared to be arguing, though under their breath.

"It's your fault," Arash heard.

"No, it's not."

"But you allowed her into the weaving room after hours."

"She was not missing until this morning. Thus, she was your responsibility."

Slowing his pace, Arash watched one eunuch squint at the other.

"How do I know she even came back to the harem last night? Wait a minute…she gave you the answer to my riddle, didn't she?"

"She told you that riddle in the first place."

Anahita used a riddle to help her escape? Hastening their steps, Arash and Mahan made for the weaving workshops and the merchants' gate, where they had left their horses. When Arash passed by Maman Bozorg seated at a loom, they exchanged smiles as she sponged the sweat from her forehead with her scarf. "We've been blessed," she said quietly.

"Mashallah," Arash said. He assumed Anahita's grandmother would leave with Naheed when the lock down subsided. In the meantime, he knew she would do nothing out of the ordinary to attract suspicion.

He and Mahan hurried down the stairs, breezed past the dye vats to the guards, who allowed them out of The Ark. They leapt on their horses and cantered toward the center of Bukhara in hopes of finding Anahita before the emir's men. A light wind touched their backs.

Kashf, Unveiling

I stood with my back to the door, which was now closed against the courtyard full of soldiers. A circle of dervishes sat on sheep skins in the midst of their meditation. My face flushed, having interrupted their *zikr*, remembrance of God. "I am so sorry. I—"

"Welcome," one of them said. "I am Shaikh Kabir. Please join us."

I couldn't sit quietly. "I have just escaped from the emir's palace and—" Most of the men were now looking at me.

"We know this," the shaikh, the spiritual master, said.

My expression must have shown puzzlement.

"We heard The Ark horns, and it is not often a young woman, unaccompanied, comes into our den as you have. It was a simple deduction."

"Of course," I said. The sound of boots on stone caused me to glance at the door.

"Come," the Sufi gestured. "Sit back on your heels like us. Quickly." He reached for a black cloak and placed it over my shoulders. Another dervish grabbed a felted hat, kissed it, and then motioned for me to put it on. I swept my hair inside its conical shape.

"Bend your head like us and pray." Within two blinks, the door to the dervishes' den burst open and two soldiers barged in.

"Pardon us," one said. I sat with my back to them. The militiamen hovered in the doorway, as if surveying the room.

"Hoda Hafiz," the shaikh said, suggesting that the soldiers leave. After a few long moments the men retreated, everyone in the room remaining silent until I spoke.

"I must hide," I said. "I would like to climb Kalyan Minaret and stay there until the emir's men are no longer looking for me." A few of the dervishes eyed each other. "I know that it is said to be haunted, but that may work to my advantage. If my fiancé, the governor of Marv—his name is Arash—comes to you, please tell him where I am. But perhaps it will be my father or grandmother or tribesman or cousin or schoolmaster who comes." I hushed when I saw the shaikh smile. A brilliance shone through his dark pupils.

"Ah," he said to the others. "This is the person to whom the naghal referred—'the much-traveled one,' followed by a hundred caravan loads of hearts."

I looked at my hands.

"We will take care of everything, *dokhtaram*." He addressed me as "my daughter," as did my mullah back in Hasanabad. This made me feel closer to home. "Come," he said, lifting a water skin from beside him and handing it to me. I began to take off the cloak, but the shaikh gestured for me to keep it on.

We walked through a low door into the gallery of the mosque beneath hundreds of arches and domes. I marveled at the play of light and shadow. I gasped when a soldier entered. The Sufi led me through a door near the front portal and up a spiral staircase. I could hardly keep from slipping on the stairs, so polished were they by centuries of muezzins' slippers. The soldier's boots tromped at the base of the stairs.

From the roof of the mosque, I could see nearly the whole of Bukhara, including an unobstructed view of The Ark. May I never lay eyes on it again. Holding onto my dervish hat, I craned my neck to see the top of the minaret and swallowed. "It must be twenty floors high," I said.

"Forty-five-and-a-half meters," the holy man said, "and it has fared well in every earthquake since it has been built."

A huge stork's nest sat on top. I admired the inscriptive bands wrapping around its exterior. I hadn't thought about what it would be like to be up inside the tower in an earthquake. The shaikh handed me a flint. "There is no light inside. Only use this if you absolutely need it. We will bring you food tonight after *azan*, under the cover of darkness. And be careful, the stairs are in poor condition."

Again I tried to give the dervish back his cloak. "Keep it. You might need it," he said. Despite that I had heard the soldier's footsteps so near, I experienced an unusual sense of calm in this man's presence. Perhaps this shaikh might help me. "My father and tribesman are held captive in The Ark, and so are many women and girls from Quchan who were sold into slavery... I wish I could figure out what to do to help everyone, I—"

"Sometimes the better option is to stop weaving and watch how the pattern improves."

I closed my mouth and listened. What he told me somehow helped to lessen my anxiety, my obvious worry about circumstances I could not change. The muscles behind my brows softened. Letting go gave me more strength to tackle the task at hand—my several-hundred-step climb up this ancient minaret. A structure, as legend goes, built upon a murdered man, and one from which the emir and emirs before him had tossed people to their deaths. A tower full of ghosts.

I hesitated before crossing the skybridge. When the dervish opened the minaret door, it clanged on its rusty hinges. I peered inside. The light from outside illuminated the first few steps before the others curved up and out of sight. Once the door shut, I would be in total darkness. I worried about spiders, bats, maybe even rats. I wasn't sure how long I hesitated there. Perhaps it was for quite a while because the shaikh seemed compelled to say, "Don't try to see through the distances. Move within, but don't move the way fear makes you move."

I held the shaikh's gaze. After I stepped inside, he closed the door behind me. He locked me in. The space turned as black as the emir's men's turbans. I endured a tinge of panic, followed by a memory of the full-bellied laugh of Fatima, the teahouse owner from Hasanabad. "The idea of ghosts never scared me, dear girl. Why, they tell the best stories!" I smiled, picturing Fatima's cheerful round face.

"Move within," I said as I lifted my cloak and the skirts beneath it. Feeling my way, I slid my foot up the steep rise of the first step. Placing a foot on the second step, I discovered it was all but missing. I'd have to hoist myself up to the third step. Searching above with my hands, I took the next few steps with great caution, walking into a spider web. "Oh!" I exclaimed, trying to peel the sticky fibers from my face and shoulders.

I climbed on—round and round. My ascension was much like the whirl of a dervish's dance, in which movement and stillness are combined. Turning up the minaret, I came full circle, around an axis, back to my starting point. I modeled their celestial dance in which the course of their motion harmonizes with the rotation of the cosmos, drawing them to their inmost center, the point where they feel closest to Allah. A dance unlocking a path through which new knowledge is given.

I counted one hundred and twenty steps, and thought that I must have been nearly three-quarters of my way up Kalyan Minaret. Even after all this time, my eyes had not adjusted to the lack of light. The darkness pressed around me, and I could see nothing. Having broken into a sweat, I contemplated removing the dervish cloak, but realized that if I held it, this would leave me with only one free hand, so I left it on.

With my next step, the stair gave way. Tumbling, I bumped and scraped against the rough stone stairs. My felted hat flew off as I tried to stop myself. After falling down several steps, I regained my balance. Panting, my breast heaved. I heard the soft taps of the dervish hat as it continued down the stairwell. Wiping myself off, I shook from head to toe. My legs seemed too wobbly to hold me, and I lost my nerve to climb on. I sat on a step.

Sitting alone in the quiet of the stairwell, the darkness sharpened my senses. Little sounds I did not notice while climbing now became quite loud. Pebbles tumbling, wing beats of a moth, the buzz of a fly. Much as if I were a chunk of ice that melted to water and then evaporated to blend with the air, I perceived no distinction between myself and the colorless space inside the minaret. Breathing the same dusty particles as the moth and fly, my heart felt the pulse of every desert creature, tree and rock.

I recalled my backing unawares into the room full of dervishes. Thoughts of those who traveled to Bukhara to my rescue filled me with love: my family, my tribe, Pirouz. Even Shamsiddin, Mahan, and the eunuchs played a role in helping me escape. I repented for my previous smug notion that I would, and could, save myself. I could not have possibly planned such things, or the timing of them.

Stop weaving and watch how the pattern improves.

Maybe the shaikh had meant that other forces are at work. Perhaps synchronicity is not mere coincidence—it's more a complicity of multiple wills coming together for reasons we do not understand. A force in the universe that responds, guides, and unifies. It seems that we exist for the sake of everything else.

My mind slipped beyond wordy thoughts to an intuitive place. A new perception—an inner eye—awakened. Something began to churn inside me—a constellation, a starry night of galaxies. *A secret within us makes the universe turn.* Maybe this silence was offered to me by the Sufi like a thoughtfully wrapped gift, a space through which I received clarity, and the flow of Allah's grace. As a result of the shaikh's nearness, I experienced a connection with the oneness of everything.

This churning inside burned hotly like the sun, scaring me. I shrank from its intensity. Surely the whole universe tried to stuff itself within me. I wanted to run from it, escape my own body.

I started up the stairs again. For another thirty or forty steps, I planted my feet on whatever morsel each stair afforded me. Though frightened, I discerned, and was comforted by, an abundant sense of trust, friendship, perhaps even joy. From inside and outside, kindness held me.

When I could hear the faint cry of the water carrier rise from the streets of Bukhara, I knew that I was close to the top of the tower. I gained speed as the light increased inside the minaret. Ascending, a new sensation assailed me. A heaviness filled my depths, as if my essence bore a thousand sorrows. The sadness belonging to every victim from Quchan, each atrocity the world has ever known, and the longing of every soul wishing to return to Allah.

All at the same time, I felt afraid yet comforted, sad but joyful. This presence held contrarieties, a kind of harmonious incongruity.

Another five, six, or dozen steps and I could make out the shapes of the stairs. I no longer needed to negotiate with my hands, but simply step one foot above the other. Emerging into open air, sunlight spilled on my cheeks through the arched windows that encircled the minaret's balcony. No words could describe how the warmth felt on my skin. Despite the events of my life over the past weeks, I felt grateful for the tremendous gift of existence itself, the unimaginable beauty surrounding me.

The wooden flooring of the balcony moaned under my feet. I inched my way around, testing the planks and finding them quite sturdy. In the streets below, people cried out in pain as the emir's soldiers plied their sticks among the throngs to clear a passage. Stalls crashed to the ground as they upturned fruit and vegetable stands, broke into private courtyards, and even searched beneath unrolled carpets. It was as if the sun had forgotten the hour of azan and the whole town had gone mad. Even flocks of pigeons dashed to safe perches. I prayed that peace would soon come.

In the light I noticed blood on my sleeve. I must have cut myself when I fell. My cheek stung, and I realized that I reopened the wound Tamam had given me. While I shivered at the memory of him, I could only feel compassion for Tamam. *There is someone here, invisible to the eye, like an image of the heart, but the radiance of his face has taken over my existence.* I became love.

After removing my dervish cloak, I shook out the dust and sat on it. The breeze freshened me even though sultry. Remembering my conversation with my grandmother, I smiled knowing how happy she likely became having entered the palace workshop that morning to find me gone. I prayed for Baba and the others in jail. But the squadron of soldiers running about in the alleyways below indicated that the emir's men were looking for many people, not just me. Perhaps they had escaped.

South of the central square stood a cluster of caravanserais. I wondered where my family and Arash were until exhaustion overcame me and I fell asleep.

Seated the next morning in the balcony of the minaret, a point where the demarcation between heaven and earth dissipated, I listened to the trilling of starlings in the walnut trees in the neighborhood below. I imagined the birds to be lemon and peach colored, the shades of Reza's cheerful lovebirds. The burning sensation inside me—that stormy presence of love—had drifted away.

My stomach growled. The dervishes had brought no dinner the night before as the torches of the emir's men glared long after dark, past the hour when the last of the city's lamps had been snuffed out.

In the distance, someone had begun chanting the Qur'an, likely a Sufi. The unimaginably sweet melody carried all the passion of Majnun seeking his beloved. Surely, tongue and lips vibrated with the breath of Allah. I needed to get out of the city. I would ask the dervishes to bring me away from Bukhara to the Naqshbandi shrine in Kasr-i Orifan.

I gathered my cloak and skirts and ducked under the low door leading to the minaret's staircase.

A Single Ray

$\mathcal{D}$isguised as a dervish, I rode with Shaikh Kabir into the village of Kasr–i Orifan, to the shrine of Baha ad-Din Naqshband. The shaikh led the way into the courtyard that contained the tomb of the late Sufi. I squinted into the sun, inspecting the small, ancient minaret tilting over a plaza beyond. I found shade under the *ayvan*, running my fingers over the intricate carvings on the many wooden columns of this terrace surrounding the courtyard. The painted ceiling threw a myriad of color on the pool in the center.

When I glanced up, Arash stood with his back to me before the tomb, a block of white stone. I wanted to run to him as much as I wanted to watch him. He walked around the stone keeping his left shoulder to it—once, twice, three times. His action petitioned Allah's blessings. After, he sat beneath the hazelnut tree beside the tomb with a Naqshbandi shaikh, who made himself available to pilgrims. I

218

wondered whether Arash would ask a question or sit until the shaikh spoke. To ask a master a question would be like shaking a tree to force the fruit to fall. My love swelled to see Arash sitting, his head lowered and his lips still while waiting for the holy man to speak. It seemed like forever before Arash got up, touched his palm to his heart, and left the Sufi's company.

I strode toward him, trying not to run in this sacred place. I caught a glimpse of his face, just before he looked up, his lashes glistening in the sun, his expression serene. When he saw me, he paused. We gazed at each other. Both of us opened our mouths to speak, but then closed them. I ran. He opened his arms and caught me. We clung to one another—clung so tightly that not a single sheet of a scribe's parchment would fit between us.

We rode in the cart with Shaikh Kabir through the small town in the direction of the train station, passing pomegranate and mulberry orchards that bloomed alongside the Rhud Zerafshan. Bidding the Sufi good-bye, we boarded the train for Marv. My tribe, Ismail, Pirouz, and Arash's battalion would travel by caravan.

Arash checked the length of the train for the emir's men and determined it was safe. After several miles, I took off my dervish hat and cloak. Now in private, we told each other our stories of what happened since Mahan had abducted me near the desert pool.

"Your khan planned to stage a grand rescue in Samarkand and win your hand," Arash said. "Until Mahan decided to betray him."

Our poor khan, I thought, that he would turn his face so far from Allah's.

When Arash told me that Mahan had taken the job to protect me from Tamam, my pride stung. My harsh words to Mahan at the storyteller's teahouse came back to haunt me: "You're no better than the crooked officials."

"I owe him an apology."

"You owe your kidnapper an apology?" Arash asked.

"I judged him unfairly." I shifted in my seat. "And Dariyoush? He is all right?" I tensed, not wanting to hear otherwise.

"Shirin rescued him from—"

"That awful pit." Relief spread through my body, but I wanted to forget it, to ignore my wretched feelings of responsibility for having caused Dariyoush this horror. I asked Arash to tell me what happened to him and Mahan that morning I escaped.

"After visiting the scribe, I paid the emir a visit."

"Was he wearing his huge turban?" I asked Arash.

"He could hardly lift his head in it!" Arash crossed a leg, resting his foot on his knee and continued his story. He told me the emir had asked him why it was that he insisted on coming to his quarters day after day to the point of his knife—uninvited. Arash reached for my hand. "'Love,' I said."

The feel of Arash's palm against my skin sent messages up my arm, fanning throughout my body. I threaded my fingers between his.

"Were you frightened, Arash?"

"Not for my life, but for the small chance that I might be locked away in some dungeon, separated from you. This would be worse than death."

A young boy serving chai came down the aisle, his teacups rattling and tinkling with the motion of the train. While the rhythm of the ride soothed me, I did not care for the smells of food and perspiration of the other passengers. In this respect, I preferred to travel by caravan.

Arash reached for his small woven *chanteh*. "I have some things for you." First, he handed me my pink dagger. "Compliments of Mahan."

I shook my head, ran my fingers across the tiny glass beads.

Arash handed me another item. I fingered the camel bone vial that no one but Dariyoush could have whittled. It reminded me of Attar's poem, "Conference of the Birds," because surely, the bird with a smile was the face of the hoopoe. "I will treasure this." My throat tightened when I thought about the desire that likely went into its whittling.

"Anahita, I want you to know that I have great respect for Dariyoush. He said something to me last night, whether true or not, that was an attempt to put my envious heart at rest. And I am grateful to him."

We sat quietly. Deep in thought, Arash said, "When I told the shaikh back at the shrine about your plight, he said he already knew."

"He already knew?" I asked. Thinking for a moment, I said, "There was a naghal at a teahouse where Mahan and I had stopped. Maybe he sent a courier to the Naqshbandi brotherhood."

"If so, that was very thoughtful of him. But the Sufi said he received no *physical* message. And after some time he recited a poem."

I looked at Arash, expecting him to tell me the poem. But he seemed wrapped in a blanket—in the *suf*, or the wool, of this silence—which comforted him. Perhaps this shaikh had opened a space within Arash just as the one in Bukhara had opened in me. We rolled by several cotton fields before Arash shared the Sufi's poem,

From each heart is a window to other hearts.
They are not separated like two bodies,
Just as, even though two lamps are not joined,
Their light is united by a single ray.

Arash said, "I always thought this poem referred to lovers who are attuned to one another, not that people anywhere in the world might communicate without words, written letters, or messengers."

I lay my head on his shoulder, touching the letter still tucked into my tunic.

Sweet Milk

May these vows and this marriage be blessed.
May it be sweet milk,
this marriage, like wine and halvah.
May this marriage offer fruit and shade
like the date palm.
May this marriage be full of laughter,
our every day a day in paradise.

Colorful tents—black, white, and saffron—dotted the grounds circling the royal caravanserai beside the governor's palace in Marv, tents that belonged to both my family and Arash's family. Mahan, Reza, and Ismail mingled with my parents and Arash's mother. Dariyoush exchanged glances with a shy young woman from Arash's tribe. Shirin, Maman Bozorg, and others shook tambourines. There appeared no end to the music, dancing, or pomegranates.

When Arash and I turned to leave our guests, high-pitched ululations split the air. The women's voices cheered us on—now husband and wife—in our new life together. As we walked along a garden pool toward the palace and to my new weaving room where we could be alone to enjoy each other's company, I said, "You know, it seems my kidnapping brought our tribes together more readily than a mere wedding might have."

Arash held my hand more tightly. "Our friends and families are celebrating a deeply-shared accomplishment."

I thought about my journey from Hasanabad to Marv, and the wisdom of venturing forth in the company of fellow travelers. Yet truly, we learned there is only one traveler. We are the many, and we are one.

Arash sat with me on the daybed in my new weaving room. Behind him my jeweled dagger lay embedded in the target on the wall, where I had lodged it only a thumb's width from the bull's-eye.

Arash smiled as he pulled a box from his satchel that was made of khatam, inlaid with mother-of-pearl stars. Inside I found sheets of satiny mulberry paper, a bottle of walnut-brown ink, and a cobalt blue, glass-blown fountain pen.

"It is for your shabnameh," he said. "No more scratching messages in stone."

I smiled as he continued. "Not only will you write the most courageous night letters of all, they—like your carpets—will be the most elegant expressions in all the realm."

Arash brushed my hair behind my shoulder as I ran my palm over the smoothly polished box. "It is beautiful, Arash. But the shah did not respond to my correspondence."

"Anahita, he has a buffer around him the size of a battalion. His own children can't get his attention without persistence. One day, he will acknowledge your efforts."

"I will not stop writing letters on behalf of those women from Quchan until they are safely home."

We turned to the sound of something sliding into the room. A parakeet cage appeared in the threshold. "Pirouz," we both said and laughed. Arash walked over and picked up the reed cage. As he carried it to me, the bird twittered, running back and forth on its perch.

"He is wishing us good fortune." I stood and reached for a tiny fold of paper held in the parakeet's beak, upon which I found a poem by Hafiz. Arash drew close. Hugging me from behind, as if to read the fortune over my right shoulder, he kissed my neck. I let the paper fall from my fingers and leaned into him, enjoying the warmth and firmness of his chest. As he slipped his arms about my waist, I turned, raising my face to his. He pressed his soft lips against mine. I could no longer feel where my skin ended and his began. Trembling, like a strand of silk from Samarkand, I dissolved into love.

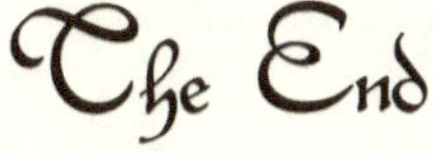

Announcement on Behalf of the Holy National Consultative Majlis

To all compatriots and all of human kind, whether residents of Iran or elsewhere, the Holy National Consultative Majlis proclaims that anyone who knows anything about the situation of women and girls who anywhere along the Khurasan border-lands have been sold to the Turkomans or have been taken captive should write their information, specify their place of residence, and send a signed copy of it through any possible means to the respected National Consultative Majlis, so that necessary actions for their release and retrieval could be taken with full knowledge.

—Actual proclamation of the Iranian Majlis from 1907 in reference to the women of Quchan

Glossary

Afshar (af-shar)—a semi-nomadic people who reside in southern and northeastern Iran near Kerman and Mashhad, respectively. Some also live in eastern Turkey. They are noted for weaving Afshar soumak rugs with geometric designs.

agha (ah-ga)—sir, a title of respect

ayvan (ay-von)—a covered porch

Alhamdulilah (Al-hum-de-lee-la)—an Arabic expression that means "Praise be to God," or "Thank God"

ankhabis (an-ha-bees)—louse; an individual who is good-for-nothing

arrêter (a-ret-tey)—the French verb, "to stop"

atelier (aa-ta-leer)—French word for art studio or workshop

azan (ah-zan)—a call to prayer

azizam (ah-zeez-am)—the possessive form of a term of endearment that means "one who is closest to your heart"

baba (ba-ba)—Farsi word for father

bas (bas)—enough

bazaar bardeh furushi (bah-zar-ray bar-day foo-roo-shee)—slave market.

bia (bee-uh)—come

caravanserai (caravan-ser-i)—a shelter built around a court to accommodate caravans along trade routes

carding—a process in which individual fibers of wool are combed or
aligned

chai (cha-ee)—tea

chanteh (chan-teh)—a small woven bag

chaploose (chop-loose)—a brown-noser

chupan (choo-pon)—an Uzbek word for a knee-length coat with extra long
sleeves, resembling a bathrobe

dervish (der-vish)—a Sufi, both are commonly known as Muslim mystics
who seek union with Allah through silence, meditation, music, song,
poetry, dance and whirling. Dervishes live everyday lives and work in
a variety of careers. They are devoted to kindness, often poverty and
acts of helping. Some of the early orders of dervishes were inspired
by the scholar, poet, and spiritual master Jalaluddin Rumi, who lived
in the thirteenth century in Konya, Turkey. Baha ad-Din Naqshband
began one of the most influential orders in Central Asia.

dokhtar (doke-tar)—daughter; girl

gabbeh (gab-ay)—a loosely woven rug

gelim (ge-leem)—a flatwoven rug in which a smooth surface pattern is
formed by the wefts; *kilim* in Turkish

gul (gohl)—a flower; also a term used to describe the pattern of a particu-
lar tribal weaving

Hoda Hafiz (Ho-da Ha-fiz)—an expression for good-bye that means "May
God protect you"

hookah (hoo-ka)—a tobacco pipe with a long, flexible tube through which
the smoke is drawn and cooled through a jar of water; it is called *ghali-
yan* in Farsi

ibex (i-bex)—a type of wild goat

ikat (ee-kot)—a fabric made by tie-dyeing the warp threads before weaving

inshallah (in-sha-lah)—an expression that means "God willing"

jadid (je-deed)—a movement in early 1900's Bukhara that called for education reform for girls and boys, among other rights.

jendeh (jen-day)—a harsh and derogatory term for a prostitute; sometimes spelled jendeh-ha

janbiya (jim-bee-ya)—a dagger

jinn (gin)—a genie or mischievous spirit

jube (joob)—a shallow trench alongside village lanes that carries water from the *qanat*

kadkhuda (kad-khoo-dah)—a headman or tribal leader

kalabash (ka-la-bosh)—commonly known as a dervish's alms bowl, which symbolizes the Sufis' receptive capabilities for divine grace, which they bestow to the world.

khan (khwan)—a tribal chief who oversees tribal affairs and represents the tribe with the government. The khan appoints the *kadkhuda*.

khanegah (han-a-gah)—Farsi word for a dervish lodge or gathering place

khatam (hat-am)—wood inlaid with thousands of triangular pieces of ebony, ivory, and gold. It is used for making boxes, picture frames and furniture.

komak (ko-mac)—help

lanati (lan-a-tee)—a Farsi word similar to, darn

lapis or lapis lazuli—a medium to dark blue stone

madder—a sprawling perennial native to Asia Minor and the Mediterranean. The roots produce a dye that gives a variety of orange, red, and brown pigments.

madrasa (mah-drah-sah)—a school

manzel (man-zel)—a small dwelling, like an apartment

markhur (mar-koor)—a Bukharan goat with long spiral horns; called a *tog echkisi* in Uzbek language

Mashallah (ma-shah-la)—an Arabic expression that means "All praise belongs to God," or "Is not God great?" Typically used when praising someone or celebrating.

meydan (may-don)—a courtyard or town square

minaret—a tall slender tower attached to a mosque, where the call to prayer is issued.

mon derriere (mon dair-ee-air)—French for "my backside"

muezzin (moo-ez-een)—the crier who calls the faithful to prayer five times a day

mullah (mool-a)—male religious leader or teacher

naan (non)—flat bread

naghal (na-call)—a storyteller who historically narrated and illustrated stories in teahouses

narenj (nar-enje)—a citrus fruit that is hard like an apple but resembles a pear and lemon

night letters—commentaries and grievances to the shah that were typically signed anonymously and either read at street gatherings or posted in teahouses and mosques

Nurooz (New-rooz)—the New Year

oud (ood)—a stringed musical instrument, similar to a lute

pahlevan (pah-lay-von)—a champion warrior-knight of ancient Shiite Islam

pardah (par-da)—a blank sheet of paper often used by storytellers when illustrating a tale. They are typically set up on an easel.

piaster (pee-as-ter)—currency used across the Mediterranean through Central Asia until about the end of the Ottoman era; often used in slave trade

polau (pee-law)—rice dish

qabaleh-ye nekah (gha-ba-lay-ye nee-kah)—an ancient term for a marriage agreement or contract

qanat (gun-ought)—an irrigation channel that often ran deep underground through the desert from the mountains

Rustam and Sohrab (Rust-am and Sew-rab)—characters in Ferdowsi's Persian epic, *The Shahnameh.*

samovar (sam-o-var)—a double-decker urn with a spigot on bottom and a teapot on top. It is used to boil water for tea.

shabnameh (shab-no-ma)—see night letters

shalwar kameez (shal-war ka-meez)—traditional clothing in the Mid East and Central Asia consisting of loose trousers and long-sleeved shirts that hang down to one's thighs or knees.

sigheh (see-rhay)—a temporary marriage in which the woman determines the duration and bride price of the nuptial agreement, often agreed upon with the purpose of raising one's status or obtaining financial security. It is a pre-Islamic custom.

Simorgh (See morg)—a mythical bird in Persian literature

soumak knot—two or more weft wraps around a pair of warp threads, a weaving technique that produces a flat weave

Sufi (Soo-fee)—see dervish

suzan (sooz-an)—sewing needles

suzane (sooz-an-ee)—embroidered cloth found in Central Asia

tamam (ta-mum)—finished

tazahor (ta-za-hor)—superficial; can also mean pretense

toman (toe-maan)—Iranian money

vizier (vi-zee-er)—an advisor, one who might oversee a palace; bears the duties actually incumbent on a ruler

warp—lengthwise threads attached to the loom that form the structure and length of a rug or other weaving

weft—also "woof." Horizontal threads worked between rows of knots in a weaving, which secure the knots in place.

yar (yaar)—soul mate, kindred spirit

yarmulke (yah-muh-kuh)—a skullcap worn by Jewish males who observe Orthodox or a conservative tradition.

Yomut (Yo-mutt)—a Turkman tribe of northeastern Iran and Central Asia

Zoroastrian—a person who follows the Zoroastrian religion, which originated in ancient Persia and preceded Islam. Its prophet was Zarathustra. Scholars believe the roots of monotheism arose from this faith.

Discussion Guide

1. How do you feel women are represented in the novel? And what about the men?

2. The approach that Anahita took in the harem is different from that which many other girls took. Can you think of situations in modern times or even in your own life when you wish people would act more like Anahita did in that harem?

3. What do you think is the overarching message of the story?

4. What are some things you learned about Middle Eastern history or culture through this book?

5. Do you see any likenesses between the Sufi poetry, perspectives and wisdom offered in the novel and other spiritual traditions with which you are familiar?

6. The author mentions in her note that in the time period in which her novel is set, over seventy newspapers were available in Tehran along with night letters, indicating diverse public discourse was at the heart of Iranian culture. How might the number of publications in Tehran compare with those of other cities around the world in that era? Do you think newspapers today represent an ample variety and diversity of voices?

7. In the Author's Note it is mentioned that "the Russians turned a blind eye toward the lingering slavery and some of the

injustices occurring under the emir so long as the czar could extract the cotton and gold from the region." Discuss countries that conduct trade with, or send financial aid to, countries that are committing human rights violations.

8. How might the tradition of sigheh be advantageous or disadvantageous to women?

9. In her book, *The Story of the Daughters of Quchan*, Professor Afsaneh Najmabadi explains that the narratives in night letters and newspapers were effective in creating a sense of national togetherness. They sparked debates in the Majlis, the Iranian parliament, over the trafficking of women and the nation's responsibility toward this issue. Do you feel that the author of *Night Letter* evoked a sense of "togetherness," or a common goal among the men and women in relation to the trafficking of women?

10. Like the Iranian Majlis of a century ago, which supported women's rights, can you identify contemporary government institutions around the world today that are promoting, preventing or even trying to take away women's rights?

For a complete classroom teaching guide visit the author's website: www.MeghanNutallSayres.com or the publisher's page for *Night Letter* at www.NortiaPress.com.

<h1 style="text-align: center;">Author's Note</h1>

(This may contain spoilers)

BUKHARA

When I was a child, names like Samarkand and Bukhara piqued my curiosity, their very sounds conjuring images of deserts, caravans, and *jinns*. These names were much different from the British names of the towns in Pennsylvania, where I was raised: Malvern, Devon, Lancaster. It wasn't until my own children were teenagers that I journeyed to these cities in Central Asia (present-day Uzbekistan) to meet the descendants of Genghis Khan, to stroll among the blue-tiled mosques and madrasas built during the ancient Persian empire, and to explore by train its vast golden sands.

"Though everywhere in the world light is shed upon the earth from above, in Bukhara the light proceeds from the earth itself." A phrase such as this would have resonated with many in the Middle East during the second half of the nineteenth century, when *Night Letter* takes place. This great city is situated on a fertile oasis beside one of the tributaries of the Amu Darya, the ancient Oxus River. In the thirteenth century, it could have been considered the Central Asian equivalent of Oxford or Alexandria, as the standard of literacy, roughly fifty percent, was likely the highest in the world. Languages including Chinese, Persian, Latin, and several Indian dialects would have been spoken in the streets.

Walking about the old city of Bukhara in the fall of 2007, I had the sense of walking in a living museum. It retained a mix of ethnic cultures and religions as well as vestiges of ancient and modern life. Old camel train shelters, caravansaries, stood alongside automobile parking lots. Men dressed in traditional, long-sleeved, knee-length *chupan* silk coats walked beside others wearing Nike tracksuits. Sun designs carved into the walls of one temple indicated the building was once used by Zoroastrians, whose religion preceded Islam. Inside this building, which was later used as a Jewish synagogue, I found carpets woven in the nineteenth century depicting the image of Moses wearing sandals. The footwear indicated that the rug was likely woven by an Armenian Christian rather than a Jewish artisan, as Hebrews rarely depicted sandaled feet in their art.

The guesthouse in which I stayed was located in the old Jewish quarter and owned by a family who had lived there for generations. The people in this neighborhood were friendly and invited me and my traveling companions to share saffron rice they had cooked in large drums in the alleys.

In an old stone building that resembled a mosque or madrasa, women sold *suzane,* cotton cloth embroidered with silk thread. Visiting these artisans and admiring their handiwork gave me an idea for the scene in the novel where Anahita hides under a *suzane* bedspread in the harem when writing her night letter. The old caravansaries in Bukhara clamored with artisans of all kinds who still practiced the ancient art of silk ikat dyeing (a striped tie-dye design), wood carving, leather work, and carpet weaving. Metal smiths, jewelers, and hat makers had overtaken the old money-changing and gold bazaars.

In Bukhara's main square, Labi-Hauz, I ate several meals of lamb kabob, eggplant, and polau beside a pool that glistened beneath mulberry trees more than three-hundred years old, the same trees Anahita saw when she rode into town with Mahan. It was in this square, soon after I had arrived, that I experienced a feeling of déjà vu—a certainty that I had an innate knowledge of Bukhara. When I asked my guide, Kamol Yunusov, what kind of building it was in which the women were selling embroidered cloth, he told me it was a former Sufi lodge or monastery. I realized that prior to coming to Bukhara, I had written in my novel that Anahita found dervishes clustered at one end of Labi-Hauz pool, in the very spot of the old dervish khanegah (Persian) or *khonaqoes* (Tajik).

In the eleventh century, Persian poet, Omar Khayyam, lived in Bukhara and so did the sixteenth century astronomer Uleg Beg, whose conservatory still stands in Samarkand. Classical Persian architecture featuring blue-tiled mosques built in the days of Tamerlane, a fourteenth century ruler who claimed to be a descendent of Genghis Khan, grace both Bukhara and Samarkand. Kaylan Minaret, where Anahita hides, was the tallest in Central Asia for seven centuries until a taller one was built in the 1990s in Tashkent, the capital of Uzbekistan. Local lore holds that the ancient minaret had so inspired Genghis Khan that he left it standing when he laid siege to the city in 1220. The ruler of Bukhara during the time of *Night Letter* was related to Genghis Khan, and part of one of the longest family dynasties in history, lasting until the Soviet takeover in 1920. During the latter 1880s and 90s, Bukhara became a protectorate of Russia. Although the emir was Bukharan, Russian soldiers amassed close by on the banks of the Amu Darya, which ran south from the Aral Sea.

Though I did not climb Kaylan Minaret, the scene in the novel in which Anahita ascends this tower was inspired by my own experience climbing a centuries old minaret in Esfahan, Iran. It was equally as dark and dangerous. When in Bukhara, I did, however, climb onto the roof of the mosque, where one could access the doorway to Kaylan Minaret. On this rooftop, I met a boy and taught him to play Frisbee.

During Anahita's time, as today, several religions were tolerated in Bukhara. In addition to the Muslim majority, the populace included Armenian Christians, Hindus, and Jews. The Jewish in Bukhara numbered about four thousand. They spoke Tajik and were mainly involved in silk dyeing. An 1897 census reported twelve thousand Eastern Orthodox Russians.

BUKHARA'S NAQSHBANDI SUFI ORDER

I learned while visiting Bukhara that it has been the center of the Naqshbandi Sufi order for centuries. The practice of Sufism, a form of mysticism, was initially left alone under Soviet rule because the Soviets assumed it was a religion that undermined Islam and, therefore, was no direct threat to Soviet ideals, which espoused atheism and allegiance to the State above any god. Apparently, the number of Muslims claiming to be Sufis in Bukhara at the time soared into many thousands. It would have been impossible not to know one. This is partly why I have chosen to include Sufi characters in my story. Just as their shrines and monasteries were ubiquitous in the region, their religion of love, their acceptance of all other paths that lead to the divine, and their unique way of seeing the world would have influenced many of the people of that era.

The Naqshbandi Sufi shrine depicted in the novel, which Arash and Dariyoush visit just before they enter Bukhara, and where Anahita and Arash are reunited, is located in the town of Kasr-i Orifan, not far from Bukhara. In 1979, after Uzbekistan's independence from Russia, President Karimov restored the shrine. Today, thousands of pilgrims come to the site every year to pray in its mosques, to circumambulate the tomb of Baha ad-Din Nasqhband, and to leave votives tied to an ancient mulberry tree to receive blessings. All the bits of threads, ribbons, headscarves, and plastic hair clips that pilgrims attached to the branches reminded me of trees similarly decorated at Celtic Christian holy sites near my grandmother's home in Ireland.

I have incorporated into my novel a local Sufi tale about a dervish and a carpet in the scene when Anahita's father Farhad, her tribesman Dariyoush, and Arash's advisor Ismail are imprisoned in The Ark. This tale was told to me by a woman named Marina Musnawira, whom I had met via the Internet while writing this book. Marina offered this story—her favorite Naqshbandi Sufi tale—unaware that I had been at work on a novel set in Bukhara that featured Naqshbandi Sufis. Some might describe this as coincidence, yet to me it feels like grace bestowed.

REGIONAL RULERS

At one time the Persian Empire spread farther north and east than Iran does now, including the cities of Marv, Samarkand, Bukhara, and Herat. This story takes place near the end the Qajar Dynasty (1787–1925), during the reign of Nasir al-Din Shah in about 1900. At this time, Iran was neighbored in the north by Russians and in the south by the British, who were protecting their access to India. At the same time, Iranian and Afghan tribes rivaled for borderlands. Travel was unsafe in this turbulent era, even for caravans like Anahita's.

At the time of this novel, Bukhara was a protectorate of Russia and Emir Abd al-Ahad was the nominal ruler. The emir depicted in *Night Letter* is a fictional character, although he was loosely based on two former regional emirs: one who took a bride every week in order to father an heir, and another who allegedly killed his brothers and twenty-eight of his relatives.

Abd al-Ahad was considered a reformer. He ended some forms of slavery, but kept domestic slaves and the women in his harem. He closed the underground prison in The Ark, featured in the novel, and he ended execution by impalement or hurling from the top of Kaylan Minaret.

NIGHT LETTERS

When visiting Tehran in 2005, I found many newspapers available in Farsi and in English. As one bookseller said, "We are a country with a history of oral discourse. We love open debate." Such was the case at the turn of the twentieth century, the time period of this novel, when no less than seventy newspapers were published in Tehran alone. The popular sentiment about newspapers in those days can be understood by these few lines by Poet Ashraf al-Din Husayni Gilani: "Newspapers aid thinking; / they illuminate the dark night. / Whenever there is a newspaper; / Danger and ill fate stays away."

In addition to newspapers, periodicals, and journals, citizens across Iran who wished to speak out often wrote or hired scribes to express their opinions in *shabnameh*, night letters. Many of these commentaries were written by women and typically signed anonymously. They were either read or posted in street gatherings, teahouses, and mosques. Perhaps night letters could be compared to today's blogging. For little cost, even the illiterate and disenfranchised could join the political discourse of the day. The wording in Anahita's night letter to the shah was derived from those featured in Afsaneh Najmabadi's book *The Story of the Daughters of Quchan.*

In Bukhara in the same era, bards recited similar personal and political expressions called *sh'er* in the form of poetry, songs, and satire. Newspapers were forbidden in public, and like night letters, underground newspapers were common. One such paper, *Tardjuman,* The Interpreter, which is mentioned in this novel when Arash meets the scribe, was distributed hand to hand. This tabloid was edited by a Russian Muslim, Ismail-beg Gasprinskii, a man who had established "new method" schools in the Crimea and brought these reforms to Bukhara. The curriculum in these schools added secular subjects such as mathematics, history, geography, and even Russian to the more basic courses of reading and writing Arabic, which was the focus of the madrasas in Bukhara at the time. The emir Abd al-Ahad remained suspicious of the new method schools, which went underground despite the efforts to keep them mainstream by a movement of intellectuals and government servants called *Jadid.* This group supported the schools along with the modernization of Islamic life and equal rights of women, a topic Anahita hears about in the harem. The Society for the Education of Children, a secret society devoted to the education of boys and girls, flourished for about four years. One of the emir's own court poets, after whom I named the scribe in this story, Shamsiddin Mahmud Shahin, was a member of this movement and a bitter critic of Bukharan morals. It wasn't until 1912 that a Persian-language daily, *Bukhara-I Sharif*, Bukhara the Noble, brought into the open for the first time, along with one other paper, *Turan*, the discussion of political order and school reform.

BRIDE KIDNAPPING

While visiting Bukhara, I met a weaver named Bakhodir Aripov who wove story carpets based on the theme of bride kidnapping. A photograph of one of his carpets is featured on my website. This image inspired the artwork for front cover of *Night Letter*. The tradition of bride kidnapping dates back centuries and was practiced in many parts of the world. The tradition in Central Asia is explained beautifully in a book by Jack Weatherford, *Genghis Khan*. One could suggest that the Mongol empire was built upon Genghis Khan's determination to end bride kidnapping and the perpetual cycle of revenge it instigated between victimized tribes. Genghis was the progeny of a kidnapped bride, as well as the victim of a bride kidnapping when his young and much-loved wife was stolen from him to settle the score for his mother's abduction. The primary factor that led to the kidnapping of women for brides was poverty, which sometimes prevented the kidnapper from raising an acceptable bride price.

Although rare, brides are still kidnapped today in Uzbekistan. In most, if not all cases, it is with the bride's consent. Apparently the tradition was more likely to be practiced by nomadic peoples in neighboring countries. A recent article on the Internet about a young actress, Aiturgan Temirova, who was raised in Kyrgyzstan, a country bordering Uzbekistan, disclosed that she was a teenager when her first husband kidnapped her. "Of course with my own consent," she said. Her parents were against it, but they eventually relented when her husband became one of the most famous figures in Soviet and Kyrgyz cinema and she starred in many of his films.

As recently as the 1920s in Fanad Head, Donegal—the hometown of my Irish grandmother—people engaged in kidnapping their beloveds, or, "stealing the stolen," as author Hugh Dorian phrases it, in his book *The Outer Edge of Ulster*.

Unfortunately, there are still many examples around the world today of forced marriages and the mistreatment and trafficking of women and girls. But these abductions are of the kind that no one feels proud to recognize.

DAUGHTERS OF QUCHAN

Night Letter brings to life a real historical event that occurred in the summer of 1905 in the village of Quchan, Iran, when women and girls were sold by their destitute parents to pay taxes to their local governor. Others were abducted by Turkmans during a raid. Both incidents involved public officials. Because the event happened during the time of Iran's Constitutional Revolution, 1905–1909, *Hiyatat-I dokhtaran-I Quchan*—the story of the daughters of Quchan—became woven into the outrage against the Qajar dynasty. The tragedy was recited from pulpits and printed in political leaflets and other literary forms, including night letters, poetry, prose, songs, satire, and cartoons, an example of which is included in this novel.

In her book, *The Story of the Daughters of Quchan*, professor Afsaneh Najmabadi explains that the narratives were effective in creating a sense of national togetherness. It sparked debates in the Majlis, the

Iranian parliament, over the trafficking of women and the nation's responsibility toward them. The letter in the epilogue in *Night Letter* is an actual formal inquiry into the matter, which the Iranian parliament eventually published.

The newly established Ministry of Justice put on trial a number of people of high station for their role in the sale of the women of Quchan, one of the first investigations and trials of government officials in the history of Iran. This trial was supported by all sectors of society, including the clergy, in the name of justice for women. This act was hugely significant, as was the fact that the shah's administrators were made to sit on chairs beside the Quchani plaintiffs.

Selling women isn't mere history. A similar account of destitute parents selling their daughters was recently reported in *The Guardian* newspaper. While the world focused on the war against the Taliban, 2.5 million Afghanis suffered from devastating droughts two years in a row. The people drank boiled water with sugar and ate potatoes, but they could grow no vegetables. The bride prices for their daughters enabled families to raise money for food for their younger, starving children.

SLAVERY IN THE PAST

Although slavery still existed in Anahita's world, according to Bernard Lewis in *Race and Slavery in the Middle East*, innumerable Islamic *hadiths*, traditions of the Prophet Muhammad, peace be upon him, quote the Prophet denouncing cruelty or even discourtesy to slaves, urging equal treatment of them, and recommending their liberation. These are found in the Qur'an in ayats 4:36, 9:60, 24:58. The early clerics who ruled the Islamic community after the death of the Prophet introduced further reforms in the eighth century. It was made unlawful for a freeman to sell himself or his children into slavery, and freemen were no longer permitted to be enslaved for a debt or crime. In Christian Europe, these practices remained legal until the sixteenth century. By and large in the lands of Islam, both Muslim and non-Muslim alike were protected from unlawful enslavement. Non-Muslim subjects of a Muslim state were permitted to own slaves, but not if the slave embraced Islam.

Although slaves such as eunuchs protected harems (as depicted in *Night Letter*) and sacred sites, others served in the military. But most slaves in the Islamic world provided domestic services and were highly regulated and protected under Sharia law. Thus, Lewis notes, their position was in most respects better than in either classical antiquity or the nineteenth century Americas.

Decades before America fought its civil war, which would eventually lead to the end of slavery in the United States, the first Muslim ruler to order the emancipation of black slaves was the Bey of Tunis in 1846. This process began in Turkey in 1830 for Greek and Christian slaves. In Iran, slavery was formally outlawed by 1906 with their Constitutional Revolution, roughly the date on which the U.S. finally enforced equal protection for slaves, some forty years after the ratification of the Fourteenth Amendment in 1868.

In Bukhara, the last two emirs before the Soviet takeover had declared slavery illegal in and around 1880s and 90s in order to be careful not to bring Russian vengeance upon their emirate. However, many still kept Persian and Russian slaves. Apparently, the last emir himself kept 134 slave women in the harem at his summer home just outside of Bukhara, which I mention in *Night Letter*. The Russians turned a blind eye toward the lingering slavery and some of the injustices occurring under the emir so long as the czar could extract the cotton and gold from the region.

SLAVERY TODAY

Night Letter brings to life an historical tragedy that occurred over one hundred years ago involving the trafficking of women and girls in the Middle East and Central Asia. While this event outraged its citizenry, it also helped to bring about a more democratic form of government in Iran that would not tolerate injustices toward women.

Sadly, the enslavement of men and trafficking of women still persists through out the world today. Modern day slavery looks different from the slave markets of a century ago in Bukhara or the U.S. southern plantation model. Nowadays people are forced into doing someone else's labor and are not compensated. If caught while attempting escape, they are treated violently or their families are threatened. In many cases workers' passports are kept from them.

The United Nations crime fighting office recently revealed that 2.4 million people globally are victims of human trafficking at any given time, and 80 percent of them are exploited as sexual slaves. Only one out of every 100 victims are rescued. National Public Radio aired a show with Reporter Peter Landesman *"The Girls Next Door"* about young women from Eastern Europe hired as nannies, wound up victims of a sex trade that took them to Mexico and ultimately the United States. Malika Saada-Saar, founder of the anti-trafficking organization the Rebecca Project has learned that between 100,000 and 300,000 children—primarily girls between the ages of 12 and 14—are victims of the sex trade right here in the U.S. Girls have even been bought and sold on Craig's List. Ernie

Allen, president of the National Center for Missing & Exploited Children explains the surge in human trafficking tends to accompany major sports and entertainment events, such as the Super Bowl. The UN goodwill ambassador against human trafficking reported that only 10 percent of U.S. police stations have any protocol to deal with trafficking.

Governments around the world indirectly contribute to the trafficking and abuse of women and girls by both the threat of war and actual combat. In advance of war, refugees leave their homes for camps, where the usual safeguards for women and children do not exist, and allows opportunities for trafficking. During war, they are at the mercy of their own people and soldiers as well as their occupiers' soldiers. The *Duke Law Journal* documents the use of sexual abuse against women as "standard operating procedure" in military culture. In 2012 a documentary "The Invisible War" debuted at the Sundance Film Festival reporting on the "epidemic of sexual assault in the U.S. Military." *The Atlantic* reported that The International Criminal Tribunal for the former Yugoslavia opened a case devoted solely to sexual crimes—a watershed moment in the development of international law regarding the intersection of women's rights and conflict.

Perhaps it would seem surprising to some that a renowned historical figure from Central Asia could be a model for women's social justice today. Under the reign of Genghis Khan—according to *The Secret History of the Mongol Queens*—women and girls could not be seized, raped, kidnapped, bartered or sold.

HOW YOU CAN HELP

We can all help end slavery by petitioning for peace rather than supporting those who advocate war. Visit the following websites to learn other ways to help work against slavery:

Not For Sale (www.notforsale.com)

The Amazing Change (www.theamazingchange.com)

International Justice Mission (www.ijm.org)

Free the Slaves (www.freetheslaves.com).

Coalition to Abolish Slavery and Trafficking (www.castla.org)

International Organization for Migration (www.iom.int)

Save the Children (www.savethechildren.org)

Rebecca Project for Human Rights (www.rebeccaproject.org)

U.N. Voluntary Trust Fund for Victims of Trafficking

Ten percent of the proceeds from the sale of *Night Letter* will be donated to the U.N. Voluntary Trust Fund for Victims of Trafficking. Also, when I return to Uzbekistan, I will contribute to the upkeep of the Naqshbandi shrine in Bukhara, in memory of that Sufi storyteller whose tale I wove into this novel.

FARSI AND UZBEK LANGUAGE

Many speakers of Farsi helped me with the language used in this story. Because the Farsi alphabet does not translate exactly into English, spellings of the Farsi words can vary. Any inaccuracies within the text are my own. The Farsi language, often referred to as Persian, is an ancient language. In Iran it predated the use of Arabic, which came with the introduction of Islam and the Muslim holy book, the

Qur'an. Later, Iran was overcome by Ottoman Turks. While many tribal people today in Iran speak Turkish dialects, Iranians retain Farsi as their national language.

The Uzbek language, which Anahita would have heard spoken in Bukhara, is a Turkic language, and its grammar is much like Uyghur. Its other influences are Farsi, Tajik, Arabic, and Russian. My Uzbek guide told me that when the Soviets took control of most of Uzbekistan from 1922–1991, locals were forbidden to speak their native dialects in the presence of a Russian speaker. Today Uzbeks are permitted to speak Uzbek and Russian as they chose.

POETS AND POETRY

The poems in this story are the work of the Persian poets Jalaluddin Rumi, Hafiz, Rabi'a of Basra, Omar Khayyam, and Mirabai of India. Please see permissions for the sources and translators of all of the poets discussed in this section.

Rumi was a poet from the thirteenth century who wrote over fifty thousand verses of poetry. He was born in Balkh, Afghanistan, then part of the Persian empire. His father was a professor of religion. Fleeing the Mongol armies, his family traveled through Nishapur near Mashhad—the setting of *Anahita's Woven Riddle*—where they met the great poet, Farid al-Din 'Attar, who presented young Rumi with a *Book of Mysteries.* After traveling to Baghdad, Mecca, and Damascus, Rumi's family settled in the land of Rum—Roman Anatolia—present day Konya, Turkey. There Rumi became the spiritual leader of a Sufi order of dervishes. The mosque in which he prayed, where he is now laid to rest, is a national museum. On my most recent visit to Rumi's mausoleum just after finishing edits on *Night Letter,* I was delighted to see that his call, "*Come, lover of leaving. It does not matter that you have broken your vow a thousand times. Still come,*" which comes to Anahita's mind and heart just before she escapes The Ark, was chosen to decorate the canvas book bags for sale in a souvenir store beside his shrine in Konya.

Hafiz, whose given name was Shams-ud din Muhammad (1320–1389) is the most beloved poet of Iran. He was born in Persia and lived about the same time as Chaucer in England and about one hundred years after Rumi. He spent his life in Shiraz, Iran, the "City of Saints and Poets," and his *Divan* (collected poems) is a classic in the literature of Sufism. Both Goethe and Ralph Waldo Emerson translated his works. Most of Hafiz's poems are written in ghazal form, which contemporary poet Robert Bly explains, "asks for a poem to begin again with each stanza." Bly, who has translated works of Hafiz with the help of Leonard Lewisohn, says, "Hafiz gives out a hundred blessings each time he lays out a poem." Hafiz's work was internationally recognized during his own lifetime. When I was in Iran in 2005 to participate in their first international children's book festival, nearly every speaker quoted Hafiz before or during their talk. I learned that people consult Hafiz in hopes of finding hints or solutions to their problems by opening a book of his poetry to a random page and interpreting his words of wisdom. Years later, when I visited Hafiz's shrine in Shiraz, Iran, the narenj trees were in full bloom. The festive mood among the pilgrims—mostly young Iranian couples holding hands—was as palpable as the sweet scent in the air. Hafiz's joyful verse, which often pokes fun at our presumptions, compulsions, and vanities, made me feel as if I had stepped into the home of a good friend.

Rabi'a al-Adawiyya, was born in about 717 CE and lived in Basra, in what is now Iraq. Rabi'a was a freed slave who later in life became widely recognized as a saint. She preferred to remain single and spent her time in prayer and receiving others. Her stories and poems were transmitted orally over the centuries before being written down by Sufi writers such as al-Ghazzal and Attar, who hailed from Nishapur, a town near Anahita's hometown in my story.

Mirabai was the most renowned poet-saint of India and lived from 1498–1550. Her songs are still sung today by Hindus, Muslims, and Sikhs alike. Born a princess in the area of Rajasthan, she renounced this life and sought the company of wandering sadhus, with whom she traveled most of northwest India on foot. She was a champion of women's rights, exposing the faults of politics, orthodox religion, and the caste system. She spent the last part of her life caring for the destitute near the Ranchhorji temple in Jodhpur and writing poems.

Omar Khayyam was an eleventh century Persian poet, mathematician, and astronomer who was born in Nishapur, Iran, near Anahita's fictional home Hasanabad, before living for some time in Bukhara. He became known in the West in the nineteenth century when Edward Fitzgerald published a translation of his rubaiyat (quatrains in a style popular among Persians of his day).

THE ARK, THE ART, AND ARCHAEOLOGY

The Ark, which translates as "the column of the state" is an ancient citadel, originating in about the fifth century C.E., and still stands today in Bukhara. During the eighteenth and nineteenth centuries, it was the core of Bukhara statehood. This fortified walled "town" was the residence of the emirs, or rulers, and their guests.

The Ark included a mint, a mosque, artisans' workshops, stables, an arsenal, and a prison. It covered roughly 34,675 square meters. Archaeologists found flues for heating passages and pipes for carrying water underground, which indicates the citadel had a secret water supply system in case of siege.

The Ark was attacked long ago by Genghis Khan and again by the Soviet Red Army in 1920, who bombed it. It is now a museum, which I visited when writing *Night Letter*. I was elated to find out that there had indeed been two entrances to The Ark, as I relied on this fact for my plot. It was thrilling to walk inside, imagining how Anahita might escape.

The map in *Night Letter* was created by the book cover designer Lindsey Wells. Much of the symbols were derived from old Russian maps of the region.

The rock art figures Anahita sketches of two men dancing in chapter one are actual figures from the bronze age found in a cave about one hundred miles from Samarkand at a canyon called Sarmish-say. This site contains about four thousand petroglyphs. The image featured in this novel is a watercolor copy painted by Annette Farrell of Spokane, Washington.

The other watercolors in this book are original pieces from Uzbekistan. The image of The Ark fortress was painted by Ulugbek Muhammed. The image of the village of Bukhara with Kaylan Minaret in the distance and a rider and donkey in the foreground was painted by M. Estatov and is entitled "Winter in Bukhara." The sketch of the whirling dervish is by a friend in Istanbul, Onur Göker.

The tapestry of Omar Khayyam that Anahita sees in the bathhouse is a weaving I discovered in a rug shop in Doha, Qatar, although it was woven in Iran. A photograph of this can be found on my website. A photograph image of an actual embroidered *suzane* textile sewn in Bukhara follows chapter 26. It is an example of the bedspread that Anahita hides beneath in the harem when writing her night letter.

The political cartoon about the women from Quchan at the end of chapter 9 is an actual sketch from the time period. It featured as cover art for the journal *Azarbayjan* in May 1907.

The Farsi calligraphy on the book cover are words from the night letter Anahita writes to the shah, and was penned by Rashin Kheiriyeh, an Iranian artist from Tehran, who also drew the cover art. This image of horse and rider was inspired by a carpet woven in Bukhara depicting a bride kidnapping.

For color images of the art in Night Letter, photos of the Kaylan Minaret, and many other photographs from Uzbekistan that pertain to the setting of the novel, please visit the Central Asian and Iran pages on my website at: www.meghannuttallsayres.com

The ancient rock art from Uzbekistan can be seen at: www.advantour.com/uzbekistan/sarmish-say.htm

Acknowledgments

Foremost I want to thank Nathan Gonzalez at Nortia Press, who risked going against the trend to publish this novel at a time when little historical fiction is acquired by mainstream young adult book publishers. As a political science professor, Nathan understands the importance of deepening today's conversations with wisdom from the past, particularly when it comes to understanding Middle Eastern cultures. It has been a pleasure to work with a publisher who believes that books set in the Middle East and Central Asia can be about love and compassion. Nathan treaded with me into unknown waters with the help of Sufis and Persian poets in hopes of conveying a glimpse of the Persian heart and mind.

Every novel seems to take a village to write, and so many people gave to me of their time and expertise. I'd like to thank Spokane writers Mary Cronk Farrell, Mary Douthitt, Claire Rudolf Murphy, Lynn Caruso, Beth Cooley, and Kris Dennison for their thoughtful critiques of this novel; Eastern Washington University MFA graduates Laura Ender, Elizabeth Moore, Ericka Taylor, and Lisa Frank (now cofounder of Doire Press, Galway, Ireland). Marilyn Carpenter, PhD, gave the manuscript a final read and offered invaluable input.

My husband Bill, my daughter Maeve, and my friends Manda Jahan, Laurie MacMillan, Kristina Rice-Erso, Sarah Swett, and Janet Stewart also made suggestions to improve my story, commented on the book cover design, and offered their support in so many other ways. Author Susan Fletcher helped me sort out the viewpoints for this novel.

Marina Musnawira shared with me her favorite Sufi tale, which I incorporated into my novel. She, and Dr. Alan 'Abd al-Haqq Godlas, University of Georgia, helped me with nuances of Naqshbandi rituals. Manda Jahan and Dominic Parviz Brookshaw corrected Farsi terms, as well as several other Farsi speakers who are contributing authors to my anthology *Love and Pomegranates: Artists and Wayfarers in Iran*. Mahfuza Sobitva, a Tajik student at Western Washington University helped with Uzbek words.

Steven Roxburgh, publisher, namelos, llc, for his initial editing and suggestions. A big thank you to my copy editor, Vinnie Kinsella, an accomplished poet, for his ear for words and attentive eye. Annette Farrell, graduate of Whitworth College Business Arts program for heading up my social media platform.

I am grateful for Rashin Kheiriyeh, Tehran, for her generosity and the beautiful cover art. Lindsey Wells, a graduate of Spokane Falls Community College graphic arts program and current visual communications student at Eastern Washington University for designing the cover and interior graphics, as well as Annette Farrell for her rock art drawing. For input on the cover design, I'd like to thank avid teen reader Samantha Yoder and Book Rat blogger Misty Braden, along with my favorite bookstores: Aunties in Spokane, Washington, The Kings English in Salt Lake City, Utah; University of Washington Bookstore, and, Elliot Bay Books in Seattle. My appreciation includes Bob Greene, the most talented hand-seller of books I know, founder of Book People, Moscow, Idaho.

I'd like to thank my Uzbek guide Kamol Yusunov for his suggestions on my manuscript and my traveling companion Jamila

Gavin, both of whom made every minute of my time in Uzbekistan a joy while researching this novel. Many thanks go to Rustam Muslimov at visit-uzbekistan.com for arranging our trip. I'd also like to thank Eastern Washington University (EWU) Fullbright fellow from Uzbekistan, Bahodir Pasilov, who helped with historical background along with two other professors at EWU, Michael Zukosky, PhD, Department of Anthropology and Geography, and, Jerry R. Galm, Director of Archaeological and Historical Services, both of whose research focuses on Central Asia.

Again, I wish to thank all the people I mentioned in the acknowledgments for *Anahita's Woven Riddle*, as everyone who informed that book indirectly informed *Night Letter*. I wish to remember the late Hussein Elvand Ebrahimi, Founder of the House of Translation for Children and Young Adult Books in Tehran, who first invited me to Iran, showed me his country, introduced me to his friends, and taught me about Persian culture and heritage.

My son Gaelen helped me with character nuance, graphics, and inspired this story many years ago on a family backpacking trip when he asked, "When will you write something with action in it?" Over the miles we walked on that desert trip, my family and our former neighbor Patrick Runkle, helped me brainstorm possible plots for *Night Letter*.

Lastly, I'd like to thank readers of *Anahita's Woven Riddle*, who encouraged me to write a sequel. I hope you have enjoyed the journey.

Permissions

Quotations / Attributions

Sufi Poetry

Rumi

The verse in Anahita's letter to Arash, which opens the novel, is a translation of E.H. Whinfield or Indries Shah with permission of the Sufi trust. The sequence of verses Anahita thinks of when she first enters Bukhara which ends in the minaret: *"Someone is here, invisible to the eye, holding on to me / Someone who does not show himself has seized the front of my robe,"* can be found in a book by Fatemeh Keshavarz, *Reading the Mystic Lyric,* University of South Carolina Press. Anahita's thought in the scene with Mahan and the Sufi storyteller when she reprimands herself, *"If your thought is a rose you are a rose garden. . ."* is from *The Knowing Heart* by Kabir Helminski. The line by the dervish who unlocks the minaret for Anhita, *"Stop weaving and watch how the pattern improves,"* and *"move within, but not the way fear makes you move"* as well as the epigraph that opens the novel, can be found in *The Soul of Rumi,* and, *The Essential Rumi* by Coleman Barks. The wedding blessing in the last chapter comes from line 2667 of Rumi's *Kulluiyat-I-Shams,* as found on www. kamush.com.

Hafiz

Some of the dialogue in the first two chapters of *Night Letter* given to Hawk beginning, *"Kiss by kiss. . .,"* *"It is all just a love contest. . .,"* and, *"I'd give Bukhara for the mole upon her cheek. . ."* were derived from verse in *The Gift: Poems by Hafiz* translated by Daniel Ladinsky. So was a comment made by the tinsmith that begins, *"Blame keeps the sad game going. . . ."*

The riddle mentioned in Anahita's letter to Arash that opens the novel, *"What is sovereign and ceaselessly moves?,"* is also from *The Gift*, as well as the poem Maman Bozorg recites to Anahita's mother and cousin, beginning, *"How did the rose open its heart...."* The following lines that are repeated by the dervishes in the story, *"May God protect that much-traveled one, followed by a hundred caravan loads of hearts,"* appear in a book by Brian Murphy, *The Root of Wild Madder*, however, this author did not specify which of three possible sources he cited.

Rabi'a

Words attributed to Rabi'a in the scene where Anahita is trapped in a cave with her kidnapper Tamam are translated in *Love Poems From God*, by Daniel Ladinsky. The quotation begins, *"What a place for trials and transformation did my Lover put me."*

Mirabai

When Pirouz tells Arash about Anahita's capture, he speaks words derived from Mirabai's poem translated by Daniel Ladinsky in *Love Poems From God*, which begins, *"Three men stole them (a woman and daughter) while they were camping. / They were brought to a city and sold as slaves; each to a different owner."*

Khayyam

Anahita recites Khayyam's verse in the scene after she is re-kidnapped, *"We come and go, but for the grain, where is it..."* This verse is cited in *The Wine of Wisdom* by Mehdi Aminrazavi. Anahita recalls the line *"And then the Tulip for her wonted sup of Heavenly Vintage lifts her chalice up"* from *Rubaiyat of Omar of Khayyam*, translated by Edward FitzGerald, when viewing a tapestry in the harem bathhouse depicting Khayyam holding a cup up wine to a woman's lips.

Anahita's thoughts on Queen Esther, *"Her beauty brought her queenship, her courage brought her freedom,"* were quoted from a story written by Claire Rudolf Murphy, "Return to Hadassah," in the collection *Daughters of the Desert: Tales of Remarkable Women From the Christian, Jewish and Muslim Traditions,* by Murphy, Sayres, Farrell, Conover and Wharton.

The riddle stated by one of the eunuchs in *Night Letter* that begins, "When a carpet is chewed by a goat," is from *Paper* by Bahiyyih Nakhjavani.

The notion that there is a force in the universe that responds, guides, and unifies, which Anahita realizes in the minaret, was inspired by Kabir Helminski. The concept that humanity is one traveler, was derived from words of Pir Zia Inayat Khan.

A phrase Arash's uses when recalling his dream, "a mourning dove surrendering its nest," is from a poem by Philip Levine, *The Names of the Lost.*

The political cartoon appearing after chapter 9 is from *The Story of the Daughters of Quchan* by Afsaneh Najmabad, with acknowledgment from Syracuse University Press.

Anahita's thoughts when watching Arash at the Sufi shrine, "To ask a master a question would be like shaking a tree to force the fruit to fall," might be the words of Coleman Barks.

The quote from the Qur'an, which Anahita tells the emir about chastity and emancipation, is from *The Illustrious Qur'an,* edited by Allama Abdullah Yusuf Ali, SH. Muhammad Ashraf Publishers, Lahore, (24:33), p. 289.

References & Further Reading

My sources for Bukharan history, both in the novel and in this author's note, include the following books, articles and radio program. I also gathered information from my Uzbek guide, Kamol Yunusov, the local artisans, museum employees and U.S. Embassy Cultural Affairs personnel with whom I spoke while visiting Central Asia. At home I consulted Eastern Washington University (EWU) Fullbright fellow from Uzbekistan, Bahodir Pasilov, who helped with historical background along with two other professors at EWU, Michael Zukosky, PhD, Department of Anthropology and Geography, and, Jerry R. Galm, Director of Archaeological and Historical Services, both of whose research focuses on Central Asia.

BOOKS

Abbott, James. *Narrative of a Journey from Heraut to Khiva*, Volumes I and II, W. H. Allen and Co.: London, 1843, and Adamant Media Corporation: Boston, 2005.

Adonis. *Sufism and Surrealism*, Saqi: London, 2005.

Aminrazavi, Mehdi. *The Wine of Wisdom: The Life, Poetry and Philosophy of Omar Khayyam*, Oneworld: Oxford, 2005.

Becker, Seymour. *Russia's Protectorates in Central Asia*, Harvard University Press: Cambridge, 1968 And 2004.

Carrere d'Encausse, Helene. *Islam and the Russian Empire: Reform and Revolution in Central Asia*, University of California Press: Berkeley, 1988.

Helminski, Kabir. *The Knowing Heart: A Sufi Path of Transformation*, Shambhala Press: Boston, 1999.

Keshavarz, Fatemeh. *Reading the Mystic Lyric: The Case of Jalal al-Din Rumi*, University of South Carolina Press: Columbia, 1998.

Lewis, Bernard. *Race and Slavery in the Middle East: An Historical Enquiry*, Oxford University Press: Oxford, 1990.

Mertus, Julie H. *War's Offensive on Women: The Humanitarian Challenge in Bosnia, Kosovo, and Afghanistan*, Kumarian Press: Bloomfield, CT, 2000.

Murphy, Brian. *The Root of Wild Madder: Chasing the History, Mystery, and Lore of the Persian Carpet*, Simon & Shuster: New York, 2005.

Najimabadi, Afsaneh. *The Story of the Daughters of Quchan*, Syracuse University Press: Syracuse, 1988.

Nakhjavani, Bahiyyih. *Paper*, Bloomsbury: London, 2004.

San'at. *Masterpieces of Central Asia*, Tashkent, 2006.

Weatherford, Jack. *Genghis Khan and the Making of the Modern World*, Three Rivers Press: New York, 1984.

Wolff, Joseph. *Narrative of a Mission to Bokhara in the Years 1843-1845*, Harper and Brothers: New York, 1845, and Adamant Media Corporation, 2005.

Lonely Planet: Central Asia, Lonely Planet Publications, June 1996.

MEDIA AND JOURNAL SOURCES

Beaumont, Peter. "Starving Afghans Forced To Sell Their Young Daughters As Brides," *The Guardian*, January 12–18, 2007.

Dick, Kirby (director), and Blush, Douglas (writer). "The Invisible War," documentary, Chain Camera Pictures and Rise Films, 2012.

Elison, Jesse, "The Hidden Epidemic: Child Trafficking in the U.S.," The Daily Beast, March 11, 2011. http://www.thedailybeast.com/articles/2011/03/11/a-hidden-epidemic-child-trafficking-in-the-u-s.html.

Landesman, Peter. "The Girls Next Door," National Public Radio, Fresh Air from WWHYY, January 26, 2004.

Lederer, Edith M., "Human Trafficking Victims: 2.4 Million People Across the Globe are Trafficked for Labor, Sex," Huffington Post, April, 3, 2012. http://www.huffingtonpost.com/2012/04/03/human-trafficking-victims_n_1401673.html

Radjabov, K.K., "Struggle for Independence in Turkestan and Muslim Clergy," Instituto per l'Oriente C.A. Nallino—Roma, OM, XXVI (LXXXVII), 1, 2007, p.177–188.

Wueger, Diana, "Women in War, Women in Peace," TheAtlantic.com, November 8, 2011, http://www.theatlantic.com/international/archive/2011/11/women-in-war-women-in-peace/248078/

"The Bukharan Princess in Brno," www.kultur-multur.org, 14 June 2007, http://kultur-multur.org/index.php?option=com_content&task=view&id=147&Itemid=2

About the Author

Meghan Nuttall Sayres is a tapestry weaver who has traveled in the Middle East and Central Asia, where she has met with scholars, carpet weavers, dyemasters, and merchants to study the age-old techniques, symbolism, and Sufi poetry that infuse many rugs woven throughout the region. Her debut novel *Anahita's Woven Riddle* has been translated into several languages. It was chosen as an American Library Association (ALA) Top Ten Best Books, an American Booksellers Association Book Sense/Indie Pick, and an ALA Amelia Bloomer Feminist Choice Book, among other awards. While researching *Night Letter*, Meghan traveled by train across the deserts of Uzbekistan to the ancient cities of Samarkand and Bukhara, plotting scenes and imagining Anahita's possible escape routes. Her other books include, *Weaving Tapestry in Rural Ireland; Daughters of the Desert: Tales of Remarkable Women From the Christian, Jewish and Muslim Traditions* (co-author); and the anthology *Love and Pomegranates: Artists and Wayfarers on Iran*, which she edited. She lives in Washington State. For more information about the author and this book, including discussion and classroom guides, please visit www.meghannuttallsayres.com and www.writingandwandering. blogspot.com

Other Books by This Author

Anahita's Woven Riddle
First published by Harry N. Abrams, NY, 2006
Re-issued by Nortia Press, 2013
Re-issued by Wayfaring Press, 2020
Available at Amazon and from your favorite bookstore.

Daughters of the Desert: Tales of Remarkable Women
From the Christian, Jewish and Muslim Traditions
Skylight Paths Press

Weaving Tapestry in Rural Ireland
Cork University Press

The Shape of Betts Meadow: A Wetlands Story
Lerner Books

Love and Pomegranates: Artists and Wayfarers on Iran
First published by Nortia Press, 2013
Re-issued by Wayfaring Press, 2020
Available at Amazon and from your favorite bookstore.

A Word from the Illustrator

The atmosphere of Meghan Nuttall Sayres' novels, *Night Letter* and *Anahita's Woven Riddle*, are full of Persian tradition, so in designing the cover art I decided to paint in the Persian miniature style—one of the most enduring styles of Persian art—using colorful characters and oriental patterns. The most important elements of Persian miniatures are the dominance of light and the use of pure color. They are vibrant, like the stories themselves, like a Persian carpet full of adventure and mystery. I worked with handmade paper, pencil, and acrylic.

Rashin Kheiriyeh
Illustrator, Painter, Animation Director
www.rashin-art.com
YouTube/rashinart

A Word from the Book Designer

It has been a pleasure and a challenge to design book covers for *Anahita's Woven Riddle* and *Night Letter* using the work of an award winning artist, Rashin Kheiriyeh. Her rich color palette, whimsical style and Middle Eastern images set the tone for the font lettering, which is CiviliteMJ.

I attempted to capture Ms Kheiriyeh's playful mood when designing the interior map for *Night Letter*, which I drew by hand using a Wacom Tablet and examples of old Russian maps from the setting of the novel. Similarly, the interior graphics on the title pages of *Night Letter* were derived from a traditional Bukharan rug pattern and a design painted above an interior door in the Mehmet Pasa Cami, a mosque located in Sultanahmet, Istanbul. The backdrop to Rashin's cover art piece on *Anahita's Woven Riddle* is an Iranian Afshar carpet. I used Adobe™ PhotoShop® and Adobe™ Illustrator® to create the layouts.

Lindsey Wells
Graphic Designer
Designedbylindsey.com